The Ravens

Leah Thompson

Copyright © 2024 by Leah Thompson

All rights reserved.

No portion of this book may be reproduced in any form without written permission from the publisher or author, except as permitted by U.S. copyright law.

Contents

i. the minefield

The Grove Forest was a minefield. From the moment the ostracized teenagers took over, one wrong step, one wrong move, could be the cause of war, yet that never seemed to drive people away. One might think that a logical person would run, find a place where they were safe and accepted, search for the legendary City of the Forgotten. But that's where the problem was: the city was merely a legend, and people were not always logical. No, despite the looming threat that hung over the forest like a heavy cloud, many had found their home in those woods. These were the people who took each other in after the fortified cities denied their acces. These were the camps they built, the places where their new families declared their existence. The Grove Forest was a minefield, but it was all they had.

Sebastian Harlem—a tall boy whose eyes were weighed down with responsibility, causing him to look older than his nineteen years—exited the room he shared with two other boys in the cabin situated near the Northern entrance of the Ravens' camp. He could hear the rest of the camp waking up, and the first people entering the center area. He scanned their territory, making sure everything was in order and safe. Sure enough, he could see the scouts on patrol, their shift having started two hours earlier. Everything seemed to be fine.

"Let's go!" He called, walking down the staircase. His building, B1, was situated higher up than the other cabins. This was to his benefit, since it allowed him to have a solid view of everything in the camp. He watched as people slowly began to move. There was Hayden, the lanky scout who'd injured his knee two weeks back, walking with Serena, the medic, and Emma, Sebastian's younger sister who he was constantly trying to protect, although that did not fit her agenda.

"Sebastian!" Serena called to their leader. He smiled and ran down the stairs, approaching her and the boy with a limp. "I have good news. That stomach bug that was going around is pretty much gone. Everyone who was still sick is definitely getting better now."

"That's great!" Sebastian said, "How's Hayden's leg doing?"

"It's fine," Hayden interrupted. He hated being referred to as though he wasn't there. "I can be back out there today, I think." He was still limping though, and Sebastian knew better than to send him out that quickly. At the same time, Dylan, the group's other leader, approached the circle.

"We're running low on food. Some of the scouts should go out hunting," Dylan said, her voice serious and mature.

"I'll go!" Hayden volunteered, but he was quickly turned down by all three others. They agreed that he would stay back in the camp and help fix the holes in the surrounding fence, and perhaps he could be cleared by nightfall.

"Are we sending messengers out for any reason?" Dylan asked, turning to Sebastian, who simply shook his head.

He was met with a cold glare from his little sister, as it was her job in question. "I'm not staying in camp," Emma said, "I'll go out with the hunters." Sebastian sighed, knowing there was little point in arguing. He agreed to let her go, on the condition that she stayed with Nathan Maxwell.

Nathan was an actual scout, which Emma was not. The latter accepted this requirement, as she was friends with Nathan and would have much preferred having some company throughout the day. The two hunters approached the weapons vault and swiftly exited the camp, Emma leading the way.

"Ellie, come help me fix the fence," Dylan decided. She was generally more hands-on in camp life than Sebastian was. Sebastian, on the other hand, was often found guarding the camp at any hour of the day. The first leader led the younger girl, as well as scouts Yasmin and Corey, towards the broken wall.

"Hayden, come back to the Med Hut," Serena said, "I'll check your leg again."

"Can I get the all clear?" Hayden smirked. It had been two weeks since his leg had been injured hunting, and he was sick and tired of being confined to the camp. It made him feel useless, especially since he wasn't exactly skilled in any field of camp life. He was a strong fighter, and he was determined, yet impatient. He wasn't a cook or a nurse by any means.

"We'll see," Serena sighed. The two of them entered the Med Hut, where a couple of the camp's members had fallen ill. A slight stomach bug had gone around the camp recently, but these two seemed to be the end of the sickness.

"Sorry, but I'm perfectly capable of moving around camp like a normal person again," Hayden laughed, "I'm bored." Serena did not respond, but began her routine checks. The boy was able move his leg, but the knee was far from perfect. She had a suspicion that it was never going to be perfect again, but she didn't want to tell him that. Besides, he was able to walk again now. He didn't need to stay in the Med Hut anymore, that was for sure.

"I think you'll be alright," Serena smiled softly, "Just don't run, and I'd still stay in camp. Not much use having a guard who can't protect the camp, right?" At that, Hayden nodded. He knew that she was right, but he was frustrated with how restrained he felt.

"I hate hunting," Emma muttered, fiddling with her spear. Her dark hair was pulled back into a tight ponytail, a typical style for the girl, and her brown eyes were filled with a vivacious intensity. The resemblance to her brother was uncanny; they had the same defined cheek and jaw, the same nose. However, there was no mistaking the two. Upon meeting Sebastian, you knew that he was kind, he was mature. Emma, on the other hand, was a wild card. She and Nathan had been hiding behind some shrubs a half mile away from camp for approximately thirty minutes, and they had yet to find a real animal to kill. "It's so slow. I just want to stab something in the neck already."

"Still think it's slow?" Nathan gestured to the clearing. A horse had just entered the area, a perfect shot. As the animal began to nibble on the dried up grass, the two hunters examined it, making sure it was safe to kill, that there were no rival hunters pursuing this same beauty.

"Can you get close enough to make sure its neck isn't branded?" Emma whispered to Nathan. She hadn't answered his question, but the new gleam in her gray eyes was enough of an answer. There was one tribe on the eastern side of the forest who had begun to domesticate animals. The Ravens had never been in contact with that group, yet occasionally they would come across their livestock.

Nathan nodded and approached the animal, "I'm not going to hurt you, I promise." He inspected both sides of its neck, looking for any symbol that it may belong to an enemy tribe. Killing an enemy's horse was one of many ways the Grove minefield could explode. He made eye contact with Emma and backed out of the way as she threw her spear. It landed in the animal's throat, and Nathan gulped as it fell over. Emma closed her eyes and sighed. She didn't enjoy killing, but she didn't feel any real guilt about it either. It was all in the name of survival, right?

"Don't worry, I hurt her, not you," Emma smiled, standing up and cracking her back, "Now let's get back to camp. We'll need help getting this girl back." She retrieved the weapon, as it belonged to the camp, and not herself, from the dead animal It was ironic though, truly, how Emma Gail Harlem insisted on examining the horse, making sure it would not be the powder keg. See, the powder keg had just exploded regardless and the minefield was slowly becoming more and more dangerous.

♥♥ ii. xenia

At the western fence, Dylan was working alongside a general named Yasmin and Ellie, the youngest member of the camp, to fix the holes in the barrier. Ellie was irritatedly cooperating, as she was training to be a messenger and felt that the restrictive work inside the camp was far too tedious. In the blink of an eye, the youngest girl had climbed onto the other side of the hole she'd examined."Ellie, come back in," Dylan warned, "It's safer behind the fence."

"But I want to explore!" Ellie complained. The leader frowned, running a hand through her hair, a nervous habit that resembled someone older than her eighteen years.

"Fine," Dylan gave in, "Just stay close enough so we can see you." Ellie smiled excitedly. Of course, as a young girl will, she soon wandered off behind a bush, and into an area she knew the Ravens at the fence couldn't see. All she wanted was some freedom, someone to trust that she was mature enough to handle the forest. She was training to be a messenger—she'd have to start somewhere. As soon as the members at the fence realized they couldn't see her any longer, the panic there began to settle.

"I'll go out there," Yasmin said, "Someone ought to protect that kid." With that she squeezed out of the hole in the fence and instructed the others to keep working on its repairment. Yasmin wandered in the direction she believed Ellie had travelled in, calling the younger girl's name as she went. What she did not expect, however, was the large tree branch located at the top of the hill behind her. With one step backwards, she took a quick tumble downhill, landing on the opposite side with a bloody gash in her leg. Yasmin was able to stand and walk, but as she had not expected this new mission, she was unequipped for this situation.

"Great," Yasmin muttered, touching her fingers to the wound. She gulped as she felt the wet bloodstain her hands. No matter how much time she'd spent in the forest, the sight always made her slightly nauseous.

"Are you alright?" said a voice behind her. She turned around instantly, hoping it would be Ellie. However, it wasn't. It was another small girl, around the same age as the one she went after, but ultimately a stranger.

"Yeah, yeah, I'm fine," Yasmin smiled to the girl, "Are you? Are you out here alone?" She ignored the stinging pain coming from her shin, and tried to avoid staring at the blood.

"My name is Hannah," the little girl smiled. She did look strikingly similar to Ellie, although there was no mistaking the two of them. "I'm a Rogue." This surprised Yasmin, seeing as how the girl could have hardly been over twelve years old. To be living completely on her own at that age, that child must have gone through a lot of hardships.

"Well, Hannah, I could use your help. Have you seen another girl around your age come around here?" Yasmin asked.

Hannah nodded, "Yeah! I can help you find her, but only if I can stay at your camp for a little bit. That's how a deal works. I help you, if you help me."

The general paused before deciding, "I'm not qualified to make that decision. But if you help me find Ellie, then you can come back and talk to one of our leaders."

There it was. The powder keg had been set off, but it would be a couple days before its effect began to kick in.

Unknowing of the fuse they'd lit, the two girls continued their search. They came across the missing child sitting in a little field of wildflowers, innocently looking around and taking in the view.

"Who's this?" Ellie asked, her eyes landing on the stranger.

"I'm Hannah," smiled the girl, "Because I helped find you, your friend said that I might be able to stay at your camp!" At this, Ellie's eyes widened excitedly, and she began to run towards the camp. It was obvious that she was thrilled that there might be another girl in camp around her age, and who could blame her? There was only so much for a twelve year old to do when everyone else had at least four years on her, if not more.

The trio returned to the camp, entering from the main eastern gate. It was a strange sight to see an unarmed general with a bloody shin walking alongside two giggling little girls, especially one of them being a stranger. Upon their arrival, Serena came rushing out of the Med Hut, an audible sigh of relief expressing her contentment with the younger girls' return. However, her eyes were drawn to the blood on Yasmin's leg, and quickly ushered the general into the Med Hut.

"Hayden, come help me out!" Her assistant and recently cleared patient came over, waiting for her further instruction. She began to cauterize the wound, while Hayden passed the doctor supplies. After spending so much time in that room over the past couple weeks, he now knew exactly where everything was located, and could actually be a surprisingly big help.

"Serena, it's just scratch, I'll be fine," Yasmin protested. She was more anxious to talk to Dylan or Sebastian about what to do with the new girl. The medics refused, however, insisting that her tumble down the hill resulted in a much deeper cut than she'd anticipated, and it could very easily get infected if left untreated.

"At least you didn't injure a bone or muscle in any way," Serena smiled calmly, "As long as you keep it covered and it doesn't get infected, it shouldn't have any permanent damage."

At Serena's comment, Hayden said, "You got lucky Yazzy, all you're going to get are some sick battle scars from your fight against topography." Of course he received glares from both girls in the room for his remark, but he shrugged it off and added more seriously, "You said there wouldn't be permanent damage. She got out lucky." To this, the medic looked down worriedly, since she had decided not to tell Hayden that his own injuries would likely never heal fully. The truth was, the boy didn't need her expertise to know that he wasn't going to heal entirely. He could feel in the way he walked that his slight limp wasn't going away anytime soon.

The door to the Med Hut opened wide as Dylan and Sebastian entered, the former asking, "Yasmin, what happened?"

"What part?" Yasmin asked, sitting up. The medics backed away slightly, opening the circle so that the leaders were included.

"The girl," Sebastian said, his expression cold and serious, "Who is she?"

Yasmin sighed, "She said her name was Hannah and she was a Rogue. She'd agreed to help me find Ellie if she could stay at our camp for a bit, and I told her that we'd get back here and talk to you guys."

"Smart move, any idea if we can trust her?" Sebastian asked, looking to the whole group for an answer. Nobody really wanted to say that they didn't trust the girl, and it just felt too cruel to send a child back into the woods by herself again. Is that not what the adults had done to all of them? Sent them away from the cities to fend for themselves in the wilderness?

Hayden was the first to speak, "She's a Rogue. We can't just trust them."

"She's not even thirteen, Hayden," Serena said, "And we can't just label all Rogues as bad. I know some are, but they aren't a united group."

Hayden shook his head, "Sebastian, your sister's not gonna like this." He had had a dark history with the Rogues. Before finding the Ravens, he had gotten himself into some sticky situations where everyone wanted him dead. This was at the beginning of the P.D. era, as he liked to call it: Post-Death. He was only fifteen years old, but kids his own age and older were after him. The reason why was buried deep down inside him, haunting him constantly, but never surfacing.

Sebastian sighed, "My sister talks to Rogues all the time, and so far she's been alright. We'll talk to her when she and Nathan get back." It was beginning to get late, and the hunters would likely return soon. Some pairs had made stops in the camp to drop off their findings, and the food supply seemed to be replenishing.

Outside, Ellie and Hannah were quickly becoming the best of friends. Ellie gave her a tour of the camp, explaining exactly who slept in which building, where the weapons were kept, and which entrances were her favorites to sneak out of. There were some holes where only a girl their size could fit through, and these were the ones Ellie was most excited to show off. She was proud of the escape routes she'd discovered over the past two years, and now she finally had a friend to share them with. There was nothing that Ellie refrained from telling Hannah. Every secret of the Ravens that the former may have known was at the second girl's access. Of course, Ellie didn't know any of the tribe's real secrets, or anything that could truly be of importance to an enemy.

"It was awful here before you came," Ellie sighed, "I was all alone, and the older kids don't trust me at all. There are a couple girls who are a lot younger, but it's no fun to play with them. Please tell me you're staying here."

Hannah smiled sympathetically, "I'd love to stay, but your people aren't going to let me. You know that."

"Yes, they will!" Ellie encouraged her, "I'll convince them. I promise."

"But what if they don't listen to you?" Hannah asked.

"Then I'll leave with you!" Ellie said, "If my people don't trust you, then they won't be my people anymore, because I know they'd be wrong." Hannah looked up, tears glistening in her eyes, and she smiled softly. The plan was set, and to the younger girls, it seemed they had a whole new future ahead of them.

iii. to trust a stranger

It was about two hours later when the hunters all returned to camp. They had been extremely successful that day, and the food supply was fully restocked. Of course, they'd soon have to start preparing for winter. They were lucky that the climate of the Grove was fairly moderate and consistent, so the slightly colder season was not too grave a threat.

"Emma!" someone called as the group entered the main gate, "Go find Dylan and Sebastian, they've been looking for you!" The huntress nodded and left her team at the entrance. She found the two leaders alongside Nova, the camp's resident mechanic.

"Who's the new kid?" she asked, her gaze glued to the young girls giggling across the camp. .

"That's what we were gonna ask you," Nova said, "She said her name is Hannah and she's a Rogue. Do you know her?" Of the whole camp, Emma was the most likely to know this girl, or at least have heard of her.

"She's not a Rogue, no way," Emma shook her head, almost laughing a little bit, "Did you just let her in this camp?"

"How do you know? Are you positive?" Dylan sighed, hoping the other girl might be wrong. Her brow creased at the prospect of a new potential threat plunged into her stomach.

"She's too young, she'd have been either living on her own since she was ten or something, which is highly unlikely, or she'd have to have been living with someone else that she just abandoned by coming here. Even if that was a possibility, then we'd still be in trouble," Emma said.

"But she's just a kid, right?" Nova asked, "She can't cause that much damage by being here." The final solution they came up with was to let her stay there overnight, as it was dark out, and nobody was cruel enough to send a child into the forest alone at night. Hannah would stay in the open cabin above B7, the room that used to be shared by Dylan and an old Raven who had gone missing a year earlier. After her heroic disappearance, Dylan stepped up to be a leader and moved in with Emma and Nova.

The circle agreed that Dylan would take the first guard in front of Hannah's room, and the rest would take whatever measures were necessary to keep her and Ellie apart. The first job fell on Sebastian, and the older boy sighed as he approached the children sitting near the western wall.

"Alright, Hannah, we're going to have you stay in one of the empty cabins for tonight; I'll take you there," Sebastian said, "Ellie, you're coming with me. We're on guard tonight."

"No!" Ellie frowned, turning from her newfound friend to her leader, "I'm staying with Hannah." Sebastian shook his head and repeated his previous instruction, but the younger girl stood her ground. After enough of this back-and-forth, he was able to persuade her to join him at the southern border. Hannah was brought up to the empty B7, and the other two left for their post.

"I don't get why you're making me do this," Ellie said, "I'm training to be a messenger, not a scout."

Sebastian paused, as this was the truth. Standing guard was never going to be his sister's responsibility, and they all knew it. So he lied, "You have to be a scout first if you ever want to be a messenger."

Ellie frowned, seeing right through him, "That's not true. Emma wasn't ever a scout." She was right, again. As the Ravens were beginning to form this allegiance, she was the one who refused to stay put. Emma was bored by the confining walls of the camp, and after having her first taste of freedom when the Plague hit, all she wanted was more. She invented the role of the messenger, using it as her way into the forest, her means to the natural drug she found so addicting.

"You just want me to stay away from Hannah," Ellie said, "Because you don't trust her. You don't trust anyone."

Sebastian sighed and looked off into the forest, "First rule of being a messenger, you can't trust any person you meet."

"That's not even your job, you don't know what you're talking about," Ellie shook her head, refusing to listen to her superior.

"I do know, actually. And if that truth is too much for you to handle, then your training is over. Is that what you want?"

"Yes, it is. You'll regret it when you see I'm right." With that, Ellie turned around and walked back to the camp, her blonde ponytail swinging behind her angrily. Sebastian sighed, and looked up at the night sky. There was a time when he would drive away on weekend nights to a place where there was no light pollution to hide the stars. He could have stared at them for hours; the pure enormity of the universe used to make him feel powerful, it made him feel like he was floating. But now? Now it only served to make him smaller than ever. Here he was, sitting underneath a tree in the middle of a dying planet, trying his hardest to keep his people safe, but really what for? Because in the middle of the cosmos, what did forty scrappy teenagers have to add?

iv. resurrection

It was in the middle of the night when Hannah and Ellie had managed to sneak away. The latter was angry at the rest of the camp, thinking it was unfair that they didn't trust her newfound friend. Well, if they didn't trust her before, now they would have a reason to. Besides, it's not like there was much for a twelve year old to do in the camp. To Ellie, Hannah's mysterious life as a Rogue seemed fascinating and inviting. All she wanted was to join her.

When the sun rose, Sebastian left his position from the previous night's patrol and returned to the camp. He hadn't slept all night, and so he consistently fought to keep his heavy eyes open. Of course, when he entered through the gates, he was instantly drawn to the door of B7, left unguarded. He sighed and marched up to Building Five, where Dylan slept with his sister and Nova.

Nova was the one to open the door, "It's like, five in the morning. What do you need?" Her hair was pulled back in a messy bun, and she was only wearing a dirty white sports bra and black shorts.

"Is Dylan there? It's urgent," Sebastian said. Right on cue, his partner entered the doorway.

"Are you alright?" she asked, concern in her eyes.

"You look dead, Seb," Emma called from the back of the room. She had not left her bed, but simply rolled over to face the door.

"Thanks," Sebastian nodded, and then led Dylan outside, "Hannah's door is unguarded."

"What?" she asked, eyes shooting towards the now empty room in the pale light, "Is she still here?"

"I haven't checked," Sebastian admitted.

Dylan turned to the boy and examined him closely, "Were you on guard all night?" He nodded, causing her to sigh, "I'll deal with this. You need to get some rest. Now." Sebastian smiled, thankful that Dylan could carry his burden when necessary. That was the perk of having two leaders; they could bear it for each other.

After Sebastian had returned to his cabin, Dylan sighed and approached the room where Hannah was last seen. Unsurprisingly, the door was left unlocked and the girl had disappeared. Her next move was to visit the cabin where Ellie generally slept with the other younger kids. She highly doubted that they'd been playing together in there, and sure enough her hunch was correct.

"No luck?" Nova asked, coming up behind Dylan. She was joined by Emma, as the two were able to overhear the leaders' conversation.

"What did you expect?" Dylan said, a dejected look taking over her round eyes, "Let's not tell Sebastian though. He's exhausted, and he's gonna freak."

"Wasn't Ellie supposed to be on patrol with him all night?" Nova said. The three girls looked to each other, and the general consensus was that things hadn't gone as planned. That much, at least, was obvious.

"I'll go talk to some of the Rogues, see if they know anything," said Emma. She had only just woken up, but was already alert enough to head out. There was a constant energy that manifested inside of her. She never seemed to need to rest, require time to refuel. She was moving, all gears running at all hours of the day as though she could outrace her own reality.

"Go," Dylan nodded. Emma smiled; she'd always preferred Dylan as a leader over her brother. One of them was far too over-protective. As the messenger turned to get ready, the leader added, "Just don't do anything stupid, and don't go too far."

"Yeah," Emma said as she ran back to the cabin to change. Soon after, the rest of the camp slowly began to wake, and the news of Ellie and Hannah's disappearance spread like a wildfire. That was the thing with the Grove forest. News spread quickly. By the afternoon, all the Rogues in the area would know, and by nightfall, the whole forest would have heard of the two little girls who ran in the night. Of course, that was assuming the Ravens were the first to know. The rumor may have already spread.

With Sebastian asleep, Dylan was left alone to divvy out the day's work, "We need scouts guarding each wall, and everyone else needs to be patrolling the forest. Look for anything that might give us a clue as to where they went."

"Hayden!" Nova called. The boy shot up from his seat on a step outside the Med Hut and approached her and Dylan, "You're in charge of the walkies today. I'll go patrol instead."

"I'm fine, Nova. I can patrol, really," Hayden pleaded. Although her position as resident mechanic did not provide her the authority to permit him to leave, he was hoping she might accidentally break the rules. Clever as she was, Nova, of course, realized this, and gave him an apologetic smile as she and Dylan turned to leave. Now Hayden and Serena were the only waking people inside the walls.

"This blows," Hayden muttered, taking a seat next to Serena outside, "How are you doing?"

Serena, who seemed a little distant, didn't turn to look at him, "Oh, I'm fine." She was staring up at the blue sky, eyes following the wispy white clouds overhead. The sky looked peaceful, as though it was in direct contrast to the stressful conditions of the forest.

"If you're worried about Ellie, she's going to be fine," Hayden said, "They'll find her."

The medical assistant frowned and turned her attention to the ground, "That's not what I was thinking about."

"What were you thinking about?" Hayden asked, trying his best to be comforting and sincere.

"Do you know what the date is?"

"September fifth, right?" The boy answered, and then he paused, "It's your birthday."

"Yeah, thanks for being the only person to remember," Serena said, "I'm sorry, I'm being selfish. There are more important things to worry about than my birthday getting ignored."

"It's alright," Hayden leaned back, resting his body weight upon his forearms, "You're allowed to think about yourself sometimes."

Serena smiled and leaned onto his shoulder, "Thank you, Hayden." They sat there in silence for a couple of minutes, but then they heard the gunshots.

"What was that?" Hayden shot up, eyes turning serious and fearful. Serena's were wide and nervous, "Get inside the Med Hut."

Sebastian came out of his cabin at the same moment. "Make sure that wasn't one of our scouts," he instructed, running towards the duo. Hayden called into the walkies, asking if any of them were hurt, if anyone shot the gun. Every response he got was negative; the shots were fired by somebody else. At least it wasn't aimed at any of the Ravens, as every group had confirmed they were alright. Still, groups were quickly returning to the camp, everyone's blood rushing with adrenaline.

"Some birthday, huh?" Hayden smirked to Serena, who only frowned at him and shook her head.

"Too soon, Hayden. Too soon."

"Dylan!" Sebastian called as his friend made it back to the camp, "Where's Emma? Is she back yet? Who was she with?"

"I haven't seen her, she was going to talk to some Rogues," Dylan shook her head. Sebastian was about to protest this decision, argue that she should not have been let out alone, but Nova quickly alerted him that the girl in question had returned. Of course, he had good reason to be: she often kept herself in dangerous company.

"Are you alright?" Sebastian asked her, hugging his sister. She hugged him back as well, but quickly. He was clearly more worried about her than she was for him.

"I'm fine, but we're not. Someone's shooting up Condor territory," Emma said, avoiding eye contact with her brother and tapping her foot impatiently, "They're gonna think it's us."

"Why would they think that? They're always the ones who attack us first, we've never made the first move onto them," Dylan said.

"Because some little Condor girl has been running around the forest as a spy," Emma snapped, "Well, at least we got our answers." The other three looked to each with concern, as the messenger backed away from the conversation. They didn't have time to discuss this, though, because a masked figure had just climbed over their walls, landing in a clean, squatted position.

At her landing, Sebastian whipped around, taking out his knife. "Get out," he hissed at the stranger, "Get out or I swear to God I will kill you."

"Oh Sebastian," they snickered, standing up calmly and brushing the dust off their knees, "We both know you wouldn't hurt an old friend, now would you?"

"You know her?" Dylan whispered, looking to her partner in shock. Sebastian, however, was unsure of who the stranger was.

"Nice knife, buddy," she continued, coming up and standing right in front of him. He recognized her voice for certain, as well as the swagger in the way she moved, but the girl he was thinking of was gone. She easily removed the weapon from his hand, although he could not register any of the happenings.

"All of my old friends are dead," he said, hesitantly.

Emma looked at her brother, almost in horror. He was never one to say something that morbid. For that reason alone, she glared at the stranger, "Take off the goddamn mask."

"Emma, stop," Sebastian warned. His sister stopped talking, but definitely gave him an angry look as if to ask "What do you think you're doing?" The hairs on her arms crawled with anticipation, and a deep resentment had settled in her stance.

The stranger responded to this by taking tossing Sebastian's knife into the air playfully, catching it every time. Suddenly, she was right before him, holding his own knife dangerously close to his body, "They're not all dead, Sebby. Have ye so little faith in all your friends?"

Along with the rest of the camp, Emma's right hand was wrapped tightly around her own knife, waiting to throw it the second she saw blood come from her brother's neck. The Ravens all stared with the same conviction and fear, ready to fight if the stranger dared attack.

"Drop your weapons!" Sebastian called out, a strange calmness sweeping over him. This surprised everyone, including himself, but he knew somehow that this girl was not going to hurt him. He had an inkling suspicion of her identity, and if he was somehow right and she hadn't died a year before, he knew she wouldn't dare.If he was wrong, and she was truly an enemy, then he did not deserve to lead these people after such a careless decision.

Before anyone could react, the stranger had managed to pin Sebastian onto the ground, his own blade right at his throat. She stared him dead in the eyes, and he stared right back. At this point, his fingers began to shake, his only sign of fear. The camp, having listened to his previous instruction, glared at the stranger, knowing their leader's life could be on the line if one of them tried to attack her. They had to put their faith in her now. At that moment, the stranger pushed the weapon into his neck, but then dropped it, surprising everyone. An even bigger surprise, she lifted off the mask revealing her face, but in an angle where her hair covered it from every surrounding them.

"Good to see you too, MaiLinh," Sebastian smiled once the events registered.

"Missed me?" she whispered into his ear. Sebastian pushed her off of him and stood up, laughing now. He was genuinely laughing. The two embraced in a long hug, confusing everyone.

"Didn't she die?" someone asked as murmurs began to flood the crowd. Everyone stared at the girl in shock. MaiLinh Walker, in the flesh. When the Ravens were first formed, back when they were a bunch of scared teenagers who had lost everything they'd thought impossible to lose, it was Mai and Sebastian who stood up to bring them together. It was the two of them who built up this camp, who established the rules, who built this tribe from nothing.

"Sorry for the rough arrival," Mai shrugged, "Things got a little out of hand."

"Was that you shooting Condors?" Dylan asked bitterly, the first thing she'd said since Mai's arrival in the camp. As the answer became clear, across the circle, Emma was on a different agenda. She had a plan, albeit a risky one, but she knew that if she discussed it with anyone else, it would quickly become prohibited. And so, in the midst of the commotion and the happy reunion, she snuck out through a back entrance of the camp as always, disappearing into the woods, and getting caught by no one.

v. coup

As far as the world was concerned, Coby Harris died on the day that the Cabener neighborhood took over the City of the Forgotten. The city, having been formed by the teens ostracized from the fortified metropolises, was easily the most organized area in the post-plague world. Divided into five different neighborhoods, the original format of government included a representative from each sect who would all come together to make the best decisions for the city. But that all changed the day Cabener seized the power.

The neighborhood used to pride itself on their miraculous team of six: Harper and Phoenix Smith, their cousin Cameron Dawson, Kamai Wells, Donovan Mayler, and Coby Harris. These six were notorious for their rebellious attitudes, their tendencies to wreak havoc wherever possible. So it was unsurprising that they were behind the coup that put Harper at the top of the hierarchy. The surprise was what came after.

In the week following the mass rebellion, Kamai had disappeared. The word on the street was that she had been captured by some other group from a different city. Donovan had also set himself on fire. He had set off an explosion, one that would change the course of the city forever, but in the process put himself into a coma. Finally, Coby was gone as well. He had changed his name, grew his hair out from a buzzcut, and cut all remaining ties to the team that destroyed everything.

The moment Harper took power, she divided her neighborhood in half. There was Fidelus, the side where everyone involved with the rebellion and supported her fully stayed, and then there was Paricida, the dilapidated side that never truly got built to begin with. In Paricida lived all her enemies, anyone who she thought might threaten her power. The name itself meant traitors. Of course, she wasn't about to kill those people off. Not because she was merciful, but because she was smart.

Jacob Hart had a small hut in the busiest part of the loyal Fidelus side. It would have been far too challenging for him to request to move to the side of the enemies. Although it had been over a year since he last spoke to Harper Smith, news of him moving would reach her quickly. Jacob lived with Donny, his best friend. The two had met as children, and grew up side by side. When the plague hit, they ran away. They were from nowhere near the city, same as everyone else, yet somehow they all ended up there together.

Following the coup, Donny was comatosed for five weeks. In this time, he had been referred to in the neighborhood as a hero, he was honored and praised like never before. Jacob knew that he would have loved the attention. If only he had been conscious to see it. When Donny finally woke up, he was confused to see the way his best friend had changed. He was going by a different name now, and his hair was growing out for the first time in a decade.

"Harper's insane. We can't be associated with this any longer," Jacob had tried to explain on their first night back together in his hut.

"Slow down," Donny said, "Let me try and talk to her. I almost died for her, she'll have the decency to listen." The following day, the two boys waited nearby Harper's office in the building where they had once lived when they were members of her inner circle. The tan walls gave them flashbacks, reminding them of the people they used to be. When the city was first being formed, life seemed so exciting to the boys. They had their first real dose of freedom, as there were no teachers, no small-town adults telling them where they could or couldn't go, what they could or couldn't do, who they could or couldn't be.

After knocking on the office door, it was soon opened by Cameron Dawson, the cousin. There was a time when these three boys, along with Harper's twin Phoenix, were practically inseparable. They were in constant trouble during that first year. Since the coup, Jacob had hardly seen Cameron, as he was always stuck alongside the twins. Seeing him in the doorway reminded him of the bittersweet memories of the time the City of the Forgotten felt so good. He could tell that Cameron was thinking the same thing.

"Donny! You're alive!" Cameron exclaimed, eyes widening. It seemed that the news hadn't yet made it to the tyrant, or at least she hadn't chosen to share it with her kin.

"Cameron!" Harper had snapped, "Get back here, we have work to do." She had turned around and looked straight at Jacob and Donovan, but if she recognized them, she didn't provide any sign. Instead, she acted as though they were strangers, as though she'd never met the boy who pushed her out of a grenade, taking the force unto himself. That was enough to prove to Donny that his friend was right, and while the first year in the city may have been the best time of their lives, their old friends had become strangers.

"So now what?" Donny had turned to Jacob, "We just stay in your shabby new hut in the middle of Fidelus?"

"I know some girls in Paricida. I've been crashing on their couch practically every night since the coup," Jacob shrugged. Donovan nodded, realizing this was a likely explanation. His friend's home was too clean for him to be sleeping there every night.

"You? Finally sleeping with a bunch of girls?" Donny laughed, "You're a riot, Coby Harris."

"Jacob Hart," he corrected. But oh, how Donovan was right. What a riot he was.

vi. the powder keg

- -

"Good work, Cora," the older of the two girls smiled down sweetly, a mixture of anger and excitement swirling behind her eyes, "You brought us our bait."

"It's wrong," replied the little one, "She really trusted me."

"Then you did it right," the first one said. She tucked her dark hair behind her ear and added, "Soon it will all work out, and your brother will be avenged."

At that, Cora smiled. Through all the guilt she felt over her actions the previous night, ultimately she wanted justice, and she wanted to make her leaders proud. Like Ellie in the Ravens, Cora Hannah Marks was one of the youngest people in her own camp. But unlike the Ravens, her leaders used her innocent appearance to their advantage.

"Mason," the older girl turned to her partner standing by her left side, "Go seek out Adrian Daroll, the Rogue. He'll know the moment they send out a search party. Or if we're lucky, the slut will come by his camp by nightfall. She'd be perfect." With that, the boy nodded, planting a kiss on the girl's forehead and leaving the two others in the small room.

"Once we have someone else, will we let my friend go?" Cora asked hopefully. She truly did feel immense guilt about the little girl they had trapped in a cell underneath the camp's ground, felt her heart weigh down whenever she remembered what she'd done.

"It depends," the leader said, "While we're at it, I really do wish you would stop using your middle name when you go undercover. It makes you too easy to track."

Cora frowned, "But it makes me feel like less of a liar. At least Hannah is part of my name."

"We're human beings, Cora," the older girl smiled, "Lying is in our blood. As Condors, we acknowledge it."

"You still haven't told me what happened," Sebastian sighed, turning to look at Mai. It was dark now, and the two were sitting alone on a couple of rocks near the back entrance. After the hectic events of the day, the two had yet to really talk. Everyone was confused, some even left unsettled, by her quick reappearance, as well as the added stress that one of their own people had just massacred an unknown number of Condors. Not to mention the fact that Ellie was still gone— in other words, the camp was a madhouse.

"You remember that battle, don't you?" Mai muttered, looking at the ground. A pit dropped in both of their stomachs as they remembered that gruesome fight and the horrid memories began to seep back in, "Well I failed everyone. So the next morning, I went to look for survivors, and the Condors were angry. Held captive for three goddamn months. And when I managed to get out, I couldn't face this camp again. I couldn't do it, Seb."

"You didn't fail them, Mai," Sebastian shook his head, putting his arm around the girl's shoulder, "Nobody ever blamed you. You should have come back."

"Sebastian, listen to me. I did fail them. I was the leader, and twenty of them died because I wasn't able to save them. My sister died because I made one bad call in battle. I cost them their lives," she snapped, angry tears filling her eyes. She wasn't about to cry, though. MaiLinh Walker would give her own life before she ever let somebody else see her cry. She sighed and looked up at the impossibly bright moon shining through the trees and wiped her eyes. When she was a little girl, her grandmother told her to look up at a bright light to stop the tears. She didn't know if it worked or not, but it was habit.

"I was their leader too. Whatever guilt you feel is on me. Whatever you did wrong, I did wrong. We worked as one, remember?" Sebastian reminded her, looking straight ahead towards the wall. He felt the girl's head resting against his strong shoulder, and they needed no eye contact. Despite having been separated for a year, their old chemistry was instantly rekindled, and their eyes were once again not needed for them to speak. "We saved a whole lot of people too that night. Every single person in this camp today was saved because of you. I know you don't feel like it, but you're a hero."

"Maybe I was once, but not anymore," Mai said, "Because of what I did this morning, the Condors are going to just come after this camp again. That's my fight to deal with though, not yours." She grabbed her black bandana and began to tie it around her neck as she stood up.

"Mai, you aren't leaving," Sebastian turned his head quickly, fear flashing in his eyes as he realized the girl was planning on saying goodbye to this camp. "We need you. You can't just go." As she began to walk towards the front entrance, she felt his firm grip wrap around her wrist, but she didn't do anything. She just continued to walk.

"Close the gate!" Sebastian shouted, and at this Mai turned back around.

"I don't need the gate!" she yelled, "I came in here over the fence, I'll get out the exact same way." The flustered attitude that always appeared when she was under stress was beginning to seep out.

"If you climb that wall, you're killing us all," Sebastian threatened, staring down into her brown eyes.

"If I stay, I'm leading the Condors here. If I go right now, they will never know I came back, they won't have any reason to attack this camp. You'll all be safe," Mai said, rambling now, and avoiding eye contact.

"Look at me," the leader glared, "Whether you're here or not, the Condors still sent a spy into our camp last night and kidnapped Ellie. No matter who the killer was, they are bound to think it was one of us. The only difference is whether or not we have our best fighter here when the war comes."

"I can't protect you all," Mai looked down again, "I'm like the Grove's angel of death. Do you have any idea how much blood is on my hands?"

"All our hands are stained," he responded grimly, "It's the price of surviving."

"Seb, please...."

"I can't lose you again," He whispered, letting go of the girl's wrist, and instead wrapping his arms around her in a tight embrace. They stood there, him supporting her, for about thirty infinite seconds before Mai broke the silence.

"I should go talk to Yasmin," she said before walking away. Sebastian smiled, knowing that was her way of saying she would at least stay the night. Yasmin had been her best friend at the start of this whole deal. The two deserved to catch up.

"God, I have so much to tell you!" Yasmin smiled once the two girls were alone in their cabin, "I've missed you so much."

"I've missed you too," Mai said, "The hardest part about being away for so long was not being able to see you."

"Promise me you'll stay? I don't want to lose my closest friend again."

"You know me, Yasmin. I don't make promises."

The sun had long set by the time Emma approached her destination. As far as she could tell, none of her people had noticed she was gone. At least, they hadn't sent anyone out to look for her yet. Then again, they probably wouldn't have known where to look. Regardless, they weren't on her trail, and that was good enough for her. A cool breeze whistled through the trees, the forest feeling more silent than usual. It was as though the birds and the crickets had disappeared, and the typical howls from nearby Rogues were nowhere to be heard. This put a visceral fear in Emma's stomach, warning her that something bad was soon to occur, but she put the thoughts out of her mind and kept on walking. Perhaps she should have listened. Survival instinct was real, but she was on a mission, and she could not be deterred. Ellie was in danger. She could not turn back.

"Adrian!" she called out when she reached a certain spot in the forest. She thought she heard a twig snap behind her, and she whipped around, gripping onto her knife. Seeing nobody nearby and hearing nothing, she took a deep breath and tried to slow her heartbeat.

"You called?" a boy asked, coming from the opposite side of the small clearing. He was bigger than most of those from Emma's camp, both in height and weight. Before the plague, he was the starting quarterback on his high school's varsity football team— a golden boy who ended up making it his life's mission to kill the kid that shot his uncle. He had at least two years on Emma, and was well over a foot taller than her as well. Using Adrian for help was a risky gamble, but she always had her tabs on him. Staying on his good side was a gamble she was willing to take.

"I need your help," she smiled, "Information."

"What do I get in return?"

She closed her eyes and sighed, "Whatever you want." With that, he approached so that he was standing right on top of her, staring down into her gray eyes. Putting his hand on the back of her neck, he leaned in and kissed her, a favor she returned. They continued for a few minutes, a flood of loveless connection, until Adrian began to unzip his jeans and Emma pulled away. "After you help me."

"Humor me," he sighed, stepping back, "What do you need to know?"

"Two girls. One a Condor, one not. What have you heard?" she said coldly. Emma hated Adrian with a passion, but he could be useful. Besides, he was one of the only Rogues she knew well who lived this close to the Condors' camp.

"Yeah, I know some things," he smirked, "But you'll find it all out for yourself."

Emma looked up at him, her eyes a blend of confusion, surprise, and maybe even fear, "What do you—." Before she could finish her sentence, another pair of arms had grabbed her from behind, covering her mouth with their palm. She tried to scream and get someone else's attention, though her voice was silenced. She clawed at the arm that was strapped tightly around her chest, trying to kick behind her, anything to get away, but it was no use. The sight of Adrian holding a bar up to her head was the last thing she saw before the darkness took hold.

vii. the anniversary

"Happy anniversary, Donny-Boy," Jacob yelled as he turned on the lamp in him and his friend's one-room hut. He was crouching on Donovan's bedside table, holding the string that turned on the light and staring down at the sleeping boy.

"What are you doing?" Donny muttered, barely opening his eyes. He turned away so that he wasn't facing his friend and the exposed light bulb, and pressed the thin pillow over his face.

Jacob laughed and got down from the table, "Wake up already! The girls want to see you!"

"Why?" the other boy groaned.

"It's been a year since you woke up. You were in a coma, remember that little detail? And then you woke up? Yeah, it's been a year, get out of bed!" Jacob called loudly, stomping around the hut, being as annoying as he possibly could.

"I wish I didn't wake up," Donny said grimly. His voice was still tired, and clearly irritated that his friend had chosen to wake him up so unnecessarily early. Despite surviving the end of the world, Donovan Mayler was still an eighteen year old boy who would stay up until the earliest hours of the morning, and opt to sleep until the mid-afternoon.

"Well I wish you didn't set that grenade, and then proceed to push Harper out of it," Jacob laughed. He then took a seat on the edge of his friend's bed and his demeanor got serious, "For five weeks, I thought my best friend was gone, and I didn't know how to handle it, or what to do with myself, or anything. And that was in the midst of getting excommunicated from Harper's posse. Am I not allowed to celebrate that you're alright, and you've been alright for a year?"

At that, Donovan sighed and sat up, realizing there was no use fighting his friend on this matter, and also that this day really did mean something to Jacob. "What do you have planned?"

"Nothing," Jacob smiled, "But the girls do. Get dressed and we can head over to Paricida."

"The land of the parasites," Donovan said, running his hand through his dark hair as he sat up, "How come we ended up on the side that literally translates to loyal?"

"We wouldn't have if you had let Harper get blown up," Jacob said.

"That's not funny. She was our friend once," Donny said.

The other boy turned around as he began to get ready for the day, "The key word in that sentence is 'once'. She didn't bother checking in on you once when you were comatosed. She didn't acknowledge you once when you woke up."

"I'm sure she was busy," Donny said.

"Yeah, busy having twincest with Phoenix," Jacob smirked.

"I was going to say setting up her dictatorship, but okay." Donovan had now stood up and was beginning to get dressed. He combed his hair with his bony fingers so that it stuck up near the front. There was a time he would have used some product to keep its shape, now he could not care less.

"Why are you defending her?" Jacob stepped back, seeming almost offended by his friend's position on the matter. Donny, of course, claimed he wasn't on her side, and suggested that they leave for Paricida as an excuse to change the subject. The other boy agreed to this, and they embarked on the thirty minute walk. There was always the option of taking the old bus across the neighborhoods, but for someone to travel from Fidelus to Paricida was rare, and they often received strange glances. Nobody ever paid much attention though to two boys walking around in tank-tops and broken flip-flops in the earliest days of September. As long as they seemed like they knew what they were doing, they were clear of questioning.

"IDs?" A guard asked as they reached the border between the two sides of the Cabener sect. They pulled out the plastic cards that marked their residency, and their names were jotted down on a piece of paper. "What are you two doing here this early in the morning? It's not like there's anything to do in this area." The guard was from Fidelus. They had seen her around often; she used to always follow Harper around, trying desperately to be a member of the Six. Jacob wished he could have given her his spot in their group, then he wouldn't have to deal with the repercussions of having once been up at the top.

"We're visiting my girlfriend," Donny said confidently, "We're filming a sex tape." This was all a lie, of course, since neither of the boys were dating any of the girls across the border, and they were definitely not creating any form of pornography, but the guard just nodded and let them through with no more questions. They soon arrived at Rachel Greenesfelt's home. She lived in a two-room shack without running water alongside two other girls. Despite having more rooms than the boys in Fidelus, the latter's home was still more spacious, and they were lucky enough to have water as well. Ideally the girls could come hang out with them, but it was too hard for members of the side labeled as traitors to travel to the capital of the city.

Rachel opened the door, "You're here!" Natalia Sanchez and Marley Dennis were seated on the torn up couch in the front room. One of them looked up and smiled, while the other didn't even flinch. Jacob and Donny were practically always at their shack, so their arrival wasn't really anything special.

"Jacob here said that you all planned something for today? It better be worth him waking me up this early," Donny said. At that, Rachel raised an eyebrow towards the boy next to him.

"It's eleven in the morning," Natalia called from behind, "You can stand to wake up before noon for once in your life."

Donovan smiled and let out a breath, "So we're chilling on your couch as usual. Great."

"Get in here!" Marley snapped. Once the boys were inside, Rachel closed to door behind them and the other girl continued, "I stole some beers. Well, I didn't steal them, since Johnny Kristen saw me take them from his booth, but I didn't pay for it."

"What does Johnny Kristen want in return?" Donovan said. Ever since his accident, there was always a little more caution inside of him. He used to run around setting things on fire, pulling pranks on the people who were responsible enough to get jobs in the community. He used to be fearless, and there were no limits to what he would do. But now that boy was gone, and in his place was someone who wanted to keep the few people he cared about safe. He had grown up during his coma.

"Not sure yet. Probably some weed, maybe some painkillers. I can score those easily," Marley said casually, picking the dirt out from underneath her painkillers.

"How have they not caught on to you yet?" Natalia laughed, turning towards the girl next to her. Marley Dennis was technically a nurse in Paricida's makeshift hospital, and rarely showed up for her job, although she didn't need to. She was able to cash in favors illegally, and Natalia and Rachel could both provide some slight income when necessary. Jacob and Donovan were lucky enough that their old associations with Harper meant that most of their expenses were covered. They didn't understand the economics behind Harper's rule, but they didn't question it either.

"We're in Paricida. All the nurses are drug dealers," Marley said casually.

"Can we smoke tonight?" Jacob asked hopefully, although this was quickly turned down by his best friend. They had tried weed once during the earliest days of the plague, and for awhile Jacob made a habit of it with Phoenix and Kamai, before the coup. Donovan and Harper were morally opposed to the drug-use, and they all figured Cameron would be allergic, since he seemed to be allergic to everything.

It was through weed, actually, that Jacob met Natalia. He was lonely in the early nights after the coup, and she was high, so he joined her. She was the oldest member of their group, nineteen while the rest were one or two years behind her, but they all had a suspicion that something more had happened between the two of them that night. They had both been drinking too, though, so neither of them remembered it clearly. Regardless, any spark that had been there that first night was long gone, and neither of the two had any problems with a relationship that was strictly platonic.

And so, the five delinquent kids set out on their fascinating plan to spend the day on Rachel's couch, an activity they were so accustomed to by now that they fell into their typical patterns in moments, despite it technically being a celebration. A guard came by and knocked on their door at around three in the afternoon, the same girl who had carded the boys on their arrival.

Donovan opened the door, and the two looked each other up and down. This girl was one of the few people left who still associated him with the Team of Six. At least she didn't recognize Jacob with his grown out hair.

"Harper's making a newscast in a couple hours," the guard said shortly, "I recommend you listen."

"Great. Thanks," Donovan nodded, preparing to close the door.

"You should listen, Donny," she continued. The room had suddenly become significantly more awkward, as that nickname was reserved for people he was actually friends with, not just girls who had chased after him once, "It's all about your friend."

viii. wake of giants

When Emma opened her eyes, a faint light blinded her, striking an acute pain in her temples. She squinted to make out her surroundings, and saw that she was in some sort of cell. She was seated on a dirt floor, leaned up against a pole, although when she tried to move, she found her hands were bound to it. Her ankles were tied as well, and a wet rag around her mouth gagged her. A slight panic began to settle when she thought back to the last thing she remembered. She had gone to Adrian for help, but he had unsurprisingly betrayed her. That asshole, she thought.

The light came from a small skylight in the ceiling of the cell, but based off what she could see, they seemed to be underground. There was a door on the wall to the right, but she figured it was locked. Besides, she was still bound and had no way to test it. As her eyes continued to adjust, she eventually saw a small figure in the corner of the room, and her heart began to race. The figure appeared to be asleep, and judging by the strength of the light, Emma figured the sun had only recently risen. The girl's blonde hair, however, gave away her identity. It was Ellie.

A newfound adrenaline rushed through Emma's body, as her instincts to reunite with the girl ran rampant. She struggled against the pole, trying desperately to break away, but it was no use. Luckily, Ellie appeared unbound, which would be a good thing for them both. Emma sighed, leaning back against her restraints, and stared up at the faraway light. She knew what she would have to do.

When Dylan and Nova awoke that morning, they turned to see an empty bed in their room. They were aware that they'd gone to bed far earlier than Emma the previous night, but it appeared she never came back.

"She left the camp again, didn't she?" Dylan sighed after the events had registered.

"Maybe she spent the night with Mai?" Nova suggested, "They were always friends."

"You don't believe that for a second," the first girl shook her head, "How come we're always the ones who get stuck discovering someone in our camp is missing?"

"Let's go outside. Hopefully she'll be in the camp somewhere." The two girls took a deep breath and exited their cabin. It was late enough now that most of their friends were awake, but there was no sign of a small teenager in a black bomber jacket with her long, dark ponytail. Sebastian was across the center, talking casually to Mai. He seemed relaxed, or at least as relaxed as he ever was. If he'd sent his sister out earlier that morning, he would undoubtedly be more nervous—he always was when Emma was gone.

"Corey!" Dylan waved a scout over, "Have you seen Emma this morning?"

The boy shook his head, "Is she not here?" He didn't need a spoken answer to understand. All three knew the truth. He added, "Both of her knives are gone from the weapon's vault."

"Is that unusual?" Dylan asked, "She always has a knife with her, it's Emma."

"At least one of them is always missing, usually both. She didn't take anything else with her, though. No swords, spears, guns even. Does she usually only arm herself with two knives?" Corey looked to his leader, hoping for an answer that could suggest the girl was still there.

Nova shrugged, "Depends on what her motive is." Although nobody in the camp knew the extent of Emma's tactics to gain information, Nova was one who had a fairly confident idea. Of course, she was never going to confront her friend about how many people she'd slept with, but she had a feeling it was a number Emma wasn't proud of. Or even if Emma was proud, Nova figured it was best to keep it a secret, as Sebastian would be beyond ashamed of her.

"Who wants to break the news to Seb?" someone sighed. Of course, he'd led Mai and Yasmin over to their circle, since he was able to see the palpable tension from across the field.

"Break what news?" he asked, and the sound of everyone else's stomach dropping was almost audible. They all looked down towards their feet, nobody wanting to tell the boy his sister was missing. That action, how-ever, was enough to tell him everything. "Oh, God." he muttered, shaking his head and walking away. The other five looked to each other in silence, unsure of how they should react.

"It's the Condors, isn't it?" Yasmin muttered, "Those goddamn snakes."

"We don't know that," Corey said, "She's a smart girl, she has friends all over the place. She could be just fine."

"But the Condors have Ellie, which we do know, and Emma would chase after her," Yasmin said, "Besides, does nobody care about Ellie being miss-ing?"

"We can't exactly send out a search party," Dylan said, "Not after Mai's run-in with them yesterday. They're going to want to kill any Raven they see." Mai frowned when Dylan mentioned that, but she didn't say anything. She wasn't proud of having become a killer.

"All the more reason to get Emma and Ellie out of there now," Yasmin snapped.

"But we have no way to know she's there," Dylan refuted.

"Ellie's there!" Yasmin shouted, "It's not all about Emma!"

"It's a trap, right?" Nova added, "They got Ellie for information purposes, but she's young so she doesn't know anything. Mainly, she's bait. They're hoping they can lure us out and capture or kill someone who actually matters. They won't kill Ellie because they know we'll do anything to protect our people."

"Emma's walking into it, isn't she?" someone else muttered.

Corey frowned, "She's the perfect target. She knows everything, and she's Sebastian's little sister. He'd do anything for her, and if he were to fall, everything else would fall."

"Now what?" They all turned to Dylan, waiting for her to make the call.

Mai, however, the old powerhouse, was the next one to talk, "It's too risky to send out anyone else. They're hostile enough that they'd kill anyone on sight, and we have no proof that Emma's actually there. Besides, if she is there, they won't kill her just yet. They'll use her to their advantage first, so we have time. She's more valuable to them alive."

Dylan nodded, "Mai's right. Nobody is going towards Condor territory." They all nodded and began to disperse for whatever jobs they had assigned that day. Mai was patrolling the southern border, while Yasmin and Corey were heading towards the east. Nova, as always, was taking over communications. Dylan sighed and looked over towards Sebastian, who was discussing something with Serena, obviously trying to hide his anxiety over his missing sister. She was desperately hoping that Emma would avoid the enemy camp, as she knew Yasmin was right that it would destroy her partner mentally, and she feared it could lead to something even worse.

She turned towards Mai, who was heading out to her position with a certain confidence, as though she knew exactly where she belonged, as though she was meant to be there. Even after disappearing for a year, Mai seemed like the perfect fit for this camp, and Dylan saw the comfortable way she interacted with Sebastian. Who was she kidding? She was sailing in the wake of giants.

"Step up, Dylan," she muttered to herself, "It's time be a leader."

<h1 style="text-align:right">ix. her mantra</h1>

Trigger Warning: This chapter deals with torture and abuse, especially in the second half. It is not very graphic, but if this puts you at risk, please don't read it.

Ellie woke up a couple hours after Emma's arrival, and the smaller girl was shocked to see another person in the cell. She didn't recognize her companion at first, as she was in a weakened and vulnerable state foreign to the child. A bloody Emma was uncommon, but it had happened before. The difference now was how defeated she appeared. Ellie had never seen the other girl lose. Besides that, her dark hair had been released from her ponytail, and since her hands were bound, she was unable to stop it from covering her face.

"Who- who are you?" Ellie asked nervously. At that, Emma's head snapped up, and Ellie was able to see her clearly for the first time. As the older girl suspected, her younger counterpart was unbound, and she quickly ran over to her friend. "Emma! Are you alright? What happened? Why are you here?" She removed the gag from the girl's mouth and sat across from her.

"Ellie, quiet down," Emma whispered, "I'm going to get you out of here. I have a plan, okay?"

"Did they send you here? Are they coming to get us?" Ellie asked, a hope-fulness rising in her voice. She'd been so frightened over the past day, and the prospect of a possible escape was wonderful.

"You mean the Ravens?" Emma said, "No, they didn't know I left. But you're alright? Did anyone hurt you?"

"I'm okay, they didn't do anything too bad," Ellie said. She had plenty of new scratches and bruises, but everything would heal. Emma smiled, extremely relieved that the girl she came to rescue was healthy enough. At that moment, however, the door to the cell flew open, and in walked four people, two of them carrying guns. The two left unarmed, Emma figured, were their leaders. Still, the pounding in her head prevented her from gaining a clear image.

"Back away," one of the leaders snapped at Ellie. This girl had a soft face framed by soft, brown curls, but it was clear from the edge in her voice that she was dangerous. Emma knew exactly who this girl was back before the plague. She was the high school bitch that almost everyone hated. Poor girl, even her old friends would have turned against her in a heartbeat. Now it seemed that her cruelty had found its calling. There was room for wickedness in the wild.

"So who do we have here?" the girl hummed, walking slowly up to Emma. A staring contest proceeded between the two, as the prisoner was not about to give up a single piece of information, nor would she look away and suggest that she was scared. It didn't matter how nervous she truly was, she was set on maintaining this aura of confidence. The Condor was the one to break the eye contact, nodding to the guards behind her. On cue, they seized Ellie by her arms, pushing her against the other wall. The younger girl looked to Emma in fear, eyes wide and terrified.

"I'll say it again. Who do we have here?" the Condor threatened. Emma looked up at her younger friend in a pinned position.

"Let her go," Emma said with a cool confidence behind her words. She was glad her hands were bound behind her because it meant that the Condors couldn't see them shaking.

Her captor laughed, "Emma, darling, that's not how this is going to work." By including the prisoner's name in the sentence, it became clear that she knew more than she was letting on, and that she would likely know if she was being lied to. Even then, by no means were these two girls strangers. They had never been allies, but they had long known of each other's existence and allegiances.

"Then you're wasting your time," Emma said, "As long as she is in this camp, you won't get anything from me. You let her go, you take her home, and I won't try to fight you. I'd say it's a good deal."

The leader paused, considering Emma's offer. She knew that Ellie was there purely as bait for a more important member of the Ravens, and Emma was just the girl she desired. Having Ellie in their camp only meant there was another mouth to feed, and she was not worth their resources. Besides, young Cora would feel better knowing her friend was freed. If anything, it would show her that becoming a spy was not wrong; it would push her to be a better Condor.

"Megan, you can't actually listen to her," the unarmed boy said. It was his first words since entering the room.

"Quiet, Mason," Megan snapped. Without consulting her partner, she whipped around to the guards, "Let her go." They obeyed, loosening their tight grip on Ellie, and causing her to stumble a tiny bit.

"Ellie, listen to me. Tell them I'm alright," Emma said, enunciating her words as clearly as possible, as if to emphasize how important this was. She looked at Megan, who was waiting for her to continue, "Tell them not to come after me. Promise me you'll tell them that?"

"No!" Ellie shouted, "No, I'm not leaving you here!"

"Go, Ellie," Emma directed, her voice stern and stable. The younger girl was in tears, but she listened. One of the guards dragged her out of the cell, and they disappeared from Emma's sight. She closed her eyes and sighed, questioning whatever decision she'd just made. She moved her right toes slightly, and felt an uneven bump underneath the sole of her shoe. That was the most comfort she'd felt since arriving in the Condor's camp. Almost two years earlier, her shoes had begun to fall apart, and so she created her favorite contraption, a secret compartment that was just the size of the smaller of her favorite two knives. She knew the first one, which had been secured in her belt, was confiscated upon her capture. This was alright though, since they were unaware she was still in control of a second blade. As long as she kept her weapon, she knew it was a fair fight. She knew that she would survive.

It had now been two weeks since Emma first awoke in the Condor cell, and her condition had changed slightly. She was no longer tied to the pole, for one thing. That was good. Her ankles were unbound as well, but she still lacked full access of her hands. The Emma in that cell though, after a fortnight, appeared to be much weaker than the girl who had arrived. This girl had been tortured: burned and whipped and cut so many times one would think she'd have to have broken. She hardly had the strength to move anymore. Although this may have been the most vulnerable state Emma Gail Harlem had ever experienced, her focus was crystal clear. Her mission, her silence, and her duty to protect her brother and their friends, were the only things she could truly manage to think about. Throughout every grueling, painful hour, her purpose was all that swarmed her mind. She understood fully that her being in the Condor's camp, her refusal to provide accurate information, was keeping them at bay.

The door opened, and in walked Mason alongside two guards. Emma realized by now that there were always guards outside of the cell as well, but it wasn't like like she'd have anywhere to run if she could manage to get out that way. Besides, her presence was keeping them at bay. Her presence was keeping them at bay. Her presence was keeping them at bay. It had become her mantra over the past two weeks; that line was all that kept her sane.

The guards grabbed her weakened body off the ground and hoisted her up against the pole, retying her wrists to the rough wood. This position was nothing new. It was where they could interrogate her, and where she couldn't move to fight back. She closed her eyes and moved her foot slightly, checking to make sure her handy blade was still present in her shoe. It was, and she knew it was, but remembering it was there provided her some strange sense of comfort.

Your presence is keeping them at bay.

"We're going to try this again," Mason said coldly, "How many people are in your camp?" Emma just stared at him, raising an eyebrow slightly enough, as if to ask if he was really going to repeat the same question he'd been asking every day since she first arrived. She had never given them any sort of answer. Mason nodded to one of the guards next to him, and she promptly slapped the prisoner hard along her left cheek. Emma grunted slightly, but turned back to her captors with gritted teeth, the guards handprint having left a red mark along her skin.

"How many people are in your camp?" Mason repeated, hissing into the girl's face. Mason always appeared to be more merciful than Megan. While the girl was just plain heartless, Emma always had an inkling suspicion that Mason only wanted to make his partner proud.

"How does it feel to be your girlfriend's bitch?" Emma muttered. As always, she showed no signs of fear. She knew this little line would only cause her pain, but it would also portray the image that she was unafraid. Soon

Mason was right up against her, his own knife pushing against her throat, threatening to make the final cut to kill.

Your presence is keeping them at bay. Sebastian will live.

"You don't get to say that to me, you slut," he snapped, pressing his blade harder as Emma gulped.

"At least I'm aware of what I am," she said, not breaking her eye contact with her attacker. They stood there for at least a minute before he backed away, and Emma let out a breath she didn't realize she was holding.

"I need the name," Mason demanded.

"I don't know who you're talking about," Emma said. She did know exactly who he meant, but she had developed a story that she was sticking to.

"The shooter," he repeated, "But I know you knew that."

"I told you what I know. It wasn't one of us," the prisoner lied. It was, technically, the truth, since Mai had not yet returned to the camp and was acting as a Rogue. Emma didn't care about that loophole, however. She wasn't afraid of lies. Mason came upon her again, placing his knife on the exposed part of her chest. He drew a deep line of blood, causing her to gasp as the incision was made.

"You and I both know that's not the truth," he said, "We can keep playing this little game for as long as you want, or you can tell us who the murderer in your camp is."

"Don't sound so high and mighty, you're guilty of murder too," was all Emma said back. This was followed by another hard attack from one of the guards, but she didn't seem fazed. She hardly even reacted anymore; it had all become protocol. It was all a routine. She couldn't help but notice just how uncomfortable Mason appeared after that remark. Could it be that he felt guilt? Emma doubted that, instead she predicted that perhaps he'd never taken someone's life directly. If he was truly a killer, she was sure she'd made enough comments that she'd be gone by now.

Your presence is keeping them at bay.

"You really want a killer living around your people? How long before they attack your friends? Your brother?" Mason was seething with anger now, as she had effectively attacked his honor twice now in the span of five minutes. This was the most entertainment Emma could get. How far could she push him before he broke? How could she make his life as miserable as possible? It was a cruel game, no doubt. But she had found herself living in a crueler world than she'd ever believed could exist. Survival came first, always.

"I told you," Emma restated her claim, "They weren't a Raven. I'm sure the woods are just brimming with news about it, too bad you're too busy with me."

"You lying bitch!" Mason screamed, and Emma almost smiled. It seemed that she'd won, she'd broken him first. He began to hit her repeatedly, and she took his shots cleanly. With no defenses, she had no choice but to let this boy beat her.

Another guard handed him a lighter, which he pressed up against her stomach through the rips in her dirty t-shirt. The fire burned her skin, and she let out a scream. No matter how many times they used this punishment, the flame was one thing that could always destroy her tricky arrogance. It was one of the few times it became clear who had the real power, who could toy around with their enemies, who was in control.

As Emma screamed in the dark room in the middle of the night, she pushed to the forefront of her mind an image of Sebastian, and she managed to regain some composure. All of this pain she suffered was in order to protect her brother and the rest of their people. The pain was worth it, the pain was manageable. She could handle it. If it meant her friends could live, she would not break, no matter how much agony she would have to endure. Whether or not her precious mantra was the truth, it was all she had.

Your presence keeps them at bay.

Oh, how she wished it was true.

X. sacrifice and martyrdom

Ellie had returned to the Ravens' camp around midday after being in the Condor's prison for two nights. When Megan agreed to let her go, the little girl ran as fast as she ever had in her life, desperate to make it home before her captors changed their minds. The gate was closed, but Nathan and Corey, the two scouts outside, let her in instantly.

"Thank God you're okay," Nathan smiled, hugging her. At this moment, in his embrace, Ellie began to cry for the first time in two days. She had been so frightened, so tired, and now she was finally back with people who made her feel safe. "We've all been so worried." She was quickly ushered into the Med Hut.

"Someone get Sebastian and Dylan," Serena called as the girl entered. "I'm so glad you're back. Are you alright? Did they hurt you?"

Ellie gulped, looking up at the medic. Those were the exact same questions Emma had asked her when she arrived in the cell. And now Ellie was home and Emma was still there and it was very, very clear that Emma had to stay there and what did Ellie do to deserve it? Was she not the one who trusted someone too quickly, had she not ignored Sebastian, and Dylan, and every other person in the camp, including Emma herself? Why was Emma the one who had to pay for her own naivete?

When the leaders came running into the Med Hut, it was clear that an overwhelming relief had spread over them both, as well as presumably over the rest of the camp, but all Ellie felt was guilt. Both Sebastian and Dylan hugged her and expressed how pleased they were that she was back, and while she didn't doubt it was genuine, she knew exactly what they were both thinking in the back of their minds.

"And Emma?" Sebastian asked quietly, afraid of what he might hear next.

"They have her," Ellie whispered, "She negotiated with them to get me out, but they still have her." The culpability began to wash over her body, causing a small relapse of tears.

"If they still have her, then we can get her out, right?" Dylan said, "That's a good thing. She'll be alright, Sebastian."

"No," Ellie muttered, "We can't do that."

"What are you saying?" Sebastian frowned, eyes having gone cold, and his voice growing curt.

"She made me promise that you guys wouldn't go after her. Her terms were clear. The Condors would be satisfied as long they had her. I'm so sorry, this is all my fault." She was crying now for sure, real tears falling down her cheeks rapidly. Serena hugged the frail child, but it didn't calm her. Sebastian had left the Med Hut, clearly looking for fresh air, desperate to purge his mind of the thoughts that currently plagued it, and Dylan had stormed out after him.

"Put this camp on lockdown!" she screamed, "Nobody leaves these borders!"

"What's going on with him?" Nova asked Dylan as the guards proceeded to shut the gate. It was too late. Sebastian had just run out of the camp, clearly not thinking straight.

"The Condors have Emma," Dylan said, "He's gonna go after her, isn't he." Although she was technically asking her friend a question, it was clear she already knew the answer, or at least she thought she did.

Nova said, "He wouldn't by himself. He'd do anything for her, but even he knows he can't take on our biggest enemy alone." Dylan shook her head, although she agreed to trust her friend and carry out this lockdown. Still, she felt that she was putting her partner in grave danger by allowing him to run off like that. He wasn't in the right frame of mind whatsoever to go after his sister, and she couldn't gauge if he could make the rational decision to leave her.

Nova, however, was the one who proved to be right. Sebastian had no intentions of saving his precious sister just yet. Well, he did, but it would not be that day. He had to get his head cleared first, he had to free himself from the words running rampant in his mind. He jogged for almost an hour, heaving heavily, but whenever he stopped, Emma's face appeared in front of him. He could only imagine her in the cell: tortured, bloody, and broken. This distorted figure of his sister seemed to loom behind every tree, he thought he saw her dark hair hiding behind every shrub.

Eventually, his body gave out and he fell right onto the forest floor. He stayed there, huddled on the ground for almost ten minutes, shutting his eyes, begging the images to go away, but they were even painted underneath his eyelids. It was there that he began to cry. At first it was just the little tears, the raindrops that dripped down his cheeks like glass and glimmered in the afternoon sun. But then he began to shake, and his voice got caught up in his throat and the pretty tears turned to sobs, and soon he was on his knees, cursing at the sky, screaming at whatever god might still be watching them. Had anyone seen him, they'd have thought he'd gone insane. They'd have thought he finally broke.

And so Sebastian Harlem stood in the center of the forest, wailing into the endless void, desperately hoping some other-worldly being would take pity on him for once in his life and save his sister. He screamed and screamed until his voice grew dry and he let his muscles relax. Suddenly, it all seemed so quiet. All that was left was the wind rustling through the leaves, and the ringing in his ears; even the chirping birds must have been frightened by his outburst. He turned around, observing the empty wilderness around him, and his breath began to return. He could see clearly now— he could see he was alone.

Never before had he felt so powerless.

The overwhelming feeling of their incapability to help their friend was beginning to resonate within the members of the camp as well. Everyone was on edge, glaring at whoever they thought could be to blame. They were all mad at someone, although nobody could discern exactly who they felt was responsible. In a way, weren't they all at fault?

There was one girl, however, who knew exactly where to point the finger: herself. Mai had overheard the entire conversation within the Med Hut, and she'd seen the devastated Sebastian fleeing the camp. She knew that the Condors were looking for blood to repay the lives they'd lost the day before, and she knew who was the fool that pulled the trigger. If blood was currency, she knew who deserved to pay. She sighed, staring up at the fence, and tied on her iconic mask. It was time to go.

"What are you doing?" a voice said from behind her. Mai froze, not expecting someone to have seen her. She was in the back corner of the camp, hidden behind one of the cabins. This was the spot she always used when sneaking in and out of the camp; nobody would see her go.

Mai did not turn around, but she recognized that the voice belonged to Hayden. "Making things right," she muttered.

"No, you're really not," Hayden said, shaking his head. Beside him was Yasmin. The two of them had always been close friends. Ever since the first day he arrived at the Ravens, Yasmin was one of the few he felt like he could trust. She was cold when she first met him, as the rest of the camp had been together for almost half a year already. That's why he was drawn to her; she didn't try to lie to him about her intentions. He'd made that mistake one too many times.

At that, she whipped around and glared at him, "And how am I not? I pulled the trigger, you dumbass. They'll take me instead."

"You think they'll stop with you?" Hayden scoffed, "Sorry, but they're in it for the kill. They want to cut us where we're weak, remember? If they get you and Emma in the palm of their hand, you're both gone."

"I was in the Condor's camp for three months," Mai said, "They honor their treaties, they're not going to break the terms of this agreement. If I'm the one they want, they'll just want me."

"Emma's agreement was that nobody would come after her," Yasmin said, "Hayden's right, you can't leave us now." By now a crowd had begun to form around the group, as all of their voices were rising with frustration.

Mai sighed, "What happens if I stay? They send scouts out after me?"

"You'll be here to fight when the scouts inevitably come. All they want is our heads on pikes," Hayden said, "They want us dead. That's why they sent Hannah into our camp in the first place. Like it or not, Mai, but you're one of us, and if you just give yourself up, you're damning the rest of us." This was strange for him to be so assertive. He was typically the smiling boy in the camp, the one who was willing to brighten someone's day. But now he was standing with a fire in his stare and determination pulsing through his veins. He was not about to lose Mai that easily; he wouldn't let the camp be so vulnerable again. This transformation was noticeable to the rest of the camp as well. It was so unusual, in fact, that it stopped others from stepping in. It was like they were testing him, waiting to see just what he could do.

It was at this same moment that Sebastian returned to the camp. The two guards controlling the gate allowed him in, and he stood silently a ways away from the circle. He was watching, analyzing every little thing possible, and nobody in the entire camp noticed—their attention was elsewhere.

"You all aren't incapable, Hayden. You survived six months without me before, you can do it again," Mai muttered.

"We could," Hayden began, "If it was just you we were missing. What do you think is going to happen when you and Emma both are dead?"

That was the line. That was what stopped the world from turning for a mere matter of seconds, and suddenly everything seemed to change. Mai untied her mask and took a step back; the circle began to dissipate, and slowly people were patting Hayden on the back, which felt so foreign to him and he wasn't quite sure what he did right.

"You did good," Yasmin whispered, hugging him, although he was in some sort of trance. Never in his life had he seen his actions change the path for the better. He had never saved someone's immediate life.

Sebastian stepped back, hearing Hayden's last line. Something had unlocked in him, a truth he hadn't realized before, but the other boy was right. What was going to happen when he lost both Mai and Emma? Nothing, that was the answer. He'd have nothing left.

xi. thanatos

I t was almost dawn, yet Megan and Mason were wide awake in the bed they shared. As the Condor leaders, their room was by the far the most decorative in the camp. Megan had insisted that their authority be shown everywhere, even in the interior design of their bedroom. She believed that in order to keep her power, the world must know it belonged to her. If she was kind, or if she appeared weak, then it would be snatched right from her fingertips. Kindness was weakness, she'd learned. It was better to be feared than loved. If her people feared her, they wouldn't threaten her. It was an age old philosophy, dating back to the days of the Renaissance. How ironic that it originated in a time known as the rebirth of beauty. Here she was, following that same principle in the rebirth of the world.

"I've heard their camp is still a mess," Mason said, breaking the silence. He could hear his girlfriend breathing beside him, although neither of them had spoken in hours.

"Good," Megan nodded, "But you haven't gotten her to talk yet, have you?" She hadn't had any success with getting their raven-haired prisoner to cooperate. She was surprised by how resilient the girl was. Based off her reputation, she figured this girl would have complained her way through the ordeal and broken her silence instantly. She assumed she was the type of girl who had never struggled before, the type of person who couldn't handle the pressure. Emma was one of the few people in the forest who had someone that would protect them, yet somehow she had courage on her own. Megan respected that, although it posed quite a challenge to her initial plan of using her for information. They'd have to improvise, but she had an idea.

"She'll never say anything of value," Mason sighed, "She was unconscious when we left her earlier. Her body is getting weaker, she can't bear the pain for as long anymore."

"She'll let herself go unconscious," the girl said, "If she's not awake, she can't feel anything, and she can't risk spilling information that way. It's to her own advantage."

"So what do we do?"

"If we can't use her for a way into their camp, then we'll just have to let them tear themselves apart."

Mason paused, "What are you suggesting?" He had a vague suspicion, but he questioned his girlfriend's rationality there. It seemed like it may be going too far.

"What will they do without their fearless leader?" she asked, almost as though she was talking down to a child, "What will happen when poor Sebby falls?"

"They'll all fall with him," Mason said, "I understand."

Megan smiled in the darkness, "Take your time, have fun with this one. I want her dead by tomorrow morning."

By the time the sun had made a right angle with the ground the following morning, Condor guards were finishing up cleaning out the empty cell.

The ground was still wet with blood, a sign of the warrior who had fallen the night before. Mason was standing near their water supply, scrubbing a scratchy old dish rag to his hands to rid them of their bloodstains. They were red and raw now, as he'd been working there for hours. He had done something bad. Oh yes, something very bad. And what for? She didn't even love him.

xᴉᴉ. kill order

B y five in the afternoon, the party in Rachel Greenesfelt's hut was well underway. The five rascals, as they referred to themselves, had planned to save their stolen alcohol until the evening, but if that officer who stopped by earlier was telling the truth, even Donovan predicted that they couldn't handle Harper's newscast sober.

And sure enough, at 5:30 sharp, the tv in the small living room turned on by itself, and Harper Smith's face appeared on the screen. She was sitting in a small office, with her brother Phoenix and cousin Cameron standing behind her. Her blonde hair was pulled into a tight ponytail, a style she had always worn, except now it seemed like a move for authority. Despite being nineteen years old, Harper had a young face that looked as though she may not have reached high school before the plague. The high ponytail now was a symbol of her power; she was just like the cheerleaders in her old school. Their post-plague world was drastically different than the world before, but they were still a city full of teenagers, and some symbols were universal in the language of the youth.

"Good evening, citizens of our gorgeous city," Harper began her speech.

"Gorgeous?" Natalia scoffed. The five of them were sitting on the couch in their usual formation, draped over one another as if they didn't care about this announcement, although they were all watching intently. "What part of this shitshow is gorgeous?"

Harper, obviously did not respond to the viewers at home, "We've come to you this afternoon with news of one of our lost comrades, our friend Kamai Wells."

With the sound of that name, the entire room went silent. Jacob and Donovan made nervous eye contact and sat up straighter. Kamai had been a member of their group before the coup when the city had not yet fallen to the tyrant Harper. She was one of the six, until she ran away in the night with no warning. It was only a week after the coup when they woke up and she was gone. Jacob had been so angry at her for so long; Donny was comatosed, and Phoenix and Cameron were caught up with Harper and the politics. Kamai was the only person he had left, and then she didn't even bother to say goodbye.

"Kamai was my best friend. After the plague hit, my brother Phoenix and I had been living with our relatives in a town two hours from here. But when we had to flee, we knew nobody. We grew up halfway across the country—the City of the Forgotten was full of strangers."

"Nobody knew anyone here. There's only, like, ten people here that actually grew up in this city before the death wave. She's not special," Marley muttered.

"Marley, stop talking," Donovan snapped. He was anxious to see what the news was on Kamai, as he'd heard practically nothing since he'd woken up from his month long slumber.

"Kamai took me in when I needed her most, she was a friend, a shoulder to cry on. But after the exchange of power last summer, she decided that the city was not where she belonged. We made an agreement that she'd be granted a grace period of one year. If she left the city, she'd have twelve months to decide whether or not to come back, but after that she would lose her place inside our borders."

This interested Jacob, as it was something he had not heard before. There was never any rumor of a confirmed agreement between the two girls. Everyone assumed Kamai just packed up and left, snuck around their security guards or paid them to let her leave that fateful night.

"We have held off for as long as possible, even adding a thirteenth month to our contract. From here on out, we must declare Kamai Wells to be dead. If she returns to our city now, she must be imprisoned, as she no longer belongs to our people. I know this may come as a shock, since she once helped accomplish great things for this community, but she has made her choice clear.

"Our other contacts have been trying to reach her, convince her to return home, but she has chosen to make that place the wild. We may not understand her judgement, as the forests beyond are full of savages, but we guarantee that as of two days ago, she was still alive. Kamai has had the opportunities to rejoin us, but she has made it clear to us that her loyalty does not fall to our great city. We cannot have space for traitors behind these boundaries. Thank you, and goodnight."

The five teens looked to each other in a numbed shock, some of them more affected than others. The girls barely knew Kamai; Marley had spent a few nights with her before the coup, and she was a fairly steady client. Natalia and Rachel, however, had likely never had a conversation with that girl. On the other hand, she had been one of Jacob and Donovan's closest friends, and to hear Harper disown her so quickly was unsettling. Kamai was closer to Harper than they had ever been, yet even she would face imprisonment for coming back. What was in store for the rest of them?

For the parasites, one step outside the borders would turn them into the city's most dangerous enemy.

"She's psycho," Jacob said, "She can't just kick Kam out like that." If Kamai meant this little to Harper now, he was genuinely unsure of who she'd deem more important. Other than Phoenix and Cameron, she had pushed away everyone who ever got close.

"Yes, she can, actually," Natalia muttered, "She's our tyrant. She can do whatever the hell she wants."

"That doesn't mean she can just give up on her morality," Jacob continued, clearly frustrated and upset. He was pacing the living room, brushing his hand through his dark uncombed hair, his pale skin turning pink with anger. "If she can ostracize her best friend for doing nothing, she's no better than the fortified cities that kicked us out!" He was fuming now, kicking the wall in desperation. He knew Harper well—he realized that she did nothing to deserve her power.

"Coby, calm down," Donny muttered, but this didn't stop his friend. Jacob continued to grunt and attack the furniture, which almost offended Rachel, as it was her hut. Donovan sighed and stood up from his seat on the sofa's right arm rest and grabbed his best friend's arm, "Kamai's alive, okay? Isn't that what matters?"

"We don't," Jacob whispered, slowing down slightly.

"What?"

"We don't matter. If Kamai can't even be saved, then what are our chances?" he elaborated, taking a deep breath.

"Good news is we don't need saving," Donovan said, "I've already come close to dying, I don't need to do it again." He wrapped his arms around Jacob, who was trying to so hard to seem composed but undeniable fear and stress was dancing around him like horses on a carousel. The two boys stood there hugging in the center of the room, their three feminine counterparts watching them with interest. Marley was always surprised to see two teenage heterosexual boys who weren't concerned with their fragile masculinity. Ever since the plague, it became more and more acceptable for boys to show emotion; everyone was struggling the same.

"How can you be so calm?" Jacob asked, looking up at his friend.

"Because Kamai found something better. Otherwise, she'd have come back by now," Donny explained.

"God, I wish I knew her story."

Kamai Wells was being followed. He was a Rogue named Jackson, a violent bounty hunter who had no qualms about any sort of job. If it offered a reward, he'd accomplish any task. Even if it meant working for Harper. Kamai didn't fully mind it though. She knew nobody in the Grove Forest. He'd been following her for almost a year now, and the two had somewhat become partners. It would be far more work to survive the forest on her own, and she did enjoy his company. It was odd, she thought, to be working alongside the man who was also providing her enemy with her whereabouts, but she knew Harper wouldn't dare go after her. Besides, she had disowned the City of the Forgotten; it was time they forgot her as well.

She was on a mission one evening. The sun was just beginning to set, causing the gorgeous orange and pink hues to brush above the forest canopy. The sunset was her favorite time of day. It was always so beautiful, and it looked just the same before the disease came and swept up the life she knew. But the sunset stayed the same, so how much could the world have truly changed?

Jackson was at their campsite this one evening, and she was sure he did not enjoy the forest's beauty the way she did. She knew the woods had been exceptionally dangerous as of late, but that did not stop her from chasing the light. She was surprised, however, to see two people approaching her. They carried few materials, suggesting they'd left the rest at their camp, or that they may have not even been Rogues. There were other tribes she'd heard of. Over the past few weeks, they'd been causing too much trouble.

"Hi," one of the people approached her. "My name is Corey, this is Yasmin. We're from the Ravens." The boy speaking was relatively tall, and had long dark hair and one of the palest faces she'd seen. The girl beside him could have easily passed as his younger sister, but Kamai had a suspicion they weren't related.

"The Ravens," she said. This tribe had been the news of the forest lately. It was such a shame, the trials they'd endured, "I'm sorry about your loss. I know it must be hard for your camp."

The boy, Corey, paused, "What loss? Our camp has been on lockdown, we're the first two people to leave in two weeks."

Kamai froze, unsure of how to continue, "So you haven't heard the news? It's all over the woods, everyone has been talking about it. Nobody told you?"

Yasmin said, "What haven't we been told?"

"That girl with the Condors? I can't remember her name, but they killed her last night. I'm sorry," Kamai revealed. Corey and Yasmin stood in a stunned silence, not expecting this sort of reveal. The banished Rogue left the duo, returning to her own camp.

"What now?" Yasmin asked, her voice merely a whisper as the shock of the death of her friend began to sink in.

"We tell the camp," Corey sighed grimly, "And we hope Sebastian doesn't lose it."

xïïi. out, damn'd spot

Trigger Warning: Deals with the death of a close family member

It was almost dark by the time Corey and Yasmin returned to the camp. They'd tried to move as quickly as possible, but at the same time were dreading having to break the news. Neither of them had been too close with Emma—she and Corey had always been rivals, but even then she was his competition. Her excellence pushed him. They may not have been friends, but he owed at least some of his new-world self to that girl. She was always there, always daring him to be better, and now she was gone. He didn't know whether or not to believe the Rogue; he half expected to see her sneaking back into camp the moment he and Yasmin returned. He couldn't wrap his shaking mind around the prospect that she might not come home.

But when they did make it back, Corey didn't see any signs that the girl had returned. There was something about her that left a mark wherever she went. He could always tell just where Emma had been, and he could tell her spark had not recently entered the camp. His heart rate began to pick up as the enormity of the Rogue's message began to sink in.

"You're back!" Dylan exclaimed, running across the center to meet them, "What's the report? Any news?"

"Where's Sebastian?" Yasmin asked, her voice flat and serious. Dylan examined the messenger and the scouts' faces, and her own expression dropped. She could tell there was something grave happening.

"Yaz!" Mai came running up behind the group, but paused as she realized that something was off. The two girls hugged, and Corey noticed that a tear dripped out of Yasmin's left eye.

"Corey, come with me," Dylan said, leading the Messenger out of the center and up to Sebastian's cabin. She knocked on his door, and they were greeted by him wearing a dirty t-shirt that once looked gray and a pair of ripped jeans. His hair was unbrushed, and it looked like he hadn't slept in days, which was likely the case. Every time he closed his eyes he still saw gruesome images of his sister in their enemy's camp. If he stopped moving or working for one moment, his incessant fear of losing her would begin to sneak back in. Over the past two weeks, he'd been working constantly. He patrolled every night, and when he wasn't on duty he was sharpening blades, assisting Serena in the Med Hut, or searching for some other way to distract himself.

One look at Corey and his heart sank, "How bad is it?" The rest of their exchange needed no words. The messenger just gave a hesitant nod and turned his eyes to the ground, and Sebastian's entire disposition changed. His face dropped, and he longer just appeared stressed. No, now he was filled with fear and anger and confusion and this feeling that his heart was ripped out of his chest and shattered like broken glass and now it was laying on the ground in front of him for all the world to see. He took a step back, almost as though he couldn't see the people in his room, or maybe even any of the room around him.

"Sebastian," Dylan said, her own stomach dropping with the news. Emma was one of her good friends, and part of her always expected the girl to survive this trial. The pain in her chest dared her to vomit, and she just wanted to scream, but was trying her hardest to maintain a calm appearance, "Seb, I'm so sorry."

"Just go away," he muttered, his head spinning. He could hardly see straight, let alone think clearly. He really just needed to be alone, and Dylan and Corey respected that. Once he was by himself in the small room, Sebastian truly lost it. While some might say he broke in the forest the day he'd heard of his sister's predicament, he now seemed like a different person entirely. He was screaming, kicking the walls and punching the furniture as he paced. It was the same sensory overload he'd been attempting for two weeks, but this time the energy was sucked straight out of him. He ended up in the middle of the empty room, just shaking and crying and screaming until he collapsed to the floor, held down by the weight of everything, yet through the pain, he realized he felt absolutely nothing at all.

Outside, the remaining members of the camp saw an upset Dylan and Corey walk away from Sebastian's cabin, and a following cacophony of screams.

Mai whipped around to Yasmin, "What's going on? I know you know what's happening."

Hayden, who had been standing nearby alongside Serena said, "Tell us everything is alright. Please."

Yasmin sighed, looking up at Sebastian's room, "I don't know if it's my place to tell you all."

"What are you talking about?" Mai said, "If something's wrong, you have to tell us."

Yasmin shook her head, "Everything's wrong."

Serena hesitated, feeling as though she knew exactly what had happened, but if she dared speak the words, they might become true, "Is Emma...."

"Gone," Dylan finished, coming up behind them. There were fresh tears in her eyes, but she was determined now to step up and fill Sebastian's shoes since he was clearly in no position currently to lead. "She's gone."

The camp was left in a stunned silence, as nobody was sure what to say or what to believe. It just didn't seem right that a girl who fought as hard as Emma could be taken over so easily. In a way, they'd all expected her to be immortal.

At the sound of a door opening, the heads of the entire camp whipped towards the figure standing in the dim candlelight. It was Sebastian, his eyes and cheeks still wet with tears. In his left hand he held the jacket that he had worn every day since being chosen as the Ravens' official leader. Since the very beginning, it was agreed upon that there would always be two in charge: one girl and one boy. At first it was him and Mai, and then Mai's jacket was passed to Dylan.

"Hayden!" Sebastian called. The boy looked up, concerned, but before he could say another word, the jacket fell into his hands. "Take it, it's yours."

Hayden looked down at the garment in his arms and shook his head, "Seb... Seb, I can't. This isn't your fault."

"Everything has been my fault. I can't kill another person," was the only thing he muttered. All he felt now was this deep regret, a pulsing guilt threatening to consume him. But this shame, although he didn't realize it, was only to cover the sadness and vulnerability manifesting in his chest. It was easier to blame himself than to admit there was nothing he could do to save his sister. It was easier to antagonize himself than to admit his weakness.

As the camp stared at Hayden and the symbolic jacket, Sebastian turned around and walked towards a rock in the back of the camp, kicking stones as he went. Failure. The word pranced around his head, teasing and taunting him for all of his mistakes. Failure. If not that, then what was he? When he was finally alone, he broke down in tears once again. He couldn't stop them; it was as though everything was falling on him now. All the stress and pain that he'd suppressed over the past two years was finally surfacing. This was the most exposed he had ever been, and what did he have to make him keep going? He bore all the responsibility for two years to keep his sister safe, and where did it get her?

"Sebastian," a voice said, coming up behind him. It was Mai, her own eyes glistening with tears. Her black bandana was hanging out of her back pocket, but she wasn't holding onto it anymore. No, she knew where she was needed. She knew where she belonged, at least for now. Mai paused when she saw her friend's shaking silhouette. She had never seen him like this. "I'm so sorry. I understand if you want me to leave."

Sebastian did not turn to look up at the girl. His eyes stayed focused on the ground, his head supported by his cold hands. "I've failed everyone."

"No, no Seb, you didn't," Mai sighed, sitting down beside him. She put her hand on his upper back supportively, but he didn't seem to notice.

"I made one bad call in battle, and suddenly twenty of our people were killed, and that almost included you. I let Hayden go out hunting by himself, and he got mauled by a panther and will never walk properly again. We don't even have panthers in this part of the woods! Ellie got kidnapped just the other day because I let that spy into our camp. And then I couldn't stop my sister from going after her. Now Emma's gone, and all this blood is on my hands, Mai. These were all my calls, and look where it got us," Sebastian snapped. It was the most he'd said since Corey broke the news.

This was also the first time he'd ever admitted to the mistakes he'd made, the first time he let the pain from the past two years loose.

"It's alright. I know how you feel, I've been there. During the plague, my father died because I couldn't save him on time. My sister got sick right before I left for the forest, and I left her behind. Those twenty people that died in that battle? That was on my watch too, I was your co-leader, remember? I know it seems like everything is a disaster right now, but look around at how many people we saved. How many people you saved. Yes, you've made mistakes, but you brought us this far, Sebastian. You'll get through this, and I'll be right by your side the whole time," Mai promised, "I'm not leaving again."

"Mai," Sebastian turned around, finally looking up at her, "You and I screwed up here. Sure, we saved some people, but how many have died because of our poor judgement? How many more are going to die? I can't do it anymore. I can't kill another person I love."

"Do you remember what happened two weeks into this whole ordeal, right at the very beginning?" Mai asked, "The Condors felt threatened, so they attacked and two of our people died. I stayed up the whole night crying, but you were right there with me saying 'Mai, look, we may have lost two, but we saved sixteen. This is going to be hard, but we're going to get through it. Day by day, Mai. Day by day.' It was the same show every time we lost someone, and you were always there to help me through it. Well now I'm going to do the same for you. We may have lost Emma, but she negotiated Ellie to safety. She negotiated terms to save all of us. We lost one, but we've saved the other thirty-nine."

Sebastian shook his head. "Well maybe I lied. Saving sixteen wasn't good enough during that first battle. Two kids still got buried. And every grave we've dug since has been on my hands." In the back of his mind, he could hear his sister's voice. He heard her whisper this quote in the back of his mind, and he muttered it along in perfect unison, "Will all great Neptune's ocean wash this blood clean from my hand?" Their parents once loved Shakespeare. How many times had he thought about Macbeth over the past two years? They were so similar, were they not? They could never wipe away the bloodstains.

"You have to stop blaming yourself. I'm responsible for just as much blood as you are, and yet we have proof of how many people we saved," Mai pointed to a dark dot in the middle of her palm, "I took a poison dart for Nova in that first battle. And look," she gestured to a different scar on Sebastian's left forearm, "You jumped in front of a dagger to save Corey's life."

"She's all I had left, Mai!" the boy screamed. He then began to whimper again, as the tears came back, "She was all I had left, and now she's gone. Emma is gone."

"I know, I'm so sorry," Mai whispered. It broke her heart to see her typically resilient partner in such a defeated state. He was always the rock in their relationship, he was her rock. And now all she knew how to do was repeat his own words back to him.

"Hayden's a smart kid. He was right about Hannah the moment she'd entered the camp. If I'd just listened to him, then all of this could have been prevented, and my sister could still be alive," Sebastian sat up, and then turned to his friend, throwing in one last punch, "But you wouldn't have known that, Mai. You weren't here."

"You're goddamn right I wasn't here," Mai frowned, taking her hands off of him, "After being tortured in the Condor's prison for three months, never giving up a single piece of information, I was too afraid to come back here. I'd have just drawn them to the camp earlier than I already have. I went through hell this past year, all to protect you and the other Ravens. Don't you dare accuse me of not caring about this camp."

Sebastian looked up at her, eyes still and unmoving, his heart aching. All he had left to say was, "Hayden and Dylan would do a better job than either of us ever could anyways." The two sat there in silence for the next few minutes, both of them hurting, but subconsciously relying on each other's presence.

"Am I interrupting something?" Dylan asked, walking up behind them. She was concerned about Sebastian, especially his decision to abdicate from his position. As Mai had walked off right after Hayden received the jacket, she missed the resulting confusion. Nobody was quite sure what to do.

"No, you're not," Sebastian said curtly. He wasn't truly in the mood to talk to either girl, if he was being honest. As Dylan took a seat to his left, Mai nodded and got the message to leave. She walked up to her room, desperate to be alone. She was hurt by how Sebastian had closed her off; she wanted to be the one he'd listen to, and she despised the idea of Dylan making him feel better than she had.

"You gave Hayden your jacket?" Dylan asked, trying to sound composed. She too was extremely shaken by Emma's demise, but she was trying to hide it. She knew that whatever pain she was going through was felt ten times worse by the girl's older brother.

"He deserves it," Sebastian muttered. He then paused before adding, "If you're just going to tell me it's not my fault, I don't want to hear it."

"Then what do you want to hear?" Dylan sighed.

The boy paused, closing his eyes for a moment, "That she's alive. That this is all some twisted dream and I'm going to wake up tomorrow morning and she'll be back in the center, drawing attention to herself as always. But that isn't going to happen."

Dylan smiled softly, "That's what we all want, I'm afraid."

"It's impossible. So now I need to be a leader for once in my life and give the position to someone who isn't going to destroy everything," Sebastian nodded. It was clear that through all the messy tears and guilt, there was more anger building up inside of him. "Everything I do ends up with someone getting killed. I trust you, though, and I trust Hayden, more than I could ever trust myself." There was nothing else to say, as it became clear that nothing Dylan or anyone else could say would change his mind. He was steadfast and stubborn that way, just like his precious little sister.

"Sebastian—" Hayden said, approaching him as he walked back into the center.

"Don't make the same mistakes I did," Sebastian said coldly, and walked right out of the camp. With the hectic events of the night, nobody had been guarding the gate. He looked up at the night sky and felt the weight of the galaxies falling down on him. How could he feel so much, yet be so impossibly small? He stared at all the stars in the clear night sky, and a dark truth came upon him. No other beings in that entire infinite universe would ever know about him, Mai, the Ravens, or Emma Gail Harlem. They all meant so little, even Emma meant so little. So what was the point of even trying anymore?

Meanwhile at camp, the remaining Ravens were turning towards Hayden and Dylan, looking to them for some sign of comfort or an explanation.

"So what do we do now?" Serena sighed, turning to the boy she'd healed just weeks before.

Hayden sighed, looking back down at the garment he refused to put on. It made him feel like a fraud; who was he to be a leader? But he felt the eyes of the camp on him, and realized he was forced into a position he didn't deserve. "We keep breathing." There was nothing else to do.

xiv. flight of the nightingale

A /N

Since a lot of people started school today, I thought I'd update!

WARNING: This is the most gory chapter so far. There are detailed descriptions of blood. If this makes you uncomfortable, but would still like a recap, please let me know. Do not read if it makes you uncomfortable.

When Mason entered Emma's cell that fatal morning, he was met with three other guards in the midst of a torture session. Although he and Megan were technically in charge, of the prisoners, there were other guards who shared the responsibility of forcing information out of the most disobedient hostages. He saw a black belt in the hands of one their hands, and a glaring prisoner.

"Clear out," Mason instructed, and the guards stepped back. He now had a clear view of Emma: she was tied to the pole at her waist, and her wrists were tied above her head. He could see from the paleness of her hands that they were losing circulation, but if Emma noticed, she didn't provide any sign. "Are you alright?" Mason asked, untying her waist. In response, she spat at him, which of course included blood. He shut his eyes and frowned; could he really blame her for actions? If anything, it was to his own advantage. Her disrespect might make it easier for him to take her life.

Emma noticed that this was the first time any Condor had entered the cell without backup. Mason was alone, and so she understood perfectly well what was about to happen, "You're here to kill me, aren't you?" Mason sighed, fingers brushing the top of his knife. It was Emma's knife, actually, confiscated upon her capture. He figured that would be the most poetic way to carry out this task, to kill her with her own blade. At the same time, he couldn't look her in the eyes and admit the truth of what he had been assigned to do. "You don't have to."

"You're right," Mason nodded, "I wouldn't have to if you would provide us with any information."

"Too bad, you'll just have to become a murderer," Emma said. She then added, "That is, unless I can provide you with something else."

"All I need is your information, or your life. Either will benefit us, your choice as to which helps you most," Mason said.

"Untie me," Emma directed. When she saw Mason snicker at her absurd direction, she continued, "It's not like I could attack you." It was true, the girl had somehow managed to appear even weaker than when he'd last seen her. He was surprised she had this much force in her voice even, he'd have expected her to barely be able to speak.

Mason sighed and listened to the prisoner. Killing her in such a vulnerable position seemed a little too cruel. If she was able to move herself, theoretically run from his blade, and he conquered her, then it wouldn't have all been his fault, right? The second Emma's arms came down, he found one clinging onto his shirt, drawing him closer to her. Before he could even react, his lips were on hers and the two were connected. At first he was surprised, but he found himself kissing her back, passionately. For Emma, she had never kissed a boy so hard in her life. It was the first time she was kissing for her life. She felt him reach down to lift up her shirt, and she allowed him to see the battered body underneath.

"You don't want to kill me, Mason," Emma whispered into, lightly biting his lip in the midst of their kisses, "You don't want to become a murderer."

It was then that the boy broke away from their embrace, shaking his head. "We shouldn't have done that."

Emma frowned, "But your girlfriend does all the time. You should ask her." At that, Mason turned away. He knew of Emma's old connection with Megan, and he had a vague suspicion that what Emma alluded to was true. At the same time, Emma took a single glance at her arms, freed for the first time since she arrived in the cell. She gasped when she examined her left forearm. Carved into it was the number 37. The blood there was dried, and what was left was a deep scar she realized would likely never fade completely.

"I'm sorry," Mason sighed, looking at the weak girl across from him. Seeing her reaction to the truth of what her body had become was agonizing. It forced him to see exactly what he had done wrong, and it caused a sharp guilt to stab his heart.

"You branded me," Emma muttered bitterly, eyes fixated on the number etched into her body, "Like I'm an animal." Ever since she came to the forest, her body was under her command. It was her weapon, her key to all the secrets of the forest. But now the evidence of the Condor's surmount would live upon her skin.

"It's protocol," Mason responded. He stared at Emma's body for a moment, as she still had not put her shirt back on. He wasn't quite sure what to think. He could see this headstrong girl's heart breaking, the confusion and shock dancing in her eyes. All he knew for sure was that he had created this beaten and broken girl before him, and now was his one chance to do the right thing. "What do I have to do?"

Emma had been on the run for two days when she found herself climbing up a tree to avoid being spotted by two incoming Rogues. She knew that she couldn't return to the Ravens just yet, no, it was far too soon. News in this forest spread quickly, and she realized that her entrance would have to be as inconspicuous as possible. Ultimately, that meant her friends couldn't find out that she'd survived until the entire forest had forgotten about her. Until then, she was going rogue.

"You heard about that Raven chick, right?" one of the Rogues said to the other, "They didn't find her body."

"Yeah, they probably burned it," said the other, "Do you have any idea how much blood was in that cell? I heard it was insane, and she was tiny. No way she survived."

"But imagine if one of us found her," the first smirked, "They'd pay us good money if we brought that scoundrel back. Besides, I've heard she'll spread her legs to anyone who asks. It would be perfect." The second boy smiled and nodded. The rest of their exchange was inaudible to Emma, as all she could hear was her racing heartbeat pounding in her ears. The boys then proceeded to set up a campsite, and she realized how dangerous her current predicament had become. There was no way for her to escape the tree without being noticed, and they were clearly after her. She had one remaining option, and it would have to be executed perfectly. Luckily, Emma was the sort of girl whose focus improved under high-stake circumstances. She pulled out her first knife, the one that had been kept hidden in her sneaker throughout her stay at the Condors, and promptly threw it into the back of the neck of one of the Rogues, killing him instantly.

She covered her mouth as she saw him fall, and reality began to set back in. She'd just killed a man, but then again, he'd have tried to kill her. Was murder not justified when it was to save yourself? And after all she'd been through, did she not deserve to save herself now?

"Who's there?" the other Rogue's head shot up, fear resonating in his eyes. Emma took a deep breath and jumped out from the tree. The second blade, the one Mason had stolen but ultimately returned to its rightful owner, was gripped in her dominant hand. She realized that most likely, neither of the Rogues would have recognized her face as the Condor's ex-captive, but there were still an abundance of cuts along her exposed skin, giving her away. And if they were to see the number carved into her arm... that made Emma angrier than anything else. How easily they'd degraded her, claimed her as one of their own. She was disgusted.

The Rogue was the first to attack, quickly pinning Emma onto the ground, since she was small to begin with, and had not yet regained all of her strength. He recognized her, though, and leaned in to kiss her. This was the worst part of her reputation, she'd come to realize. People thought they could take advantage of her; they didn't seem to understand that her use of her body meant that she was the one taking advantage of someone else's desire to feel. That it was her power, that it put her in control. When the Rogue leaned down onto her, she managed to whip out her second knife and slice his throat, his blood squirting out like fireworks. Emma gulped and pushed his body off of her, and, examining their now abandoned campsite, stole a red bandana that had once belonged to one of the boys. Tying it around her face to hide her identity, she ran.

One sudden idea came to Emma about two hours later. She hadn't yet had a chance to really think about what she was going to do, but she remembered that there was one person who might help her. There was one Rogue who lived alone in a stable cabin one mile from the Ravens' camp. It was closer to home than she'd like to be, but Lily Wilder was one of the few people in the forest who had helped Emma because she wanted to, not because sex was involved. Lily would likely be Emma's best bet at survival. Besides, Emma Gail Harlem was a messenger, and oh, did she have a message to send.

Emma arrived at Lily's cabin the following morning, and knocked on the door hesitantly. She prayed that Lily was the only one home, as she was certain there was no other person in the forest she could trust with the secret of her survival.

"Hi!" Lily opened the door, smiling. Lily was one of the few remaining people in this forest who always appeared to be happy. She still managed to find light in all the darkness of the world before them, and Emma admired that greatly. "Can I help you?"

Emma untied the red bandana, revealing her face, "Are you alone?"

Lily stared at her in shock for a second before embracing her in a tight hug and ushering her into her home, "I thought you were dead! How did you get out?"

"It doesn't matter," Emma frowned. She didn't want to think about the two boys she'd killed the previous day. Besides, Lily wouldn't have respected murder or seduction, both of which were techniques she'd used. "I need your help. Can I stay here for a little bit?"

"Of course!" Lily said, "Honestly, it's been so lonely here lately. Mai was with me for the longest time, but she's back at your camp now. You knew that, right? That she's back?"

The other girl laughed, "Mai was here? And you hid her for that long? You're really good." She had been around Lily's cabin multiple times since Mai first disappeared, and never had she suspected her friend to be hiding in that very building. When Lily first mentioned Mai, Emma was almost surprised. She had practically forgotten about the girl's sudden return. She had fled their camp in the midst of the resulting chaos, so she wasn't used to the idea of Mai being a member of the Ravens again.

"Thanks! I'm more than happy to take you in, and I'll fill you in on all the news with the Ravens," Lily promised.

"You're a lifesaver, Lily," Emma sighed, taking a relaxed breath for the first time in week, "Could you do me a favor?"

"What do you need?" Lily asked, pouring Emma a glass of water, "Drink. You need it."

"Could you get a message to my camp? For their leaders only?"

"Easily. What do you want me to tell them?" Lily pulled out a piece of paper and a pencil. Emma was always confused by how Lily had that many practical resources. Her cabin was the only spot in the whole forest that actually resembled the sort of home they'd all grown up in. But that was a question for another day; Emma was first intent on sending this message to her people.

"The nightingale awaits."

xv. blood, lies, and tyranny

Cameron Dawson was in the in-between, as he liked to call it. His position in his city's political affairs was on a pedestal, but when it came to the truth, he wasn't quite sure he mattered. He was Harper and Phoenix's cousin. He was connected to the two of them by blood, a bond that he could never break. When the plague hit his cousins' town in California, they moved in with him and his family. He was there when the disease took his uncle, and they supported him through the news of his deadbeat dad's death. Only their mothers were left alive, but they instructed the trio to run to the woods. They promised that it would be safer, that they'd avoid the sickness altogether. As far as Cameron was aware, that was the last any of them had heard from the sisters who gave them life.

At least, that was what he thought. One afternoon, he went off of his typical trail, and decided to visit the corridor where the Team of Six first met. It was all for the nostalgic value, of course. It made him a little bit sad to walk down that cold white hallway. It was now just an empty corner on the middle floor of an apartment building in Fidelus. He and Phoenix had shared the room on the left, across the hall resided Jacob and Donovan, and between them lived Harper and Kamai. They were put together so perfectly back then; they thought their friendship was fate.

He overheard a small voice in that hallway, however, and decided to approach it. As he got closer, he recognized the distinguishing tang in the girl's tone, and based off the door from which it came, he knew exactly who was speaking. It was Harper, sitting on the floor of her old dormitory. There was a second voice there too, one that Cameron couldn't instantly place. He could tell it was a woman, a real grown up woman. This puzzled him, as the oldest person in the City of the Forgotten was only 22 years old. He put his ear to the door, trying to make sense of this conversation, and he realized they were speaking over a video call. Cameron didn't fully understand how this city managed to maintain their technology. The devices all worked when they arrived, and somehow they hadn't stopped.

"I'm not sure what else you want us to do," he heard Harper say, "We told them that we'd kill my best friend. Was that not enough?"

The woman on the other line sighed, "Did they react? Has this left any mark on your people?"

"I don't know," Harper said, "I don't want to hurt Kamai."

"Harper, darling, listen to me. You must keep your people inside the boundaries, or else we cannot track them. This is the world's greatest social experiment, remember? We need to work together to learn, sweet child. You and I could discover something amazing about the human race, wouldn't that be great?"

"I'm not the one discovering," Harper murmured, "That's all you. I'm just condemning my people to this fate at your hands."

The woman responded, "Yes, but in return we finance your city. We pay for your water, your supplies, your technology. If you refuse to help us, then you lose everything. Is that so hard to understand? You are saving your people, Harper."

"I get it, mom," Harper said softly. At that, Cameron took a step back, shock and confusion manifesting inside of him. Harper was speaking to her mother, his Aunt Jeanette. The details of their conversation confused him, and while he longed for clarification there, what he mainly wanted to know were the details of his aunt's survival. The next immediate question was there as well: what had become of his own mother?

However, he did not get the answers he desired. Within the next minute, Harper and his aunt hung up on their conversation, and he realized that if he stayed in his current position, he'd soon be discovered. So he ran. Although unsure of what his next objective should be, his feet seemed to have an idea. He found himself in front of the office he shared with his cousins.

When Cameron barged into the room, Phoenix's head shot up. The moment he entered, the room seemed to get significantly cooler. He was clearly confused, and a look of betrayal resided in his eyes.

"Your mom's alive," Cameron said, breathing heavily, "Did you know that?"

Phoenix's face dropped, realizing exactly what his cousin had somehow discovered. He'd kept this secret from him for over a year now—Harper insisted it was best if the information stayed within the family. He'd pointed out that Cameron was family, but apparently everyone outside the nuclear bloodline was off limits. Phoenix had to admit, he was surprised that his sister had trusted even him with this valuable news.

"How long have you known?" Cameron asked, understanding that this was nothing new for his cousin. To be completely honest, he didn't want to know the answer. He didn't want to acknowledge the secrets being kept from him. He was in some strange predicament now: Harper and Phoenix were the only two people he had left, but did they even count? If it turned out that they were hiding from him the survival of their other relatives, did he really have anyone at all?

"That doesn't matter," Phoenix muttered, "I'm sorry. We should have told you."

"You think?" Cameron snapped. His face was serious now, as he was about to ask the question he feared most. "And my mom?"

Phoenix sighed, "I have no idea. Harper and our mother have the most communication, I haven't been allowed to talk to her once since the coup. I barely know anything. I'm sorry, Cam, really."

Cameron took a deep breath and sat down in the ratty black swivel chair at the desk that was technically his. Phoenix's answer was better than it could have been. He could have told him she was dead. But his vagueness, his apparent oblivity, striked Cameron as odd. He couldn't imagine what system was in place that would somehow allow for a daughter to speak to her mother, yet ban the son.

"Can I ask how you found out?" Phoenix asked after an uncomfortable minute of silence. He hated this tension between him and his cousin. Like Cameron, ever since the coup he'd been separated from the boys he was once friends with. Harper made it exceedingly clear that Coby and Donny couldn't be trusted anymore. Coby had even changed his name, obviously trying to dissociate himself from any remaining ties to the Team of Six. Cameron was truly his only friend over the past year, so this uneasiness in their atmosphere felt foreign and wrong.

"I overheard Harper," Cameron began, "They were on a video call, talking about Kamai. It sounded like your mom had something to do with it. Almost like she was behind it or something." As he spoke, he began to realize for the first time the severity of what he'd heard. His dear Aunt Jeanette was involved in Kamai's death sentence. She had referred to the city as the world's greatest social experiment.

"That's cause she was behind it," Phoenix sighed, "She's been behind this whole damn city. Harper didn't want to tell you."

The other boy shook his head, running his hand through his hair. It was an old habit, one that always came out when he was under stress, "Why didn't you tell me, Phoenix?"

His cousin looked down, "I don't know." He hated keeping these secrets from his cousin, and he realized now that Cameron deserved to know the truth. If they were both supposed to stand behind Harper, they both had to know everything. "But there's more I should have told you. Kamai is in that forest, and my mom wants our city to take it over. It'll be all the remaining teen survivors under one government. They'll study us, watch how we interact, examine our different cultures. I don't even know if we have different cultures yet, it's only been two years, but they've been living in some the wild for awhile now."

"Who is your mom to declare this?" Cameron scoffed, gaping at this new information, "She was a pediatrician, not a sociologist." His Aunt Jeanette had always been a little bit extreme, so this didn't seem unrealistic. Harper had to inherit her ambition from someone.

"I don't really get it. All I know is they're going to pit us all against each other. As far as I'm aware, the three of us are the only ones legitimately safe," Phoenix frowned. "I don't support it, but I don't have a say. And you can't tell anyone about this or else you're risking your own safety."

Cameron shook his head, "So what becomes of everyone else? They're your mother's lab rats? I won't let her put my friends in danger with any of those Rogue people." As having been a member of the core trio, he did know some vague information about the Grove Forest. He knew that they were mainly composed of small, decentralized groups that always seemed to be fighting or killing one another. The idea of the City of the Forgotten trying to overcome these people seemed ridiculous. The people in that forest would only ever want freedom, and Harper would only ever crack down on those who were different than her citizens. It would lead to blood, violence, and death. They'd already escaped the plague—now was not the time to throw their lives away.

Phoenix sighed, clearly understanding that gears were turning in his cousin's mind, "What are you going to do?"

"Get Kamai out of that forest," he declared, leaving the room. Phoenix did not try to stop him. If he was being honest, that idea seemed like the best option. He worried, however, that Cameron could face the same fate as their friend. But Harper wouldn't kill her own blood, right? They were family. Did that count for nothing?

When Cameron knocked on the door in Paricida, he was met by an angry looking girl in a red sports bra and black leggings. Her dark hair was tied up in a high ponytail, and she stood in just the position where he couldn't see into the room. Cameron had spent very little time in this part of the city, and was surprised to see how dirty it was compared to everything else. At the same time, it seemed more lively than his streets in Fidelus. There, they were forced to grow up. In Paricida, it seemed that the kids were still wild and reckless.

"Are you Rachel?" Cameron asked the girl, as that was the name listed for this address. He'd seen enough records to know where his old friends had been spending their time lately.

"No, but I live here," she shook her head, "Can I help you, your highness?" She clearly recognized him from all the newscasts, but she seemed more hostile than admirative.

"Are Coby and Donny here?" he asked, immediately regretting saying the former boy's old nickname, "Jacob, I mean. Jacob and Donovan."

"Not sure they'll want to see you, but I'll ask," the girl said. At that, Cameron heard some footsteps approaching her behind the door.

"It's fine, Natalia," one of the boys said. The girl, Natalia, stepped away, and was quickly replaced by the two boys.

"For what do we owe this pleasure?" Jacob smirked, pronouncing each word in a proper and sarcastic manner. It was obvious that both boys felt some resentment towards the one who once completed their trio. Not to mention he had just appeared in a newscast that revealed a death sentence for one of their closest friends. Cameron and his cousins were by no means on the best terms with the other two boys.

"I need to talk to you guys," Cameron said, cutting straight to the point. "It's about Kamai, she's in trouble."

"Shocker," Donny muttered, "It's not like you broadcasted that she'd be killed if she ever came back here."

"There's a bigger threat now," he said, "And you two can help me save her." All three boys looked to each other, and the stoic eye contact that had once served for all communication was back. Jacob and Donovan were far from trusting Cameron once again, but they knew that he was loyal to Kamai. If she was truly in danger, the boys in Paricida realized that the privileged cousin would risk everything to help her. It was simple: the Riot Boys, as they'd once referred to themselves, were back in business.

XVI. gail

L ily lived up to her promise. Within thirty minutes of leaving her cabin, she arrived outside the Ravens' camp. Although she had connections to a few of their members, she had never actually been to their camp before. Her special hut was strangely the most modern spot in the forest, and she had her boyfriend to thank in part for that. He was known to carry out an assortment of odd jobs for unknown sponsors. He hated talking about who his employers were, and Lily figured it was better not to ask. He generally never came over bloody, which meant he wasn't hired as a hitman.

"Who's there?" One of the guards called as she approached the gates. It was Yasmin on duty that day, her dark hair french-braided into two tight plaits reaching her upper back. "State your name and purpose."

"I have a message for your leaders, then I'll leave," Lily smiled. Like everyone else in this forest, giving away her name scared her.

Yasmin nodded, "Hand over your weapon." The Rogue nodded and handed her her dagger. Lily had barely armed herself for this mission; this was the part of the forest where she lived, and so she was well-known among the Rogues. She was more worried about the Ravens than the lone rangers. Yasmin opened up the gate, and Lily entered the camp for the first time.

"Lily!" Mai screamed, running across the camp. As Lily had protected her for months before she returned to the Ravens' camp, the two girls had an inseparable bond. They had known each other since long before the plague, however. They had gone to school together since second grade, when Lily moved to their small town. They had not travelled to the Grove together, but they were beyond pleased to find each other again in the woods. "What are you doing here?"

"I have a message, leaders only," Lily explained. She then leaned in and whispered, "So do I finally get to meet Sebastian?" Over the time spent hiding in Lily's cabin, Mai had told her plenty of stories of the boy whom she was so close with in the camp. She had built him up to be a hero of some sorts. She had always admired his tranquility and heart, but after being separated from her friends for months, her stories of him quickly became glorified.

Mai hesitated, however, after this request, "Some stuff has happened lately, I'm sure you've heard about Emma, right?" Lily nodded, as suspected. It made her feel strange keeping the secret of the other girl's survival. She could see how this saddened Mai's eyes, and she hated hurting her that way. "Well Sebastian stepped down from his position. He's a wreck, understandably."

Lily's eyes widened, "I'm so sorry. I can't imagine how hard this has all been on your camp." Again, that guilt of keeping Emma's status hidden felt awful. "So who's in charge now?"

"Hayden and Dylan," Mai said, and at the same time the two leaders came over. Hayden was still getting used to wearing Sebastian's jacket. It didn't fit him right. He was tall and lean, while his predecessor had a far more athletic build. He thought that the uncomfortable size of the garment was a metaphor for how this position was too big for him. By no means did Hayden consider himself qualified to protect this many people.

"Hey, what's going on? You have a message?" Hayden asked, trying to maintain the image that he was in charge and had any idea what he was doing.

"Yeah, leaders only. Sorry, Mai. Those were my instructions," Lily explained, handing them the paper.

"Who's it from?" Dylan interjected, as Hayden unfolded that sheet.

"How'd you get paper?" Hayden asked, confused by where the resource had come from. Nobody heard this question though, or if they did, they didn't acknowledge him in the slightest.

"All I can tell you is what's on that sheet. They said you'll understand it though," Lily smiled. With that, she hugged Mai goodbye and left the camp to return home. At this time, Mai walked away as well, respecting that, despite her curiosity, this note was not meant for her. It bothered her, however, that Lily was one of her closest friends, yet Dylan got this piece of information instead of her. The two of them had no relationship, and though Mai realized that the other girl was their leader, and that Lily did not decide who would receive this message, she couldn't help but feel a tang of jealousy.

"'The nightingale awaits,'" Hayden muttered, reading aloud the sheet, "Does this mean anything to you?"

"Well it's a code," Dylan explained, "The nightingale is obviously supposed to mean something."

"Obviously, it's not like a bird told that Rogue to tell us this," Hayden rolled his eyes.

Dylan sighed, "It's a metaphor. My guess is that the nightingale is our enemy. Ravens and nightingales, both are small, black birds? It makes perfect sense."

Hayden shook his head, "We're overthinking this. It's meant for the leaders only, right? Well, I've had this job for about two days, and nobody has left the camp. It's for Sebastian."

"You heard her rules, only the leaders are allowed to see this," the girl declared.

"What's she going to do?" Hayden smirked, "Either we show Sebastian and we decode this thing, or he doesn't understand it and we're back to base zero, which is where we are right now. It's not like there's a downside here."

"Fine," Dylan snapped. She shouted the moping boy's name from across the camp, and he walked over from the rock where he'd been sitting. Just from the way he moved now, it was evident that a deep sadness weighed down his bones. He was left with only pain being pumped through his arteries. His blood was made of pieces of her: his memories, his love, the genes they shared.

"The nightingale awaits," Hayden said, almost a little too loudly. Dylan sent him a short glare, warning that he should lower his voice, but he didn't really care. He realized that Sebastian was the only one who could theoretically understand this message. And understand he did.

His face dropped, and he stared at the two leaders, "Where'd you get that?"

"Some Rogue stopped by. It was supposed to be for leaders only, but Hayden insisted we break that rule," Dylan said. She clearly didn't respect the boy's decision, especially since he hadn't considered her advice in the slightest. She'd had this position for a year; Hayden had worn the jacket for less than a week.

"But they didn't know that I stepped down," Sebastian nodded, understanding exactly what his successor had realized. "So you think I know what it means."

"Do you?" Hayden asked hopefully. Sebastian closed his eyes for a moment, and took a long look at the paper. The other boy stared at is as well, and pointed out, "They spelled 'nightingale' wrong." The others hadn't realized this yet, but it was spelled with a g-a-i-l.

"No, they didn't," Sebastian looked up, a new hope appearing in his eyes. The other two looked at him puzzlingly, desperate to know what thoughts were rushing through his head, "It's her."

"Sebastian—" Dylan began, "I'm sorry, but we both know that isn't true."

"No," Sebastian shook his head, smiling now, but he lowered his voice, "The nightingale. Our parents called her that when she was little because Gail is her middle name. It's not spelled wrong."

Hayden and Dylan made a wary eye contact, neither of them fully sure that Sebastian was right in his suspicions. It seemed like there was evidence to support his claim, but they couldn't gauge if he was stretching some truths. He seemed so sure that it was his sister, and it seemed like a little flicker of light had returned to his eyes. Neither of them wanted to bring the darkness back, as it was eating up their whole camp's morale, but they were more afraid of false hope.

"Talk to Mai," Sebastian said, fully aware of the leaders' disbelief, "She knows that Rogue. See if there's any evidence there that I'm right about this."

"I just don't want you to get hurt again if you're wrong," Dylan sighed, being blatantly honest with him. She had grown to care about Sebastian deeply over the past two years. He was the person who was always supportive, always willing to help someone else, and always willing to do whatever it would take to keep their people safe. To see such an admirable person become this broken was heart-wrenching.

Sebastian made one last comment before walking away, "I can't get hurt if there's nothing left to feel." He was past the point of sadness, he thought. He felt anger, but he mainly felt lost. The one reminder of who he used to be had been stolen from him, the one person whom he had left to love was gone. And he had sworn to protect her, had he not? Who was the post-plague version of him if his little sister was out of the picture? If he had failed his most fundamental goal?

Eventually, the leaders went to talk to Mai, see what she knew about this Rogue. She was more comfortable telling the story of her year in the wilderness now. She wasn't as ashamed of what she'd done. This transformation was massive compared to when she and Sebastian had first discussed her journey. In that first conversation, Mai wasn't quite sure she even wanted to stay. Back then, she'd felt like had dug herself into a dangerous hole, and was putting everyone else in danger just by being in the camp. But she came to realize that she was not the biggest threat to her friends, and in truth, her story was to their own benefit.

"Lily protected me for months," Mai explained, and she noticed the two leaders make eye contact again. "What was on that note? What aren't you telling me?"

"We aren't allowed to say," Dylan cut her off quickly. She was clearly a little bit pleased that she got to keep this important secret, since she felt that if Sebastian was still in charge, he'd have trusted her with it. Dylan couldn't deny that she felt a little threatened by Mai; every time she questioned one of her own decisions, she knew that the camp was comparing her to the old leader.

"What if they go visit her?" Hayden suggested, turning to his partner.

Dylan's eyes widened, "No, Mai can't. That's strictly against her rules."

"I think Mai's an exception," Hayden shook his head, "Especially if she's bringing Sebastian there."

"What are you talking about?" Mai interjected, frustrated with all the secrets.

"Take Sebastian to Lily's camp," Hayden declared, "He'll explain the rest." Dylan huffed and walked away. She hated how arrogant Hayden had become. He somehow felt that he was qualified to make all these big decisions, which only she seemed to understand were meant for them to make together. That was the point of having two leaders—it would check the other's power.

Mai and Sebastian soon headed out for this mission, although the former had no idea what she was walking into. She did notice, however, how her friend's eyes were gleaming again, and how there seemed to be hope in his steps. Nobody had to tell her what was going on; she had a vague suspicion that another girl was heading down the exact same path she once took.

Back at camp, Dylan turned to Hayden and sighed, "You can't just make the calls like that."

"Sebastian needs it, we both know that," was all the boy responded.

"He'll just get hurt again if we were wrong," she warned.

"He's already hurt. I don't think it can get any worse."

"You'd be surprised."

A/N

As an explanation to this title, which I didn't want to explain before the chapter, "gail" is a Hebrew name meaning joy. I don't think that should be too hard to understand its context to the chapter

xvii. the winter of our discontent

A/N we all need a happier chapter by now...

Lily arrived back at her cabin without any issues, and Emma was eager to hear how her mission went. She was desperate for some news about her friends and brother, and longed to know how they were doing. She had seen the way Sebastian broke when they lost their father; it was something she never wanted to witness again. She couldn't help but fear that his reaction to losing her might be similar.

"Is he alright?" Emma asked impatiently, the more she'd been thinking about her brother, the worse she felt. She was killing him slowly inside by pretending she was gone. This was why she asked Lily to send him that message—she couldn't let him feel that pain.

"It didn't sound good," Lily sighed, "He passed his power off to some other kid. Aiden, maybe? Hudson?"

"Hayden," Emma shook her head, "Why the hell would he choose Hayden? I love that kid, but he's only seventeen."

"You're only seventeen," Lily pointed out.

"And I'm not a leader," Emma added, "Sebastian can't think that Hayden will handle all that pressure. That's ridiculous." She paused after that, realizing that Sebastian didn't know everything about the boy he chose as his successor. Hayden's life during the plague had one of the most dramatic changes of anyone she knew, and he was forced into the wild a year before the cities built their walls. Before the Grove was inhabited. The details of his adventures were kept secret, and only Emma knew the entire truth. At least, she knew the most about his past. She knew there was more that he wasn't willing to share.

"Emma, it seems like your death is really taking a toll on your friends," Lily advised, "Are you sure you want to stay away from them?" The other girl did not have a chance to respond, however, as they heard a fist knocking on the door. Emma ran into the back closet, as it would be dark enough to hide. There was also a crawl space underneath the floorboards, but she didn't have the time to successfully enter the dusty small area.

"Mai!" Lily exclaimed loudly when she opened the door. She wanted to make sure that Emma could hear who the visitors were. She then turned to the boy at her friend's side. He was tall and seemed nervous, darting his brown eyes around the room anxiously. Lily could tell his breath was shaky, and the way he held himself showed that a deep terror that he may not find what he was looking for lurked inside of him. "You must be Sebastian!"

"Yeah," the boy nodded. When she heard his voice, Emma gasped. Although she knew that she missed her brother dearly over the past few excruciating weeks, she hadn't realized how much it hurt to be without him.

"Emma. Is she here?" Mai asked quickly. She too could see her partner's nervousness, and wanted to limit the anticipation. If they were wrong with their suspicions, she wanted Lily to break the news as quickly as possible.

She feared the idea of raising Sebastian's hopes any higher than they already were.

At this, Emma physically could not stand it any longer. She pushed open the closet door and ran into the main room, clutching her brother tightly. Sebastian didn't seem to comprehend what was happening at first, and was almost confused by the girl hugging him. But once it sank in that yes, this was Emma, this was his little sister, his heart raced and he nuzzled his chin against the top of her head and he was instantly in tears.

"I thought you were dead," he wheezed out, squeezing her close. Emma didn't know how to respond, since in this moment, surrounded by the warmth of her brother's arms, she had lost all her composure. Tears trickled down her face like a heavy storm, and she struggled to keep her breath under control. She was finally letting down her guard, feeling safe for the first time in what felt like forever. Mai smiled, watching the two siblings reunite, as it was an extremely moving force. It struck her that this was the first time she'd ever seen Emma cry. In fact, it was quite possible this was the first time since entering the forest where she had let another person see these emotions. Emma was tough, too tough sometimes, but there was always a breaking point. Sebastian was hers.

"Now is the winter of our discontent," Emma smiled. It was another Shakespeare quote, a piece of their childhood that neither of them could forget. If the summer was their struggle, then the seasons had turned and their pain was over.

When they finally broke apart, Emma turned to wrap her arms around Mai. Mai was surprised at first to receive this warm a reaction; when she had come back to the camp, right before the younger girl in front of her ran away, Emma had not acknowledged her in the slightest. This was their first interaction in over a year.

"I'm glad you're okay," Mai smiled, "Want to tell us how you did it?"

"Did what?" Emma hesitated, turning to face her friends.

"Live," Mai frowned, her face serious. She felt that this clarification was unnecessary.

The other girl looked towards her crying brother and laughed a little bit, "You don't need to know. I'm alive, that's all that matters." She knew for certain that Sebastian would be forever scarred if he found out the truth about her more sexual ventures. It was an image she didn't want her brother to think about. "Seb, are you alright? I'm so sorry I've put you through this."

"You're fine?" Sebastian looked to her for confirmation.

"I'm breathing," Emma smiled, "I'm okay, Seb."

"Then so am I," he smiled. He was gazing over her body, and he realized that the girl he used to know was disappearing. She was almost unrecognizable. By now, she had washed her skin, and so the only remaining evidence of her time in the Condor's prison was in the cuts and bruises that tainted her pretty face. She was dressed in a black bomber jacket, the same one she'd worn when she left, and a t-shirt and leggings that were donated by Lily. Most of her body was covered, hiding the deeper scars. Despite the fact that she looked healthy enough, Sebastian could tell that her demeanor had shifted. She seemed more independent, if that was even possible. She looked like she didn't need protection.

"Why Hayden?" Emma asked, her curiosity getting the best of her.

"He's a good kid," Sebastian shrugged, "He's careful. He's doing well so far." His sister rolled her eyes and shook her head slightly. As much as she loved Hayden, she didn't trust him to be the leader. He always came off as far too passive; he was always just taking life day by day, and even Emma understood that a leader had to maintain some end goal.

At this point, Lily entered the conversation, "It looks like it's going to storm. You all should probably head back if you want to beat the rain." Mai nodded and grabbed her small backpack off of her friend's counter.

"You coming back?" Sebastian asked his sister, his heart almost breaking at the prospect of leaving her here.

"I can't just yet. The forest has to move on first," Emma sighed. The two siblings hugged again, neither wanting to let go of the other. They were all each other had anymore. It was just the two of them. Them, and a mentally unstable mother whose condition denied them access into salvation, and two older brothers who were just old enough to be allowed inside the cities' walls. When Sebastian and Emma would have to leave each other again, they would be walking in opposite directions from the only other person in the world that either considered family.

"Stay safe," Sebastian warned, "I can't lose you again."

"I already cheated death once," Emma smirked, "Now I just get to weather the storm."

"I love you, Emma."

"You too, big brother."

Dylan had sent Yasmin and Ellie out on a mission before the storm kicked in. She understood why Emma had not come back yet to the camp; she'd have to wait until the Rogues weren't thinking about her and her death. It would make her less suspicious as she walked around the forest under a bandana. But Dylan understood that news travelled quickly in the forest, and was fully aware that some other event may have occurred, causing the people to move on faster than suspected. The only way to find out was to hear the news. Besides, Ellie needed training as a messenger. As Corey wasn't feeling too well, Yasmin had had enough experience on these sorts of missions to take his place.

Yasmin and Ellie had been wandering for about thirty minutes when they first heard other voices. They came across three Rogues, all of whom seemed older and stronger than the two girls ahead of them. Yasmin could have likely taken on the smallest of these Rogues, but still, they'd have been defenseless. They were lucky that they were two smaller girls; some ethical teachings still remained in the forest. Some rules were too ingrained in their minds. It was impolite to hit a girl, under any circumstances. Some things had never changed.

"What are you two doing out here alone?" one of the Rogues asked, "Not sure it's safe."

"We're fine, thank you," Ellie snapped. Ever since her experience with the Condors, she had become far less trusting, and significantly more fearless. It was hard to tell, however, how brave she truly was. She was trying to be like Emma, mimic the stubborn and determined girl she saw in the cell. That was a different side of her friend; it was the messenger side, she came to realize. All Ellie wanted now was to live up to the person she was. She wanted to make her proud.

"You know there's a storm coming, right?" the Rogue laughed. He wasn't used to receiving sass from such a younger girl, "Do you have shelter?"

"We're on our way back to our camp," Yasmin lied. She wanted to speak before Ellie said something else that might get them in trouble. These Rogues didn't seem like an enemy, but they could easily become one if someone uttered one wrong word.

"Stay safe," the one girl in this trio added, "There's a killer on the loose." This was news to the Ravens, and was exactly the sort of information Dylan was hoping for. Yasmin and Ellie, however, were unaware of what their leaders were hoping to hear, and were really just frightened by this prospect.

"What?" Ellie gasped, her eyes widening. Despite the strong face she'd been wearing over the past two weeks, there was still a childlike innocence about her. Although she lived in a camp full of killers, when that word became a title, the connotation became more terrifying.

"Yeah, a couple bounty hunters were found dead a couple days ago," the girl explained, "Big guys. People are saying it's the same person that killed all those Condors a few weeks ago, but these ones were killed by knife instead of sword. Either way, this dude is dangerous. I'd watch out."

With that, the trio of Rogues continued in the direction in which they were heading, and Yasmin and Ellie turned back towards their camp. They were both on edge now, afraid that this mysterious killer would be looming behind any of these dark trees. Besides, the storm clouds were rolling in faster now. It was time that they went home.

Mai and Sebastian first heard thunder a few minutes after they exited Lily's cabin, and quickly realized from the darkened sky and cool wind that the storm was closer than they'd anticipated. The rain had not started off slowly. No, the sky opened up and buckets of water began to pour onto the two teenagers. The heavy clouds obscured their vision, and within moments it became exceedingly clear that they wouldn't find their way back to the camp so quickly. Besides, the lighting that split the sky in half could easily hit them under the forest canopy.

"There's a cave nearby!" Mai screamed to her partner. It was hard to even hear her own voice against of the roaring winds around them. "We can make it if we run!" Sebastian did not say anything in response, since there was no way the girl would pick it up. He just nodded and followed her lead as they raced through the muddy ground. This was one moment where Mai was relieved she'd spent that time alone in the wild. She knew the geography of this forest far better now; she figured that no other Ravens, except for perhaps Emma or Corey, knew the landmarks in Lily's area.

When they finally made it to the cave, they both practically collapsed on the dry ground. They were freezing, exhausted, and thoroughly soaked. Although they hadn't ran far, they had used up all of their adrenaline, and now their energies were crashing. They were like the younger versions of themselves: the little who had stayed up late because they thought they weren't tired, but all of a sudden realized that they needed rest. Sebastian sat up and pulled off his shirt, not even thinking about showing skin to his friend.

"You're so lucky you're a guy," Mai muttered, "If I did that, it would be sexual."

"You really think I care?" Sebastian smirked, a small hint of laughter behind his eyes. Mai smiled, realizing that some of his old spark had come back, but she looked down a little bit. "If you're freezing because your shirt is soaking wet, then take it off."

Mai looked up and took a deep breath, removing the shirt was difficult, as the wet fabric stuck to her damp skin underneath. They both sat there for a moment, laughing and pretending not to stare at each other's bodies. They had gone through so much together over the past two years; this was the first time they'd looked at each other without all of their clothes. What started as that silent laugh where you don't want your partner to know how happy you are soon grew to the point where they were smiling and laughing uncontrollably and there was something foreign known as joy falling out of their bodies just as quickly as the rain outside. It was all they felt. Joy.

Neither of them could remember the last time they didn't feel pressure or pain weighing their shoulders down.

Before either of them knew it, they were lip-locked, Mai kneeling over Sebastian on the forest floor. Their bodies had become one, their energy pulsing through each other. The last time they were in this same formation, with Mai on top of the other boy, she had a knife to his throat, as it was all apart of her grand entrance. All she had wanted in that moment was to hold him, love him, feel his body's warmth around hers. She felt it now, and it was electrifying. Sebastian felt it too. Emma had been right, he thought. It was the winter of their discontent, the end of the all the hurting and unhappiness.

They couldn't hear the storm any longer.

xviii. after the storm

By noon the following day, every member of the Ravens, with the exception of one presumably dead girl, had returned to the camp. The storm had passed, but the entire forest floor was still wet with mud, and the air was damp and heavy. The teens were delighted to be outside again, however, since they'd been confined to their cabins for almost twelve hours as the storm persisted.

Hayden was sitting outside with Corey and Nathan, the three of them sharing notes on what parts of the camp might need to be rebuilt after the storm, as well as areas in the forest that should be examined for damage. The three boys were roommates, and they all served as scouts as well. This meant that over countless sleepless nights and innumerable inside jokes, they'd developed a particularly close bond. Hayden may have been the official leader of the camp now, but Corey and Nathan had been standing right beside him.

"Oh God," Nathan muttered, "Incoming." The other two boys turned around to see a livid Mai marching towards them. Behind her walked a reluctant Sebastian, who sent them a small smile as if to apologize for what was about to come.

"So there's a murderer running rampant in this forest? And I had to hear about this from Ellie of all people?" Mai snapped, "What the hell do you think you're doing?"

"Sorry, you miss out if you're not at camp," Corey muttered, smirking as he looked between Mai and Sebastian. Since he didn't know the details of their venture the previous night, he figured that their absence was only for sexual purposes. He was completely unaware, of course, of who they had gone to visit, since he still thought that Emma was out of the picture.

Mai shook her head and glared at him, looking like she was about to pounce. Hayden then interjected towards his friends, "You two should go. Help Dylan make a plan for patrolling." Corey and Nathan nodded, grateful for the opportunity to walk away from the impending hurricane.

"Of course, go tell Dylan to do something. Because you, Hayden, don't do anything. There is a killer on the loose and we are just sitting here. How's that supposed to save us?" Mai added before his friends had the chance to fully walk away.

"We don't even know who the killer is," Hayden pointed out, somehow managing to remain calm, "And they don't have any reason to be against us, unless you have some unfinished grief with the some psychopathic Rogue that you want to tell us about." He and Dylan had discussed their options thoroughly the night before. In fact, he'd even ended up sleeping on the floor of her and Nova's room, since the storm had locked him in there. They'd agreed that until they learned anything else about the culprit, there was no use trying to prepare for a threat that may not even be real. The best they could do was be ready to fight if the time came, and never send someone out on a mission alone.

"The Condors didn't have any reason to hate us either, you dumbass," Mai flashed, "That didn't stop them."

"You did kill ten of their people," Hayden added, "We'd have retaliated too."

His opponent glared, "I'm sorry, but I can't just sit here and let some maniac kill us off. This isn't happening." She reached down for her biker mask, the symbol of her plans to leave.

"Mai, they killed two bounty hunters with perfectly clean stabs, or cuts, or whatever it was. They're strong, and we have no idea who it could be," Hayden groaned, emphasizing the last clause.

At this point, Sebastian stepped in. He had previously been silent, but after the last comment, he'd come to realize something, "They were bounty hunters? In Condor territory?" This was new information, since Ellie had forgotten those seemingly small details.

"Yeah," Hayden nodded.

"Who would have needed to kill a couple of bounty hunters in Condor territory a couple days ago?" Sebastian asked, lowering his voice so that the rest of the camp couldn't hear him. Both Hayden and Mai's eyes widened as they understood exactly what he was suggesting.

"She's good with a knife too," Mai added.

"See, Mai?" Hayden smirked, "Nothing to worry about."

Despite the comforting fact that Emma was the secret killer, Mai's temper had not been cooled. Once she got going, it was hard for her to let go of her anger. Instead, it just kept on pouring out of her. So she continued, "Alright, so what are you going to do about this camp? This place is a mess. Why has nobody ever fixed those holes in the fence? Do you not realize how exposed we are?"

Hayden stood up, so that he was looking down at Mai. As skinny and small as he seemed, the boy was actually quite tall. He said sarcastically, "There are holes in the fence? Shocking! It's not like the storm last night just destroyed all the progress we've made. Oh, and it's not like these holes have only been around for three days when I, you know, actually became the leader. In fact, I actually think our camp has had its issues since the very beginning. What was the leader's name back then? Oh yeah! MaiLinh Walker."

At Hayden's outburst, Sebastian was taken aback. He had never seen this side of his friend. Apparently he wasn't as passive as everyone thought he was. He had a hostility that nobody had ever seen before. However, this was not the time to come forward with this different personality. Both Mai and Hayden needed to calm themselves.

But for Mai, this remark only fired her up more, "You have no idea what I've done for this damn camp. It's more than you'll ever do in your sorry little life."

Hayden shook his head; he was far passed the point of no return. There was no backing down now. "You think that I've done nothing? Do you have any idea how many times I've been the one to talk someone out of suicide? After we thought you died, do you have any idea how many hours I spent counseling half of this camp because our friends died beside you in battle? Do you have any idea how much shit has happened here over the past year? No. You don't, Mai. You left, and you don't get to come back for two weeks and think that you're still in charge when you are the one that left."

"You're right, I don't what happened here, but I know that you're all still alive because I sat in the Condor's cell for three months," Mai growled, "They tortured me every day. Every time, I either had to give up information, or suffer the consequences, and you can sure as hell bet I suffered every single time." She rolled up her left sleeve, revealing the scars on her wrist,

"They carved a number into my skin, like I was their property. But guess what? I let them do it so that the rest of you could live." Sure enough, the number 23 was written permanently on her body. It would be a constant reminder of those three dreadful months, a reminder of the time she wasn't in control.

Sebastian shuddered and his face dropped the moment he realized what that number meant. He'd seen it before, but thought it was an old tattoo from before the Plague, something he'd merely forgotten about over their year apart. But no, it was a sign of what she'd been through, and he realized that someone else he cared about had taken the same steps she had. "Emma was wearing her jacket," he muttered, his breathing heavy and body going cold.

This was enough to quiet the feuding foes beside him. Despite their problems, they had one thing in common: they cared about Sebastian. Seeing the look of terror return to his eyes was heartbreaking. Obviously, he was aware that Emma had been tortured; he'd seen brutally grotesque images for weeks. Even now that he knew she was alive, he was still haunted by the idea of her old condition. But scars would fade, and she would move on, he thought. This permanent number on his friend's wrist had to be present on his sister's as well—an unwanted memento that would never leave her. He had seen none of the damage during their visit, but now all he wanted was revenge on the person who did this. It would be payback. Not just for Emma, but for Mai. And if Mai was number 23, then for all the numbers before her. Emma had paid for a crime she didn't commit, and Sebastian was done with it. The next time he and Megan Martins came face to face, he would not back down. Never again.

Hayden sighed and stood up from the log where he'd been sitting. He sent Sebastian a small, encouraging smile, and did not acknowledge Mai in the slightest. He had work to do. Mai was right that the camp was a mess, but that wasn't his fault. If anything, they'd made a lot of progress over the past few days. The storm, however, blew it all apart.

"How are you?" a soft voice asked from behind him. Serena. The two of them had become closer over the past few weeks. Ever since Hayden injured his leg, he'd had to spend more and more time in camp, which was where Serena's work was situated. There was never much to do within the four walls, especially if most of the scouts were out, so it was often that they were each other's only companions.

"Great," Hayden muttered. Still, he shot an icy glare towards Mai, which was enough to tip off the medic that he was everything but great.

"What did she say to you?" Serena asked, "Come sit. Dylan's covering the construction on the wall right now, they don't need an extra set of hands just yet."

"The usual," Hayden shrugged, taking his friend's invitation, "That I'm incompetent and ruining this camp."

"That's ridiculous," Serena sighed, "You've done a great job so far."

"I haven't killed anyone so far," Hayden muttered, "That seems to be the definition of a 'great job'."

"Maybe," the girl shrugged, "Everything is relative."

"Mai was right, though. I don't have any place wearing this jacket."

"Sebastian chose you," Serena pointed out, "That's all the qualification you need. You've deserved it."

"He couldn't even think clearly."

"That doesn't matter. When the most skilled leader I've ever met in my life couldn't handle the weight of the world any longer, the one person he trusted most was you. His instincts told him that you were the best person to succeed him. He saw that in you, and I see it too," Serena wrapped her arm around his shoulder.

Hayden looked up at her, his brown eyes showing nothing but exhaustion. He was tired, not just of being in charge, but of managing a world where teenagers held the power. He just couldn't keep on like this any longer; he needed security. He needed structure. He needed a future where he would someday end up happy. He shook his head slightly, eyes pleading towards the girl across from him, "I have no idea what I'm doing."

"Neither do the rest of us."

Near the western fence, Dylan was leading the construction process to fix up the holes made by the previous night's storm. She had bitterly watched the exchange between Mai, Hayden, and Sebastian, although she couldn't hear a word they said. She had considered entering the conversation, but quickly realized that whatever the problem was, none of them thought that she deserved to be apart of it.

"What's your problem?" Nova asked her. As her roommate and best friend, the mechanic had heard all of of the leader's complaints over the past year. She knew better than to act sympathetic. What Dylan needed was someone who wouldn't sugarcoat the truth. Nova was just the person.

"Why does Mai go to Hayden first?" Dylan asked, "Does she actually think he has a better idea of what's going on than me?" This was what had begun to bother her over the past few days. When she was partners with Sebastian, everyone understood that she was his second. She was the backup. Dylan didn't mind that; he had more experience, and she was still learning. With Hayden taking over his position, she figured that she was going to be the one with the responsibility. Hayden would have no idea what he was doing, just like she had no idea how to fill Mai's shoes when she took over her spot. But no, it seemed that everyone regarded Hayden just as they had regarded

Seb. The man in charge. Once again, she was the second, and she was sick of it.

"Mai looks pissed," Nova pointed out, "Let Hayden take her wrath. You don't need to deal with her."

"But she still should have come to me instead of him," Dylan shrugged, "I should be the person she considers at fault."

"I don't know what to tell you, girl," the mechanic shrugged, "You wanna join them?"

Dylan rolled her eyes and went back to working on the fence. Then she added, "Hayden's not even fun to fight. You just feel bad. It's like kicking a puppy. You feel terrible."

"You would know," Nova smirked, "You're always fighting him."

"We don't fight that much," the leader frowned, a little bit annoyed that her friend saw right through her and Hayden's dynamic as co-leaders. To the rest of the camp, they had to act like their cooperation was seamless. She was determined now that they would be equals; neither of them would be more powerful than the other. Unless she was the one the one who was higher up. That, she could handle.

"He spent the night in our room, Dylan," Nova smirked, "You don't get along."

The other girl sighed, looking down, "He's the most agreeable person in this forest. How am I the only person who can't get along with him?"

"The same way Garrett can't stand Emma," Nova shrugged. Then she corrected herself, "Couldn't stand her. God, I can't get used to this. I keep thinking she's still here." Dylan bit her tongue. She couldn't tell her friend that she was right, that Emma was still alive, and was living only a thirty minute walk away.

The final scene across the camp was in the exact spot where the argument had gone down. Sebastian had walked away, frustrated and worried about his sister, as always. Mai was left at the small log, frowning.

Yasmin approached her on her way back into camp. She had been on the first guard shift since the rain had cleared, so she missed the entire fight. But just seeing an extra hostile Mai tipped her off that she'd missed out on something. "What happened?"

"I can't handle him anymore," Mai muttered, "He's so freaking annoying."

"Who?" Yasmin laughed, "Sebastian?"

"Oh, God no," Mai said, "Hayden, of all people. He thinks that I'm the reason this camp is messed up. Have you heard anything more ridiculous?"

"Something tells me that you started this," Yasmin observed, to which Mai stood up.

"I can't," she said, "I can't handle this. I'm going."

"Mai—"

"No! You're all insane. I can't put up with this right now." With that, Mai walked right out of the camp. She didn't even put on her iconic bandana; she just had to get out as quickly as possible. She was fuming. She couldn't remember the last time she'd felt this insulted by her friends—it had to have been before the plague. It was time to leave.

"Oh!" Lily exclaimed, "I forgot to tell you. My boyfriend Adrian is coming over soon. I trust him, but if you want to hide, I understand."

Emma's eyes widened at the name of Lily's boyfriend, "Adrian?" Emma knew an Adrian, she knew him all too well. She prayed that this was not the same boy.

"Yep! He's great!" Lily smiled.

"I'll hide," Emma nodded. Within the next five minutes, a knock on the door signaled his arrival. The dead girl was in her position underneath the floorboards, and she intently listened in on their conversation.

"Hey!" she heard Lily greet him.

"I've missed you, Lils," said a different voice. Emma's lungs dropped. Yes, it was the same Adrian she knew. The last time she'd heard him speak, she was kissing him. He had begun to unzip his pants when she stopped him. His face was the last thing she saw before she was knocked unconscious and woke up in the Condor's cell. Adrian was a bad man, that much she knew for certain. And she could never tell Lily that she had slept with him.

Within the next thirty minutes, there was another knock on the door. The next voice that came in sounded agitated and angry; it was Mai. She sounded beyond furious with the other Ravens, and Emma couldn't help but wonder what could have possibly gone down so dramatically over the past night.

"If I leave the Ravens, can I just join you guys permanently?" Mai asked.

"Of course!" Lily smiled, "You're always welcome. But what did they do?"

"They're just the worst. I can't put up with them any longer," the first girl responded. This was bad news for Emma, as the problems arose before her eyes. Adrian was dangerous. There was an old feud between him and one of her friends, and if Mai was unaware of their history, and she deemed him trustworthy, their entire camp would be in danger. That was the reason

Emma had begun to contact him. She had to keep her friends close but her enemies closer—tabs on him were a necessity.

As the rest of their conversation hinted that Mai was truly walking away from the camp who had loved her dearly, Emma's heart sank. She couldn't change Mai's decision, of course. Not without revealing her friend's secret, which she had sworn to keep. No, she had a different idea in mind. It was quite likely the worst idea she'd ever formed, but this message had to go to the boy directly.

Later in the evening, the Lily, Adrian, and Mai had left the cabin, as they were going to meet another Rogue who was camped out a couple of miles east. This was Emma's opportunity. She scribbled out a quick note, thanking Lily for her hospitality, and she was out. The red bandana tied around her face, she walked towards the Ravens' camp.

xix. odysseus

The masked figure snuck into the Ravens' camp through an entrance hidden in the back. This seemed to be the only escape route left, as many had been repaired. The figure felt almost insulted by how much more secure the camp had become. The stranger had relied on all the holes. It would make their life more complicated; it would restrict their freedom. They had lost their freedom once before, and they refused to lose it again. Perhaps this camp would not be the best place for them.

They hid behind a building they knew all too well. They could describe the architecture with impeccable accuracy. How many times had they crouched behind this building, waiting for the moment to run? There was a slight ditch underneath the structure, built as an irrigation system for rainwater. This was where the figure was situated, a place where only one other person could fit.

"Hayden!" a voice called from across the camp. It was a little girl who they identified as Ellie, "There's an intruder!" The figure cursed under their breath— they had been discovered. But all was going well, the one they wished to talk to would be there shortly.

"Ellie, stand back," another voice warned. It was the protective sound of the person that the stranger loved most in the world. There was more confidence in his voice now than when they'd last heard him speak; it seemed he was getting strong again. "They might be armed." The figure fingered the blade in their sheath. It was relatively small, but it was all they would possibly need. They had a secret weapon that would protect themselves, should it come to that. But this weapon would destroy all of their plans, although in this new world, plans were merely dreams.

"There's a hole underneath B5," another voice said. The figure recognized that it belonged to the boy they'd come to see. "Only one person can fit in it. I'll go, but Yasmin, Seb, you both need to cover."

"Don't get yourself killed," one of the people warned.

The last boy responded, a snicker in his voice, "That's all on you, buddy." Soon, a dirty blonde-haired boy had slid into the hole alongside the stranger. He examined them closely, trying to make out who could be hidden underneath the red bandana and black beanie. Their slim figure told him it was a girl before him, and not his primary foe throughout the forest. But his nemesis had friends in strange places, and this girl could be anyone. Neither her face, nor her hair, was visible.

"Get down, and listen to me," the figure snapped. The boy nodded, recognizing her voice instantly. All he wanted to do was hug her, hold her, know that it was truly this person in front of him and know that she was truly alive, but he was serious now. He understood that she would not have come to their camp in this manner if her message was unimportant. "Mai is with Adrian right now, and she's thinking about leaving your camp. You might not be safe here anymore."

The boy's heart sank, realizing that the threat that came with his cousin was real, and it was spiraling straight towards him. He'd been running for too long, and it seemed his punishment was finally catching up with him. The act that plagued his subconscious was ready to be avenged; Hayden James Barrels had pulled the trigger on his father, the bullet from the victim's very own gun.

Hayden was young, only fourteen years of age, and his father was sick. All he ever heard were the tortured screams as his body convulsed and the pain and illness took him over. Eventually his father had enough. He was sick of being a prisoner in his own body, and handed his son the gun. The son refused, but his father swore that he would never forgive him if he let him live any longer. And so he bit his lips and closed his eyes and vomited as he pulled the trigger. His mother came home, and Hayden ran. Now the rest of his family lived in the sanctuary cities, everyone but his dear cousin Adrian, so Adrian was the one responsible for killing him. Hayden only ever told these details to one girl, and she was standing in front of him now in disguise. He had come to realize that she was the right person to tell; she could provide him with the scariest of details, such as the ones before him now.

Hayden nodded, looking at the girl before him, "What are you going to do now?"

"I'll figure it out," she shrugged, sighing. There was no way to create a real plan in these circumstances. Her next move would be to run, and then she'd fight. Was that not all they ever did? Run from their problems, and fight when they couldn't be avoided?

"Stay safe," the boy smiled weakly. At this moment, they heard the foot-steps of more members of the camp circling the building, "They're armed. You can't get out."

"I'm not going to hurt you, just trust me," the stranger declared, after examining their situation. Before her friend even had a chance to speak, her knife was at his throat, and she was dragging him out of the hole.

"What the hell is this?" Yasmin snapped, her spear out and pointed towards the stranger. Sebastian was beside her, holding out the only gun the camp owned. Mai had stolen this weapon from a Rogue over the course of her adventurous year alone. His finger was on the trigger, ready to shoot anyone who threatened the rest of his friends. The stranger stared at him, shock resonating within her. Never had she seen this boy hold a gun. Never had he been so eager to kill.

"State your name and affiliations," Sebastian snarled, staring down this masked person. Seeing her weapon upon his friend blurred his vision red, making it hard to discern any other details.

The stranger spoke in a raspy voice, unrecognizable to those who knew her, "Put down the gun."

"State your name or I shoot," the other boy repeated, anger resonating in his vocal chords.

"You shoot," the stranger began, "And your leader dies. You put down the gun, I walk out, he lives. Understood?"

"Seb—" Yasmin nodded, and he hesitantly lowered the weapon. The knife came down from the stranger's neck.

"Get out," Sebastian threatened, "Get out before I kill your sorry ass."

The stranger smirked beneath her mask, "You'd never live with yourself." With that, the nightingale exited the camp through the hole in which she'd came, and flew into the woods.

After a brief discussion with Dylan about the contents of this meeting, Hayden understood something clearly. Adrian was a threat to his friends so long as he had any authority. It had been a strange three days, but his reign was over. This was being a good leader: realizing when you had to step back.

"Sebastian!" he called, and his friend ran up to him instantly. He was beyond curious about the contents of the leader's meeting with the stranger. He wanted to make sure the younger boy was alright, since their conversation clearly ended with the intruder's knife around his throat.

"What happened? Who was that person?" Sebastian asked instantly.

"An ally," Hayden nodded. He wasn't quite sure he wanted his friend to know that he had held a gun up to his younger sister. He had seen the look in his eyes, saw just how close that finger was to pulling the trigger. Besides, Hayden was asking Sebastian to do something massive, something he would never do if he knew who it was he came so close to killing. At that moment, he took off the jacket, "You can have it back."

"Hayden, what's going on?" Sebastian stepped back, skeptically.

"There's a Rogue that wants me dead," he revealed. By now a small crowd had gathered around them, everyone searching for answers about the mysterious debacle. "And Mai's with him."

"What does that even mean, Mai's with him?" Nathan interjected.

"I pissed her off, she walked out, now she's with him. That's all I know, they didn't give any details," Hayden explained, "Adrian won't come after the Ravens as a whole if I'm not in such an elevated position. Sebastian, you're alright, and you were a better leader than I'll ever be. It's time you take it back."

Serena, who was standing nearby, shook her head, "No. Hayden, you can't just run when it gets hard. You've already rebuilt half this camp, you're doing great!"

"I'm not running," Hayden shook his head, "I'm being a leader, and I'm protecting my people by not painting an ever bigger target on our backs."

Sebastian sighed, respecting the boy's decision, "It's just as hard to step down."

"Exactly," he nodded, and then smiled slightly, "Besides, this was too big for me anyways." Just as quickly as the jacket had been turned over only three days earlier, it had found its way back to its proper owner's hands. As Sebastian put it on, it was clear that the camp had regained the order it didn't know it lost. The jacket was built just for his arms, and no matter who tried it on, it would always and forever fit him best.

"I hate to ruin the moment," Corey added, "But what do we do about Mai?"

Rae cut in, "We can't just jump to conclusions. We need to talk to her, I'm sure there's just a misunderstanding. If she knew who this Rogue was, she'd leave right away." As Mai's closest friend in the camp, Rae was terrified of the prospect of her leaving them again. She knew in her deepest, darkest heart that a simple conversation could not clear up this issue easily, but it was what she wanted to believe. What she needed to believe.

"She walked out because she was pissed with me," Hayden sighed, "And now she's with the guy who wants to kill me. You really think that's a coincidence?" It did seem a little bit strange to him that Mai knew exactly which Rogue to seek out; he had only ever told that one girl of his nemesis. He had trusted that she would not reveal his secret to anyone else, but it seemed that somehow Mai knew. Perhaps she was not meeting Adrian for the first time. Perhaps they'd come to know each other during her wild trip, and since returning, she had known all the details of his predicament. Perhaps she had been relaying information to the Rogue for weeks.

"If she comes back, we let her in," Sebastian nodded. Like Rae, he was not ready to turn on his friend. Not now, not so quickly, not after the previous night. "Hayden, if she comes back, you cannot speak to her. You can't piss her off, or give her any information that she could pass off to this Rogue." He then turned to the rest of the camp, "If she brings Hayden up in any conversation, you change the subject. Anything that could hurt him is off limits."

"But Seb, she's our friend," Rae pleaded, "We can trust her."

"Remember what happened last time we chose to trust a stranger?" Sebastian sighed. He was thinking back to the fateful night almost three weeks before, a prehistoric time where the girl in question was dead. He chose to trust a stranger, a child, and he paid the ultimate price. He was not making that mistake again.

"You're trusting one right now," Rae frowned, "Unless you knew who that Rogue was."

Hayden shook his head, "She wasn't a stranger."

"Then who was it?" the scout snapped. She turned to the returned leader, "Do you believe this?"

"I'm not sure," Sebastian said, "Which is why we're even letting Mai back into our camp. If I trusted that Rogue, she'd be gone by now." This was the sort of hard decision that one boy was more equipped to declare than anyone else. This was what reminded the camp of why he was the leader in the first place. He provided stability, and they would all trust Sebastian Harlem.

"Glad to have you back," Dylan smiled, patting his shoulder supportively. Sebastian didn't smile, but he nodded. Oh, how quickly all these tables had turned.

The stranger had nowhere to go. It was time; she had gone rogue. She had turned her back on her friends, her family. All she could picture was the barrel of the gun pointed at her head, the gun held by a boy whose biggest fear was to become a murderer. Then she remembered, her knife was wrapped around another boy's neck. She paused, staring at her hands and the vast forest surrounding her. These hands were stained with blood. What had she become?

"Shit," she muttered, "They might as well call me Macbeth." The stranger was never one to stop and reflect on her emotions. They were manifested inside her, somewhere in the most strange and foreign corner of her subconscious. She had to keep moving. It was almost a coping mechanism. The world had burned to ashes, but the forest was her Garden of Eden. Here she was free. Here there were no limits. Here the most raw truth of mankind ran rampant.

Her raw truth was blood and sex, was it not?

There was a creek five miles off, and it separated the two sides of the forest. On the other side, she was truly a stranger. She did not know a single person who held residence on that ground. Conversely, the people there did not know her. Her name would no longer be a liability. So there she went.

The eastern side of her forest looked just like the west, but greener. Here there were no chains that could hold her down. Her name was not her enemy, her face was not her foe. That was good enough for Lady Macbeth, perhaps now she could wash her hands clean. She wandered for a while, unsure of where to go. She knew nothing of the alliances or boundaries that divided this land, but she still felt both her knives in her possession. One in her belt, one tucked away safely in the most hidden location she could imagine.

"Hey!" a voice called, and the girl's head whipped up. Sitting on the forest ground was another girl, approximately her own age. "Look at the sunset. Isn't it beautiful?"

The newcomer paused, following the other's gaze. Sure enough, the sky was aflame with painted strokes of orange and pink covering up the blue. The light tinted the clouds, causing them to burst with spectacular color. Her breath was stolen, as the overwhelming peace and harmony of nature's most magnificent hues overcame her senses. There was something beautiful there, even in the midst of all the forest's chaos. It made her feel so small, her plight purely trivial. Slowly, she untied the red bandana, and let her dark hair fall out of her beanie. The light wind pushed it towards the west, towards the camp from which she came. She was one with the world right now, and it felt so kind. It felt like absolutely nothing at all.

"You going anywhere?" the first girl asked, leaning her head against the sturdy tree behind her.

"I've got no plans," smiled the stranger.

"Who are you, anyways?"

The newcomer paused, realizing she had no answer to that question. "I'm nobody."

"Nobody, the pseudonym that saved Odysseus from the cyclops," Kamai mentioned casually, "It sounds like you've had quite the hero's journey."

Nobody smiled, "You're well read."

"I've had time."

"If I'm Odysseus, what does that make you?"

The girl paused, "There's no character named Kamai, is there?"

xx. silent anarchy

T he City of the Forgotten had tread too deep into waters they could not handle. Waters they could not justify. Monday morning, the details were shared between only two tyrannical souls, but by the afternoon, three times the original number had learned the truth. And these six were not pleased with what they had discovered. Now it was Wednesday, and it was time to start a riot, it was time that they turned to anarchy.

But silent anarchy. Peaceful anarchy. Donovan Mayler was more than fully aware of that juxtaposition, and he was the one who advocated for a more quiet approach. The last time the city turned to anarchy, they dug themselves into their current predicament. Besides, he cared little about the fate of the city. It was not his home, nothing here belonged to him. He lived in a shabby hut underneath his friend's name—his own name stood for nothing. Nothing but a reminder of the person he once was. He knew since his first glance at Paricida that this city had turned its back on its own people. He felt no attachment to these streets anymore; he felt no reason to protect them. And the forest in danger? Why, he knew no one in those woods. It would be a shame for them to fall underneath Harper's rule, but he'd feel no guilt.

"Fifty miles due southeast, " Cameron Dawson said, entering the room, "That's where you'll have to go. Fifty-two, to be exact."

"Fifty-two miles in a random direction?" Marley gaped, "We're never going to find it. She might not even be there, and it could be occupied. There's five of us going, that's nothing."

"It's our best bet," Cameron sighed, "Kamai's been off the grid for two weeks now. She would have gotten there by now."

"She's been off the grid because your contact was killed, dumbass," Marley rolled her eyes, "Or he realized that whatever you were offering him wasn't good enough. We have no reason to believe she left that forest."

Jacob sighed, "It doesn't matter. If she's in the Grove, we have no way to find her. That thing's massive, and that's where Harper's going to invade."

"So we leave and hope that we can magically find her old summer camp, risk our lives in the process, just to find out she's not there and we can't come back here? Sounds like a suicide mission," Marley groaned.

"If we're still here when Harper invades the forest, then we're committing suicide by staying. There's what? A hundred people here? The Grove has a least three times that many," Jacob said.

"They aren't centralized, they don't have the communication to unite against us."

"That's what Harper's counting on. She's also counting on nurses like you to save people's lives on a daily basis," Donovan muttered, "So far, her streak's been pretty bad, no offense."

"None taken. I don't know shit about medicine," Marley admitted. Although her job was technically in a medical field, she was completely clueless towards anything in that subject. She was a nurse because it got her access to painkillers, and painkillers provided enough cash for their little group to survive. "So, you're saying that they'd somehow come together against us?"

"Precisely," Jacob nodded, "They speak the same language. They all want their autonomy. We're trying to take that away, they'll share a common enemy. Plus Kamai might be there, in which case they know everything about this city. None of us stand a chance."

"And this isn't a place we want to fight for," Natalia muttered, speaking her first words in this conversation, "So we need to get out regardless. It's just a matter of if we trek to this camp or not." The rest of the room nodded in agreement, although this was the plan they'd decided on the previous day.

"How much time do we have?" Jacob asked, turning to Cameron. He was their plug into the city's secret political agenda. He had now become a traitor to his own family, but it was only in efforts to save his friends. Besides, they took him back in now, after he turned his back on them, but his cousins had been lying to him for months now.

"The plans will be released tomorrow evening. Harper will call for a volunteer army, and then they'll invade in two weeks. The second week of October, I think," Cameron revealed. This was new, only decided on the previous evening.

"What happens if not enough people volunteer?" Natalia asked, "She's obviously crazy. I would never risk my life for her."

"Not everyone lives in the parasites' neighborhood," Donovan sighed, "She has support from people that don't know her personally."

"It'll probably be a three day journey," Cameron said, turning his attention back to his friends' plan, "It's only fifty miles away, but there are hills, and no roads anymore. I can get you guys an old map, but everything's different now, you know? You're going to get lost."

"Then we'll get lost," Jacob sighed, "We don't exactly have any other options."

Soon, the plan was set. In two days, Jacob, Donovan, Marley, and Natalia would leave the City of the Forgotten forever in hopes to discover Camp Peregrin, the lost haven where Kamai Wells once spent her summers. Before finding the city, when Kamai ran from the plague, Peregrin was the first place she went. After living there alone for about a week, she realized that there was nobody else coming, and that if she wanted to survive, she'd have to find someone else. She couldn't live on her own. And so she stumbled upon the City of the Forgotten, and she fell into the ragtag group of friends that would so quickly become iconic, and just as quickly fall apart.

Cameron and Rachel would stay behind. They had stolen two walkie talkies that were strong enough to cover a fifty-five mile radius. The camp fell right into that limit. Cameron had to stay to send them information, as well as make their exodus seem less suspicious. If he were to vanish, then wouldn't Harper realize he knew more than he was supposed to? No, Cameron must be their spy on the inside.

And then there was Rachel. Her name held title to the little shack where they had spent so many sleepless nights and tired days. As far as Harper knew, Jacob and Donovan had no associations with Rachel Greenesfelt. Every time they checked in to Paricida, they claimed that they were visiting the residency of Marley Dennis. As a nurse, Marley technically had a home, but it was nothing more than a tiny room with nothing but a bare lightbulb in the ceiling. Still, if Jacob and Donny disappeared alongside Marley, there would be nothing there to question. Rachel would be able to pull her strings from the inside.

They realized that the moment Harper told the city of her plans to dominate the nearby forest, there would be opposition. Some people would realize that what they planned to do was wrong, and they would look for a way out. Kamai's old summer camp used to hold three hundred kids, she'd mentioned once. If it was uninhabited, it could be theirs, and it could become a refuge for the parasites. Rachel would be operating the underground system, alerting the Riot of who would be arriving soon, providing safe passage to those who needed it. This was how they would fight for their city, because their city was only made up of the people who searched for humanity. The borders of this town meant nothing; but the borders of Peregrin could.

It was silent anarchy, and Donovan Mayler called it beautiful.

xxi. turf wars

Before long, the second week of October had arrived in the Grove forest, although the inhabitants knew nothing of the threat that was to come. There was one impending threat, of course: winter. But they were lucky enough that their forest was in the perfect climate for the upcoming season. It would never truly get cold, but it would soon get dry. Winter weather was more challenging for forest survival, but manageable. Manageable was all that mattered.

"I must be coming up on a year and a half now, right?" Kamai asked, turning to her newfound companion. This other girl had been travelling with her for about two weeks now. She was beyond relieved to have some company. The old Rogue who'd been sending her whereabouts to the City of the Forgotten had been killed about a month before. She'd missed having someone else to talk to, but she couldn't particularly miss him. He was a bore, and far too slow to understand any of her comedic genius. Of course, he didn't deserve to die, but that was the way of the world now.

"Since you've come to this forest?" her new companion clarified. Kamai now knew the girl's real name, but would never speak it aloud. There were too many wandering ears in this forest. She understood the value of secrets, and this was one. She had grown to call the girl Calypso, in honor of the Odyssey's seductive nymph. Initially, she'd called her Odysseus, but it became clear overwhelmingly quickly that a nickname of that sort would only feed this girl's hubris.

"Yeah," Kamai nodded, "Actually, it's probably less than that. Maybe a year and two months?"

Calypso smirked, "That's a big difference, you know. A lot can change in four months."

"A lot can change in two days," Kamai added.

At this same moment, Calypso's head shot up, having overheard some noise echoing towards them. Throwing her hair into her black beanie and tying the red bandana around her face, she whispered, "Someone's coming." Although she had no acquaintances on this half of the forest, she was always worried that someone from her past would end up walking by. She could never be too cautious in hiding her identity. In fact, part of her still worried about telling Kamai the whole story. But Kamai had ultimately saved her, had she not? She knew better than to think this girl her enemy.

The two girls crouched behind a couple of shrubs, as a group of five walked past. One boy was in the lead, relaying information into a walkie-talkie. Calypso could not make out a word of what he said, since she was soon distracted by her friend's reaction. Kamai had frozen, staring at the posse ahead. Holding her breath, she slowly began to take in exactly what she was seeing. She did not move again until the group was so far away that she could not see them anymore.

"Who was that?" Calypso turned to her, "Are you alright?"

"Yeah, I'm fine," Kamai muttered, "But this forest isn't."

"What are you talking about? Who were those people?"

Kamai muttered, "That boy in the front's name is Griffin, but everyone calls him Phoenix. He used to be one of my closest friends, before I left the city."

"Well, maybe he's like you? Those five could have ran away the same way you did," Calypso pointed out.

"Never," Kamai shook her head, "Phoenix is Harper's twin brother. He's the second-in-command. He's here on official business, important business."

"What, you think they're trying to conquer the entire forest or something?" Calypso smirked.

"That's exactly what I think," Kamai groaned, "You're underestimating them. They are armed and militant. We're a bunch of scattered Rogues that hate each other. They'll take us down in a heartbeat."

"So what do we do?" The other girl frowned, "What happens if they take over this forest?"

"Nothing good," muttered her friend, "But there's a place we can go. It's probably a four day walk, and last time I was there it was uninhabited. I'd say it's our best bet, but we should head out as soon as possible. Tonight, preferably."

"We leave the forest tonight?" Calypso hesitated, "Not unless we go back and tell my friends. I won't leave them here."

"We can't. It'll draw too much attention if this whole group leaves at once," Kamai shook her head.

"Then I won't go. Leave without me," the first declared.

"You're making a mistake. Harper is dangerous. Whatever her brother is doing here is going to cause death."

"I'm not leaving my friends to die. It's that simple."

"They almost shot you last time you saw them," Kamai pointed out.

Calypso shrugged, "They didn't know who I was."

"And why would they believe anything I tell them?"

"Because I trust you, and they'll listen to me."

"It's too early. You'll only be putting yourself in danger," Kamai warned. She did truly enjoy spending time with this girl. It would be such a shame to lose her so quickly, and the forest still whispered about her death from time to time. Her identity was not ready to be revealed.

"The forest is changing, Kamai. I just won't be here long enough to suffer the consequences," she smirked. And so the two girls headed back to their campsite and began to pack. There would be no returning to the eastern side of the creek.

As the two girls approached the Ravens' camp by the end of the afternoon, it was clear that they were both stressed. One worried about making it out of the forest on time, the other about her friends she was about to face. Last time, she had stared straight into the barrel of a gun held by the one person she truly loved. She had held a knife at a close friend's throat. Wearing the same bandana and beanie, she knew that she'd be recognized, and that her welcome would be cold.

Alas, they reached the clearing. The girl known as Calypso took a deep breath, and gestured that her friend followed her. She felt to make sure her knife was in her sheath, where it would be easiest to reach. But she didn't plan on fighting. For once in her life, she planned on letting the others take the lead, play their little game. She knew that they would not kill her without taking off her mask first, and her face was all the protection she would need.

As they walked towards the camp, both girls raised their arms in a position of surrender, showing that they were not there as foes. At the gate stood Corey and Yasmin, who were both quick to react. Instantly recognizing the Calypso as the girl who'd previously intruded their camp, Yasmin quickly pinned her on the ground, her back facing the sky, and her head angled back towards the forest. Her sword stood at the back of the girl's neck, the tip pricking her body just slightly enough to draw blood. Corey had just as easily gotten his knife around Kamai's throat. Kamai had trusted her friend's instructions to not fight back, but she did worry about the decision they'd made.

At the sound of Corey's whistle, Sebastian and Dylan, alongside the rest of the camp came running out. The people stared at the captured girls in the center of the camp, as murmurs spread throughout the crowd. Everyone was recognizing one to be the person who'd threatened Hayden, but the other was a stranger. The Ravens didn't like strangers. They'd learned their lesson one too many times.

"What are you doing?" Hayden yelled, sprinting across the camp, "She's not an enemy!"

"She tried to kill you," Yasmin snapped, "And now she's back. Why? So she can tell you that more of us aren't to be trusted? Newsflash, Mai came back. This chick was lying to you."

"She wasn't lying," Hayden shook his head.

"Her knife was around your neck, Hayden," Serena pointed out, putting her arm on the distressed boy's shoulder, "She's dangerous."

He glared towards Sebastian, ignoring the medic's gesture, "Only because you threatened to shoot her." The entire crowd examined the body on the ground carefully. Her head was facing away from her friends, and the bandana still covered her face. She was unrecognizable, minus a small lock of black hair peeking out from under the cap.

But those few strands of hair were enough to reveal her identity to the leader. Sebastian's heart raced as he realized who it was he'd threatened to kill. How ironic? He blamed himself for her death once before, and it proved to be unnecessary. He had somehow come so close to actually being the one to pull the trigger. One second later and he may have destroyed everything. How could a person be so terrible? Oh, how he wondered.

"Let her stand," he instructed, to which Yasmin gaped.

"She's armed," the guard warned.

"Then keep your blade at her neck," Sebastian snapped impatiently, "Just take off her mask." Yasmin sighed, clearly disapproving of the boy's orders. Mai stepped in to interject her own discontent, but it was too late. The stranger was soon on her feet with a sword pushing against her throat. It was strange how comfortable she had become with this position. The looming threat of death no longer scared her. She had avoided it so many times, it seemed that it may never quite reach her. The girl raised her hands to untie the mask, and let the red bandana fall to the ground.

The camp was silent as Yasmin dropped the blade and they stared at her in shock. There, in the fading light, stood Emma Gail Harlem. Alive and slightly bloody but breathing. She reached to take off the gray beanie, letting her dark hair fall down.

"You're not dead?" Someone asked the question that almost every member of the Ravens had been thinking.

"Of course not," Emma smirked, "You can't get rid of me that easily."

At this moment, Ellie, the youngest of the tribe, came running across the area, hugging the girl tightly. Tears were swelling in the younger girl's eyes, as she was so relieved and shocked to see this girl standing in front of her. "I thought you were gone. I thought- I thought I killed you."

Emma kneeled down, holding the smaller girl closely, "It's alright, Ellie. You didn't do anything wrong, I promise." Emma then turned to Kamai, and stood back up, addressing to the camp, "We have a problem."

"What type of problem?" Dylan muttered. The rest of the camp froze, nobody moving to embrace the girl. Her news was frightening, and until she could explain further, nobody wanted to change the subject.

"The City of the Forgotten," Emma began, "We've all heard of them, thought they were a legend. Well, it turns out they're real, and they're psychopaths. That's why Kamai here left them."

"And this is affects us, how?" Dylan asked skeptically.

"They're in the Grove," Kamai revealed, her first words since entering the forest. "I left them because they changed power, and the girl in charge now is ruthless. They want to take over this forest. You all need to get out as soon as you can. I know a place that's safe. It's our greatest chance for survival."

"Why should we trust you?" Mai interjected, her voice bitter and cold.

"Because I trust her," Emma said casually. She then raised her voice and made her declaration, "We leave tomorrow morning at dawn. You can come with us, or stay here and let some army take you over. The choice is yours."

As the evening persisted, the camp was torn. Some people believed Emma right off the bat, others leaned towards remaining in the camp and fighting for their land. The weight of this decision, however, fell most heavily on the shoulders of Sebastian and Dylan. Wherever they chose to go, their friends would choose to follow.

"We don't even know who this Kamai girl is," Dylan shook her head, "Or where she thinks we should go."

"Emma trusts her," Sebastian said.

"Emma's one person. Besides, I know she's your sister, but she makes awful decisions sometimes," Dylan shrugged.

"But she knows how to get out of them," Sebastian argued, "Besides, she hardly trusts anyone."

"So you want to take her word for it?" his opponent snapped, "Just automatically listen to the girl who accidentally got herself kidnapped by our greatest enemy? Seems like a great plan, Seb. You've really outdone yourself."

"I'm trusting the girl who negotiated our youngest to safety. The girl who convinced the entire forest that she was dead, including the people that supposedly killed her. She's not dumb, Dylan," Sebastian frowned, "And she doesn't get scared easily. If she deems that the City is a threat, they're a threat."

"You don't think our camp is worth fighting for? All this work we've put into it, and you want us to just walk away from it? I didn't realize you were such a coward," Dylan glared.

"If I'm a coward for wanting to save our friends, then so be it," he muttered, "But I'd say the easy way out is just sitting and waiting for our enemy to take us over."

"You don't even want to bother fighting."

"Dylan," Sebastian began, keeping his breath under control, "The Ravens are a people, not a place. Definitely not a patch of ground we deemed survivable. Walking away means fighting for our people, not our land."

"Then walk away," Dylan decided, "Take whoever else wants to give up this easily. I'll stay here with everyone that's willing to fight."

"Fine."

xxii. vagabonds

The four kids who called themselves the Riot had embarked on a wild journey. They only had to travel fifty miles, approximately a day's walk, if they were to average twenty minutes per mile. Cameron had predicted it would take them three days, allowing for breaks, a slower pace, and of course, time spent getting lost. They arrived at Camp Peregrin at the top of the fourth night.

They had gotten horrendously lost along the way. Cameron had instructed them very clearly to avoid the forests. They were unsure of where Harper's army would be, and they couldn't risk being seen. Besides, the quickest route was by following the old highway. The signs that once marked exits, however, were long gone or had layers of festering moss, so they were clueless as to where they were. After so many wrong turns, they were shocked to discover the camp at all.

When they'd reached what they believed to be the entrance, they agreed to send one member down first. The road leading to the campsite was surrounded by trees, and their goal of going undercover was mandatory. Natalia was the candidate. She was unknown by most inhabitants of the City, so they wouldn't recognize her to be one of the runaway foursome.

She was also a smart girl, and a fighter. If there were people living in the camp, she could fend them off until the rest of the Riot could save her.

Natalia tip-toed down the hilly road until she came upon a sign. The painted wood was faded, but she could clearly make out the only word that mattered.

"We're here!" she called up to her friends.

"If there's anyone down there, they'll have heard her," Marley muttered to Jacob and Donovan. Still, the trio approached her and the sign.

"There's no footprints anywhere, and nobody's vandalized this sign or anything," Natalia observed, "I don't think anyone is here."

"They might be at the base," Jacob pointed out.

Donovan shook his head, "Look," he gestured to a field below them that was covered with weeds and overgrown plants, "That had to have been a garden when this camp was real, but it hasn't been touched in years."

"So Kamai isn't here either," Jacob muttered, "Well, at least we're alone so far. Should we head down?" He was met with a unanimous nod, and the group began to continue down the steep path towards the camp. Apparently cars and buses had once managed down this road; it seemed like they would have rolled right off. In a way, these kids had forgotten how normal driving once was. It had been years since they'd sat behind a steering wheel. Some of them had never even been old enough to drive.

Once at the base, they were overcome with silence. It was as though the camp hadn't been touched in years. There was no trash anywhere, no sign that someone was living there, no signs of enemies.

"Hands up," Donovan whispered to his friends, and they followed his instructions. He then yelled, loud enough for anyone who might be living in the camp to hear, "We come in peace. Is there anybody here?" The Riot stood at the base of this gravel path for about five minutes, waiting for some sign of life. There was nothing. They were alone.

The group began to walk around the perimeter of the abandoned camp. At the bottom of the large hill, there was a lake, still equipped with canoes and kayaks and the fishing gear the campers had once used to explore. Fishing gear was good; it meant they could find food. Along the camp sat around fifteen cabins, each of them filled with four to six sets of bunkbeds, depending on the side. The doors were all locked, but some quick finagling opened them easily. Dust filled the empty rooms, a final sign that they did not share this land with anyone else.

As the sun set that evening, the Riot sat outside by the clearing that once held a campfire. They were too tired from their journeys to find dry wood, and besides, the air was warm that night.

Marley pulled out a lighter and a joint from her back pocket, "Shall we?" On any ordinary day, Donovan would have condemned this behavior, but on that evening, he joined in. All four kids passed the drug around, smoking and getting high. As the substance reached their brains, the stresses began to dissolve, and they were left with the comfort of a world where they did not have to worry. A world where Harper couldn't touch them. Yes, finally, they were untouchable. Invincible. In that moment, they would even say they were immortal.

When dawn came to the Grove forest, some of the Ravens had packed their old duffel bags and backpacks that they'd brought with them when they first fled their hometowns. In the dim light, they turned towards Emma and Kamai, who were standing at the front gate.

"He might have chosen to stay," the latter of the girls turned to her friend, who was staring longingly around the camp, eyes searching for one person in specific.

"He would have told me," she muttered, "He'd have said goodbye." They waited out there for about five more minutes, staying longer than they'd ever intended.

"We can't hold out any longer," Kamai said eventually, "We have to start moving."

"I'll find him," Emma shook her head. She walked away from the nervous crowd, and barged into her brother's bedroom. Two heads turned to look at the intruder: Sebastian and Dylan. "Get out to the center, or we're leaving without you."

Sebastian nodded and stood up, picking up his packed bag. Before following his sister out of the room, he turned to his co-leader, "You can still come."

Dylan just sighed, "You're making a dumb mistake."

"Have fun being their pawns," Emma snapped, "I thought we came out here for our freedom."

"We came here because we had nowhere else to go," the other girl corrected.

"Sounds like the same thing," responded the first. With that, the Harlem siblings exited the cabin, leaving Dylan Alexander alone. Around twenty of their forty members had gathered in the camp's center. The rest had chosen to stay. Among this twenty were Mai, Serena, Nova, Hayden, and a multitude of scouts, including Corey, Nathan, Yasmin, and even Ellie. They had counted off their numbers at least ten times before they set out onto this new journey.

"The camp where we're going is one forest over," Kamai announced, "We're headed northeast. There's a highway near the top delta of the creek. If we can get there by nightfall, it'll be smooth sailing until we get there."

"Why do we trust this girl again?" Mai muttered to Sebastian. The two were standing near the back of the crowd, making sure that nobody would fall too far behind. Sebastian was watching his sister intently. She was at the front, right beside Kamai.

"We don't," Sebastian responded, "But we trust Emma, right?"

Mai nodded, "And Emma doesn't trust just anyone. Besides, I could kill this chick if I had to."

"It's not gonna come to that," the other boy smirked.

"I didn't say it would, just if I had to," Mai shrugged. As the group cleared a couple of miles, they approached the border of the Condor's camp. Luckily, they would not have to cross through any of their self-proclaimed territory, but scouts were still patrolling the area.

"Gail!" Sebastian called, and Emma's head whipped up as she walked back to meet him. He was careful not to say her name so close to this territory. Her hair was hidden again in the beanie, and her bandana covered her face. Hopefully, nobody would recognize her as their deceased prisoner. The leader turned to both girls beside him, "You two need to go. Take a longer route. Meet at the bridge near the creek by noon. We'll wait for you there."

Mai and Emma both nodded, understanding why they must avoid being seen by the Condors. They were too valuable to both sides, and as far as one was concerned, they were lifeless. As the two girls began to leave their group, Sebastian gripped Mai's arm.

"Stay safe," he said, gazing into her brown eyes, "And keep her safe too."

"You too," Mai nodded. Emma began to interject something towards her brother, express her discontent with needing "protection", as he'd suggested, but she refrained. A Condor had whistled, signaling that the Ravens had been sighted, and it was time that the renegade prisoners run. And so they ran.

Sebastian sighed, watching the two people he cared for most in the world as they disappeared into the greenery. So many things could go wrong. He could lose them both in an instant. But would he not lose them if they stayed in this pack? Would the Condors not see them? Deep down inside him, he knew that they would need to separate to make it through this trial.

"Ravens, huh?" said a voice from behind him. The crowd stopped and turned to the newcomers. The trio consisted of three Condors: one girl and two boys. The boy in front was the one who had spoken. He was tall, with dark brown hair and an innocent face. He seemed harmless, but Sebastian knew better than to deem any member of their clan harmless.

"We're not in your territory," Sebastian said shortly. His eyes wandered towards the forest, making sure the girls were out of sight. They were. The Condor boy followed his gaze, and then scanned through the clump of Ravens, although he was looking for someone.

"There's a whole lot of you here," he observed, "Suspicious, right?" The Ravens' leader took a step forward, but was met with Serena's hand on his shoulder.

"Seb—," she whispered, looking at him nervously. She could see the anger rising inside him just by looking at this Condor. She feared the cords keeping him in control might snap.

As she said the boy's name, the Condor's face dropped. He took a deep breath as his heart raced, "You're him."

Serena stepped forward, more protectively now, "And what's that supposed to mean?"

"I'm sorry about your sister," the Condor shrugged, "She was a fighter. Wouldn't break to anyone. She did what she had to." At this moment, Sebastian realized who he was speaking to. Whoever this boy was had seen his sister in her most vulnerable state. He may have been the killer, for all he knew. He may have thought he'd drawn the life from her lungs. The details of Emma's escape were still blurry to Sebastian; he figured that they assumed they'd killed her, and when her body was removed from the cell, she'd ran. He was utterly unaware of her means to freedom.

Serena's fear was right. Within seconds, Sebastian was on top of this boy, punching him relentlessly, and soon enough the other Condors were attacking the Ravens' leader. The Ravens stood by in shock, some of them aching to assist in this squabble, but Serena and Hayden held them back.

"Sebastian Harlem!" Serena screamed, hoping to get his attention, "Seb, if you don't calm down, the rest of us will have the same fate as your sister!" She knew this last part wasn't true, as she knew that Emma was still alive and well, and while Sebastian knew this as well, just the mention of his loved one was enough to draw him out. He stepped back, breathing heavily. His bottom lip was swollen, and his left eyebrow dripped with blood, but the boy on the ground fared worse.

He stood up shakily and sighed, "I deserved that. Now get out of here, and I won't tell Megan about this. And I know the last thing you want to do is face her."

Sebastian nodded and turned back to the Ravens, "You heard him, let's go." Just like that, the group continued towards the creek, moving slightly further from the Condor's boundaries. He remained in the back of the group, as the rest just followed Kamai. She appeared to be irritated by this slight delay, but when they were travelling along this path, it was inevitable.

Serena pulled out a small napkin from her bag and wiped the blood off Sebastian's face. "You could have hurt yourself."

"He hurt Emma," the boy muttered angrily.

The medic sighed, realizing the subject had to be changed. She said, "He mentioned Megan. She's their leader, right?"

"Yeah," he nodded, not really paying attention. His mind was elsewhere. When Emma had interrupted him and Dylan that morning, she was not wearing her jacket. For the first time since her capture, he saw her bare arms. Most of her wounds had healed by that point, but the scars still remained. He saw lashes on her back that could only be caused by a hard belt, burn marks painting her pale skin, the number 37 carved into her forearm. Emma had told him nothing of her time in their prison, but that morning, his twisted nightmares came true.

"He made it sound like you knew her," Serena continued.

"I did," Sebastian shrugged, "I wish I didn't."

"Tell me," the girl prompted, "It's a long walk, we'll run out of things to talk about."

"She's my ex," he began, "We dated for a couple years in high school. She was crazy high-maintenance, which was fine, but stressful. Anyways, she started cheating on me. Emma's the one that figured it out, she was in my sister's room with my best friend. I called her out for it, and she told the world I was the devil incarnate, or something like that. Well, now she hates me, and consequently hates all of us. It's all my fault that the Condors hate the Ravens, so that's just great."

Serena frowned, "I'm sorry. She's a bitch, you know. Mai's told me stories. But Seb, you're not at blame for any of this. They're strong, we're strong.

With Megan in charge, they were going to hate us no matter who our leader was."

"She knows my weak spot," Sebastian pointed out, "She knew to take Emma."

"Emma gave herself, remember?" Serena smiled softly, "This isn't going to help, but my brother had a psychopathic ex-girlfriend too."

The leader smirked, "Really?"

"Yeah," she nodded, "My parents died during the Plague, and so I was living with just her and Slade for awhile. That neighborhood got violent as soon as the adults started dying off and losing control. The turf wars were pretty severe. Basically, she pushed my brother in front of a bullet, and then got mad at him that he hadn't been eager to take it for her. He was only shot in the leg, so he lived and made it to a fortified city, but still. She was insane."

Sebastian cracked a smile, "I didn't picture you as one to put up with a crazy person for so long."

Serena just shrugged, "I've put up with this lot, haven't I?"

Mai and Emma had decided on a path that was far inland and filled with Rogues, but that meant there would be no Condors. Taking on Rogues would be easy. They wore masks and bandanas to hide their face, a custom carried by many of the forest's inhabitants, and carried bags as though they were looking for their next place to set up camp. Mai's gun was situated in her makeshift holster as well—a symbol that they were not to be messed with. They passed by many real Rogues throughout this travel, and nobody gave them a second thought. A couple stared at Emma for a brief moment, and she held her breath as she realized they were boys and girls she'd slept with. They recognized her shape, but with the rumors of her death and her hidden face, there was no way they could prove who she was.

"We haven't exactly gotten the chance to talk yet," Mai said at one point in their hike.

"We've talked this whole time," Emma shrugged.

"You know what I mean," Mai sighed, "We went through the same thing. Nobody else has gone through that."

Emma shook her head, "There's nothing to talk about."

The older girl paused and rolled up the other's sleeve, as well as her own, "See these numbers? There's plenty of shit to talk about."

The younger one snapped, "I give two shits about our camp, you don't. It's that simple."

Mai stepped back, alarmed by her sudden outburst. She couldn't deny this stab to her own hubris, and reputed, "Are you insane? I spent three months there, you took two weeks. You're not any stronger than I am."

Emma just laughed, "You think that measures anything? What about when my brother was a disaster and gave up his jacket to Hayden, of all people? You came to Lily's looking to leave them. They shouldn't have even let you come back. All you ever want to do is run away."

"You left them too," Mai hissed, glaring at the other girl.

"I came back after, I don't know, three weeks?" Emma rolled her eyes, "You took nine months, and then tried to leave again when they were already weak."

"Then why don't you just kick me out? Why'd you let me tag along on this trip in the first place?" Mai challenged her.

"Sebastian wears the jacket," her opponent said casually. While the older of the girls seemed to seethe with rage at this attack, the younger had been swept over with a steely resolve. She was unwavering and relentless, but under control. This Emma had grown up. She no longer thought of her emotions the way she had once before. To her now, all the world was a mess of tricky alliances and bloodsport, although the killing was something she hoped to avoid. Emma Gail Harlem was no longer weak. She added, "You better be thankful that he's the older sibling."

They reached the creek thirty minutes after the Ravens, and it could not have been a moment more soon.

XXIII. union

- -

For the first two days since their arrival at Peregrin, the Riot had avoided direct contact with any other human beings. Other than occasionally speaking to Cameron over the radio, they were utterly alone. Had anyone stayed at the camp since the Plague, they were long gone, and never to return. However, that also meant Kamai was not about to come back. They had arrived there hoping they would find her, but sadly, that seemed to be impossible.

Impossible, at least, until Jacob Hart came sprinting down the hill one morning with a warning.

"People are coming," he revealed to his friends, as they looked up at him with fear and concern flickering in their eyes.

"What do you mean?" Natalia asked, "What people?"

Jacob's heart was racing, "I don't know. There were a lot of them. Maybe fifteen? Twenty? Carrying bags and stuff like that. They might be coming here."

"Were they armed?" This was a very reasonable question, as the four of them stood no chance against an army of fifteen.

"Are we armed?" added Marley. Her cynical dose of reality was always necessary. The answer was not a surprise, but still not the best of news. They had some knives, but none of them were trained to fight.

"Diplomacy," Jacob declared, "That's what we need. Donny, take the lead."

"Why me?" Donovan looked up, startled by this newfound responsibility.

"You're articulate. Just say something smart," the other boy shrugged. All of their heads whipped up towards the gravel path, as they heard footsteps approaching. Walking down was a girl with a dark ponytail. The way she carried herself beamed with confidence and bravery, and it was clear that she believed she may have come across her promised land. She and Donovan met in the center of the camp.

The stranger's eyes scanned over the surroundings, "Is it just the four of you?"

"What is it to you?" Donny frowned, crossing his arms and trying his hardest to maintain the appearance that he was in control. That he and his friends had any true claim to this land. They'd been there for two nights now; they were foreigners.

"There would be space to share," she shrugged casually.

"Not that simple," Donovan shook his head, "Who are you, and where do you come from?"

"I could ask you the same thing," said the explorer.

A different idea struck him at this moment, "Kamai Wells. Does this name mean anything to you?" If he stuck out this olive branch, perhaps the two sides could come to some reconciliation. Besides, it seemed Kamai was the only soul in the forest who knew the details of this sanctuary. It was likely, in fact, that she sent these people.

"What does it mean to you?" she hesitated.

Donny was not about to answer, but he would respond with yet another question, "Did she send you here?"

"What's your connection?"

"Don't know who you are, don't see any reason to tell you. Go tell the rest of your group," he declared, a new assertiveness in his throat.

The stranger took a step forward, glaring at the boy, "I don't take orders from you, got it?"

Donovan took a deep breath, gulping at this powerful girl in front of him, "Bring down your people. Then we'll talk." The stranger seemed satisfied with this response, so she shoved him slightly and began to make the journey back up to the road. When she was far enough out of sight, Donny turned around and addressed his friend, "Get to the boat shed. If they're enemies, we can't take them all. If I'm standing here alone, they probably won't hurt me."

"I'm not gonna leave you," Jacob smirked, and then received a tired look from his best friend, "You're going to make my life living hell if I stay."

"Pretty much," Donny nodded. The other boy sighed and led the girls down to the dirty shack near the docks. This was likely the one place where the newcomers wouldn't look if they decided to raid the camp. Once his friends were hidden, the de facto leader turned his attention back towards the hill, and watched as the group began to descend. The stranger was still in the front, leading them down with the same tricky poise as before. By her side stood a taller boy wearing a dark jacket, worn out around the edges.

"You said we'll talk," the girl announced, repeating Donovan's words from earlier.

"Your proposition?" he challenged, waiting for the group to declare what it was exactly that they wanted. Perhaps they could work together. Four people was hardly enough to hold down this fort. As he spoke, a girl near the back of the group shot her head up. She had been distracted by the camp's surroundings, lost in the time when this place was her magnificent second home. But his voice shook her back to reality, and she pushed straight through the crowd.

"Donny?" she gasped when she could finally see him. His face broke into a relieved smile when he saw the girl's pinched face and bouncing dark curls. "How long have you been here? Where's Coby?"

"Good to see you too, Kamai," he grinned as the two hugged, "And he goes by Jacob now, for your information."

Kamai just laughed, "Jacob? Really? Too formal for my liking." By now, the group of newcomers was staring at the duo in confusion, and Donny couldn't help but notice a scowl forming on the jacketed boy's face. Kamai turned to her friends and said, "This is Donovan Mayler, an old friend. We can trust him. Donovan, these are the Ravens of the Grove."

Donovan reached out to shake the original stranger's hand, and she returned the favor. There was definitely a certain coldness in her grip, as though she didn't quite trust him. He couldn't blame her. He wouldn't have trusted himself either, nor did he really trust these people.

"I'm Mai," she said curtly.

"Donny," he smiled. Mai gestured to the boy beside her, and he clicked his tongue, as if contemplating what to say.

"Sebastian," he said hesitantly, eyeing the Rioter suspiciously.

"Is the City in the Grove yet?" Donny turned to Kamai, desperate for an excuse to break the daring eye contact with Sebastian. "Is that why you came now?"

Kamai nodded, "They'll destroy everything. We had to get out. Is that why you guys came?"

Donny sighed, "Harper's a psychopath now, if you were unaware."

"Oh, that's nothing new," she laughed, "There's a kill order on me for a reason." At this, Donny couldn't help but notice Sebastian turn to a shorter girl whose face was hidden by a red bandana. He glared at her, as though he was surprised by this information, and she was responsible for informing him.

The girl stepped forward, pulling down the mask, "There's twenty of us. Do you have space?"

"Em—" Sebastian began, trying to pull her back.

She quickly cut him off, "We don't have any other options."

Donovan looked between this new speaker and his old friend, who gave him a supportive nod. He sighed, "We have four. There's plenty of space, on the terms that we work as one team. Riot and Ravens, together."

Sebastian began to shake his head, and Mai stepped in to argue, "Alright, but since we have the majority in people, we have the majority in power. Deal?"

"No!" the previously masked girl interjected, "He's right. We share power. Two jackets, except Dylan still has the other one. You know what I mean."

"You don't get to make the rules, Emma," Sebastian snapped, receiving a sharp scowl from the other.

Donovan paused, unsure of how to assert his power. He did have one idea, although it was something he would never risk using. Still, he casually added, "We have a radio to connect to the City. If you dare tread on the Riot, our shared enemy will be here within three days time. They'll kill Kamai on spot, and imprison the rest of you for having supported her. Since we're the ones who would have turned you in, we'll be let off clear. Understood?"

"You would never," Kamai whispered, eyes widening at his violent declaration. This was not the Donny she remembered. That boy was a wild soul, afraid of nothing, yet always looking out for those he cared about. He never feared hurting himself, but hurting another person was a powerful evil. Before the coup, he would never dare make a statement so violent. She would have expected this from Harper, perhaps, but never from good old Donovan Mayler. And where was Coby all this time? Where was Jacob hiding? Why did they feel they had to hide? She feared her friends were nothing more than strangers now.

"It's up for discussion," Sebastian said eventually, and it appeared that Emma was about to protest once again. "Until then, we have a deal."

xxiv. the raven's riot

With Sebastian and Donny now on shaky terms, the Ravens moved to settle into the cabins. As there were few of them, they were split between two of the old cabins: boys in one, girls in the other. Kamai would join the four members of the Riot in a separate structure, feeling uncomfortable around her allies from the Grove.

Among the boys who had chosen this journey were Hayden, Corey, and Nathan: the old roommates from their original camp. Sebastian was the only one who hadn't shared a space with anyone else back in their forest. Since the very beginning, his room had doubled as an office. Originally, that was all it was intended to be, but he had spent so many nights in that room, falling asleep at the wee hours of the morning, they all began to see it as his own.

The others in his cabin chose their bunks based off where their old roommates would be. It was the first time he'd felt like the odd man out. There were nine boys, and five sets of bunks. Sebastian was the only one with nobody above him.

As they began to organize their supplies, Corey was the first to cheer. "Guys, we made it! The Condors ain't shit any longer!" he yelled. In response, the other boys hooted and clapped at his announcement.

However, Sebastian was far from thrilled. He simply muttered, "Great, now we're living with another enemy." As he'd learned from the encounter earlier, Kamai had a kill order on her head. This wasn't some irrelevant detail; if she had a kill order, she was dangerous. Besides, she'd said this camp would be empty, although clearly it was not. She'd lied to them twice now—what else could she be hiding?

"Lighten up," Nathan smirked, "That Donovan kid was weak. Even Marko could take him down in a second."

"You know it!" called a skinny Asian boy near the back of the cabin. His face beamed with happiness as he was laughing alongside the rest of the room. They all felt so comfortable in this new camp. Sebastian couldn't help but worry they were making a mistake. Hansel and Gretel felt this way too when they arrived at the witch's house, did they not? At this moment, the door to the cabin swung open, and in irritated Emma stormed in.

Nathan teased, "Ever learned to knock? We could have all been naked in here. Your brother could have been naked in here."

"His fragile masculinity couldn't handle that," she snapped, then turned to the moping leader, "Can we talk?"

Sebastian sighed and stood up off his bottom bunk, "Let's go outside."

"No," Emma said, "In here. They can all hear it."

"What's your issue?" he sighed, realizing he was in for his sister's wrath.

"What's yours?" she said, "I mean, welcome to Nirvana, right? We have everything here, and you're acting like we're all about to die."

"We followed a wanted criminal here, Emma," Sebastian said, his voice monotonous.

"Great," she shrugged, "I'm one too, remember? And so is Mai, and Hayden too, yet you trusted him to be our leader." Across the room, Hayden smiled, slightly embarrassed. He was one who did truly value their new location. Adrian wasn't here, so he was finally safe. The Condors or the City of the Forgotten were never his biggest threat.

"So you think we should trust the random band of criminals and drug addicts," Sebastian crossed his arms, glaring slightly, "They left three joints on the ground, who knows what else they do."

"Woah, some unsupervised teens are doing drugs. Not like that's never happened in our camp before," Emma laughed, "Besides, that one girl seems dope." That last line cracked a laugh from most of the guys in the room, since they were all enthralled by the siblings' argument.

"This isn't a joke, Emma," he sighed.

"You're the one that's not thinking rationally, Seb," she shouted, "We can't go back to the Grove. I saw the City, you didn't. They'll destroy everything. So we're stuck here in a huge camp with a garden, and a lake, where we can actually support ourselves, but we have to deal with four more people. There shouldn't be any question here."

"We don't know who these people are. I don't think they're safe," Seb said.

"There's four of them, twenty of us. What threat are they going to pose when we're running from the same group." The younger sister pulled her hair back, clearly frustrated with her brother's stubborn stance.

"They threatened to call the City here," Sebastian snapped, "Why would they do that if they were on our side?"

"The same reason I put my knife to Hayden's throat," she shrugged. Her brother did not respond, waiting for her to stake her claim, make her grand accusation. "You were pointing a gun at me."

"I didn't attack them," the other boy muttered as a wave of guilt flew through his body. He still hadn't come to terms with the fact that he had almost hurt his baby sister, even though he was unaware the masked intruder was in fact her.

"Not physically," she corrected him.

"You know you're wrong about their numbers," Sebastian said, changing the subject, "It's five to nineteen. Kamai's with them, and you know it."

Angered, Emma whirled around and walked back towards the door from which she came, "Make it six to eighteen." With that, she marched out of the cabin and out of the boys' line of sight. After a few seconds of uncomfortable silence, Sebastian stood up and followed her out, although he turned in the opposite direction. He just needed fresh air and space to clear his mind. Emma did have a point, but he couldn't bring himself to trust these strangers. Every time he chose to ally with a new person, a new group, his friends somehow ended up in danger. He couldn't just put them at risk again. The moment he let down his guard, he had a vague suspicion that everything in front of him would fall apart.

Back inside his cabin, the other boys looked to each other with surprised, and maybe even impressed, expressions. It was still strange for some of them to see Emma walking around so casually, as though she had never left. This was one of the first times they'd seen her changed personality really break through. She had always been outspoken and stubborn, but there seemed to be more now. Perhaps it was simply maturity, but as she spoke to her brother now, she was no longer the rebellious little sister with an inflated ego. Instead, she was an entity unto herself. A fighter in control of her own story, tied down to no one.

"If he's sharing a cabin with everyone, are we always gonna have to deal with his leader drama?" Nathan asked eventually. None of these boys were used to living with Sebastian, and consequently the stress that came with it. He had managed to keep a calm composure on the outside, so many of the kids who weren't close with him knew nothing of the flaming anxiety manifesting inside.

"How long until Emma steals his jacket?" Corey added, "Let's take bets. I give it a week."

"Less than that," Nathan laughed, "I bet she's negotiating with the Riot right now, and then she has the power. Tomorrow morning."

Someone added, "She already has it. She's the one that brought us here, Sebastian was just following her."

"Let's just hope Sebastian doesn't screw this whole thing up," Nathan sighed, "We're finally someplace stable, he needs to simmer down."

Hayden stepped in here, "Give him some credit, it's harder than it looks."

"Oh yes, because so much happened in your three days in power," the first boy muttered.

The ex-leader frowned, "Actually a lot happened, for your information. And Seb's been doing it for two years. He's done a damn good job."

"No one ever doubted that," Nathan shrugged, "Anyways, if two years is how long it takes for him to wear out, then it might be time for someone else to bear it. Otherwise, he's going to lose it, and then we're all screwed." To this, Hayden simply shook his head, not wanting to hear the other boys degrade their leader. Sebastian wasn't perfect, he'd made his fair share of mistakes, but anyone else would have done the same. Hayden had the utmost respect for him, but even now, he did have to admit that he could be making a mistake by not trusting the Riot. The two groups would have to collaborate, or else there would be bloodshed. It wasn't exactly difficult to predict.

Emma Gail Harlem was pissed. She had fought with her brother plenty of times before, but never had she been so disapproving of his decisions. He's crazy! she thought, He's gone mental! After storming out of the boys' cabin, she marched down the hill towards the cabin where the Riot was staying and knocked on the door. She hated standing there, waiting for them to let her in, but she still didn't know them well enough to simply barge in.

The girl Marley opened it, and seemed a little hesitant about seeing who was outside, "Are you lost? Your cabin's up the hill"

Emma rolled her eyes, "Can I come in?" Kamai was able to recognize her voice, and alerted Marley that this girl was to be trusted. Emma entered the cabin to find the other four kids sitting in a circle around a deck of cards. They seemed peaceful and simply happy to be in each other's company. This was a strange contrast compared to the Ravens' cabins—both of theirs were hectic and brimming with tension.

"So how can we help you?" Marley muttered, glaring at the other girl.

"This is Emma," Kamai explained, "My guess is that she's here to be reasonable."

Emma smirked and turned to the group, "My brother's an asshole. For whatever it's worth, I'm on your side."

Donovan smiled, "I could guess." He remembered this girl's outburst when he and Sebastian had gone face-to-face on the hill. She had protested her own people's plan of government, which he greatly appreciated.

"So what's your point, Miss Emma of the Ravens," Marley scoffed, snickering on that last part. Emma simply glared at her.

"Chill, Marley," Natalia laughed. She then turned to the Raven girl and added, "Want us to deal you in? Baby Druggie over there has decided she's too cool for card games."

"Baby Druggie?" Emma raised an eyebrow. The other kids in the room just laughed.

The girl whom they referred to sent Emma a side-eye and muttered, "Don't ever call me that."

"Got it, BD," she responded, receiving a harsh glare.

Natalia smiled, "I like you. You're cool."

"I don't," Marley said, although not in a cruel way. She was picking dirt out of her nails in a casual manner, as though nothing in this room fazed her. Her rancor was showing, of course, but when was it not?

"She makes intellectual comments," Kamai added, "Occasionally, at least."

The drug dealer just shook her head and chuckled, "Just get out of here already. I'm not dealing with smart people."

Jacob commented, "You're a doctor, Mar."

"I am not!" she protested, "I'm a nurse. There's a difference."

"Is there?" the boy laughed.

She frowned, "Why do we keep bringing this up? One knows about medicine, one's a drug dealer. We've been over this."

Jacob turned to Emma and asked, "So, little Raven princess, you at all naughty?"

"I'm the forest slut, so that counts for something," she shrugged. It seemed that she was proud of this title, honored that she got to be a little rebellious. She had never referred to herself this way; it was a secret to her friends, and a known fact to all the forest. She'd never had to explain it.

"She keeps getting better and better," Natalia smiled. And so Emma Gail Harlem took a seat on the floor of the Riot's cabin. Nobody came looking for her, and the group never did leave their room that evening. When the rest of the camp had gone quiet, as they had yet to come up with an organized guard schedule, the group stayed up for another hour more, hollering and laughing and shouting at the stars. The Riot were a wild type—free, and happy, and dancing under the weight of the universe. This lost girl felt that she had found her people. Oh, how she felt she was at home.

XXV. catalyst

T rigger Warning: This chapter includes more detailed drug use than previous ones

Through three sunsets and starry nights breaking to magnificent sunrises over the untouched lake, Camp Peregrin had not changed. Its inhabitants were not exactly friends, although some got along better than others. A shaky teamwork, however, was slowly beginning to build. When the time came to take the canoe out to fish, Jacob may be accompanied by a Raven. Often times it was Yasmin, since she had grown up going fishing with her dad. She was a natural, and Jacob was happy to have her help. They could handle conversing on the little boat, and a sort of friendship soon blossomed, as their responsibilities as fishermen provided them with a newfound respect and responsibility in the camp.

On their very first full day together, Serena had actually been the first to extend a helping hand to their new companions. Of course, Emma was the first to fully undertake the change, but Serena was the first to truly help. During the Riot's journey to the camp, Natalia had fallen, resulting in a small wound on her leg. However, Marley's medical abilities proved to be just as poor as she'd promised they were, and the lesion was on the verge of infection when they arrived. Thanks to Serena's help, the injury was soon covered, and any threat of illness was gone.

They had yet to come to concrete terms about this partnership, and some hoped that they never would. They seemed to be surviving with simply teamwork and each other's skills, the way the Ravens always had in the Grove. For some, including Emma, they wished Sebastian would never push for a change. Whatever unofficial system was underway was clearly working, and they feared that if a power structure was ever discussed, it would all fall apart.

Slowly, even the most untrusting Ravens were beginning to reach out to their new peers. Most of them, at least. Sebastian Harlem was still utterly terrified at the prospect of trusting these people; they had yet to explain what this kill order was, and the notion gave him the suspicion that they were criminals. He understood the need for teamwork on a survival scale, but as he saw relationships forming between members of the two groups, he grew weary.

One of the first surprising friendships he saw forming was between Hayden and Donovan, who seemed to be the Riot's leader. Of all possible combinations, this seemed to be one of the better ones. Hayden was mature, and he would be able think rationally about the third member to his party. If anything, he could be a bridge between the Ravens and the Riot—one that wouldn't act on their own terms. That was his biggest concern about his younger sister; she was quick to adopt the parasites, as he had once heard them refer to themselves. He knew that Emma would act on what seemed to be best for herself and nobody else. As courageous as she was, she couldn't see the big picture.

Hayden and Donovan were alright, Sebastian had decided. On this given morning, the trio was collecting firewood for the evening, as the nights had begun to get cooler. They seemed to be carrying a friendly conversation, and they were all laughing, looking extremely comfortable in each other's presences. This did concern Seb slightly, for he feared that Hayden may be letting down his guard. There was nothing he could do, however. Hayden was one of the few people in the camp whose decisions Sebastian really did trust. He had to trust him now.

There was one spurring friendship, however, that would surprise everyone, Sebastian especially. As Yasmin and Jacob developed some type of relationship, their friends were soon pulled in. Mai, the girl who threatened Donovan from the moment they'd entered the camp, had decided to turn away from Sebastian's guidance, and instead trust her best friend. Yasmin was always talking fondly about Jacob; naturally, Mai began to impede on their time together. Luckily, Jacob's partner in crime was almost always there to accompany him. Marley Dennis was thoroughly bored in the camp, and wanted nothing more than to have fun and get high. They'd ran away from the City for their freedom—she wanted to act on it.

On this sunny October afternoon, a disenchanted Marley was the one to make the first move on Mai. She approached her at a stone by the campfire, where the Raven girl was sharpening a blade.

"I'm bored," Marley declared, "Jacob is fishing with Yasmin, probably making out with her, and I want to smoke. You down?"

Mai looked up and smirked, "Isn't Jacob gay?"

"Definitely," the other girl shrugged, "But they're a couple horny teens on a canoe. It's bound to happen eventually."

"If he doesn't like girls—" Mai began, questioning this faulty logic.

"Do you want to smoke or not?" Marley cut her off, "Because I'm not putting up with you if you're going to be this uptight."

"Fine," Mai laughed, "Where to?"

"The lake, nobody goes down there," the dealer smiled. The Raven nodded, placing the knife in her backpack. The two girls began to walk down towards the sandy area near the docks, checking to make sure no wandering eyes followed them. Hayden and Donovan seemed to be the only two to notice. The boys whispered something and snickered, clearly aware of the girls' agenda, and clearly not concerned.

And so the two girls sat alongside the dock, passing a joint back and forth, breathing in the drugs and laughing as they exhaled. They were making small-talk, although neither girl could really articulate what it was they discussed. It seemed that just by asking for the other's favorite color, they were discovering the secrets of the universe. The whole entire world was at their fingertips. Mai felt that if she just reached out, perhaps she could touch it all, feel the energy of the sun rush through her veins, enlightening her mind and body and soul. This was what peace felt like, how it felt to truly be relaxed, although in this high state she was unable to realize what it was she was feeling.

Eventually, however, the only person who could ruin this beautiful vibe came walking down to the lake. He was instantly concerned when he realized Mai was no longer focused on strengthening their weapons, and even moreso when he saw two girls sitting together on the dock. He could recognize her from anywhere, he thought. How funny though, how about a month and a half before, she had entered this camp, and it took him oh so long to figure her out. But he knew her better now, did he not? He had seen her body, held her in his arms, been held in her own. Whatever they were, that label still unclear, was greater than just two co-captains.

"What the hell do you think you're doing?" Sebastian asked as he approached the two. They turned around, giggling when they saw him.

"Having fun," Mai laughed. There was a new tranquility in her eyes, the typical stoic determination having disappeared, "You should try it sometime, Seb!"

Sebastian rolled his eyes and sighed, "Is that just weed?"

"Just weed?" Marley gasped, almost sounding offended, "How dare you disrespect it like that."

The Raven's leader was trying his hardest to keep his temper down, but he was thoroughly bothered by the risky activities Mai was partaking in. He'd spent enough time in high school and this forest to know that drugs might be laced with some other substances, and while he knew Marley was a dealer, he still questioned the source from whom she bought.

"You're being an idiot, Mai," Sebastian frowned disapprovingly, although his friend did not seem to pick up his uncomfort.

"That's not nice, Sebby," Mai chuckled, "You're so mean now. I see where Emma gets it."

The boy just glared at her, not responding. He knew that this intoxicated version of the girl in front of him didn't know what she was saying, or at least hadn't really thought it through. It shouldn't bother him. It should have meant nothing. Still, his natural instincts were to fight anyone who dared degrade his family; that slight insult towards Emma was enough to hurt his honor. If Mai was sober, he'd have fought back. When Mai became sober again, they'd have to discuss this.

Within the next four minutes, Jacob and Yasmin docked the canoe onto the beach, and called on Sebastian to help them unload the day's catch. He was grateful for the opportunity to leave the high girls, and instead do something productive for the camp. They'd trusted him to be a leader because he was a worker, someone who didn't put themselves above everyone else. Getting on good terms with the Riot meant participating. It meant sweating, it meant being busy. Clearly his old friend didn't understand that anymore.

If the camp's location wasn't perfect already, its equipped amenities made it so. According to Kamai, they had never had running water there, but instead there was a complex filtration system that would provide them with water. Buckets must be carried up from the lake, and then filtered, boiled, and cooled. The system was located up by the old dining hall, which was in the direct center of the hill, so carrying the buckets of water was one of the more grueling tasks. However, their entire survival was dependent on water. Back at the Grove, they'd used a similar system from the creek right behind their camp. This version was just a little bit harder, and everyone was willing to take their turns carrying.

"What happens when winter comes?" Sebastian had asked Kamai later that afternoon, since she was the most educated about the camp's structures. The two were working the filtration system that day, waiting for Emma, Natalia, Corey, and Nova to provide them with water.

"I don't know," she paused, "It was a summer camp, nobody lived here in the winter. The creeks in the Grove never froze over, did they?"

"Never got cold enough," the boy shrugged.

"It'll hardly get colder up here," Kamai said, "And a lake will be harder to freeze than a creek."

"It better be," he said.

"We'll make it work," she promised, "I wouldn't have brought you all here if we were all just going to die."

"You thought we'd die in the forest," Sebastian said.

"That's why I got you all out," Kamai said, "I don't owe you anything, Sebastian. You just need to learn to trust me now."

"You have a kill order," he frowned, finally pointing out the detail that had bothered him since their arrival, "Why?"

Kamai sighed, realizing that this was a part of her history, and she couldn't just ignore it and pretend it could disappear. It was bound to catch up with her eventually, but she had done nothing to be ashamed of, had she not? "Harper, the leader of the City, is insane," she began.

"I know. You and the other four all ran from her and her brother. We've been over this," he cut her off.

"Shut up and listen to me. She was my best friend for the first year or so in the City. We were roommates, did everything together. It was the two of us, her brother, their cousin, and Jacob and Donny. Anyways, some things happened, there was a revolution, but you knew that. Donny pushed Harper out of a grenade, but he absorbed the impact and went comatose, Jacob was severely depressed after that, and then I realized just how mental Harper was. I had no choice but to leave, and we'd made an agreement that I had a grace period of one year. When I decided after that not to come back, I was excommunicated fully, and declared an enemy," she revealed, turning away from Sebastian.

"That's it?" he asked, raising an eyebrow slightly, trying to gauge if the girl in front of him was telling the truth.

"Yes, that's it," she snapped, "We're not dangerous. Everyone knows that except for you."

At this point, Emma and Natalia arrived at the system with their next buckets of water. They paused for a moment, reading the discomfort between the two.

"Please don't tell me you're trying to kill each other," Natalia said, "That's unproductive."

Sebastian smirked, "We're all good, actually." Kamai side-eyed him slightly, unsure of his own honesty this time, but he sent her a small nod to signify that yes, he was being truthful.

"It's about time," Emma muttered, "Welcome to Peregrin, big brother." The two girls emptied the buckets into the tub above the filter, and returned down towards the lake to retrieve more.

"Do you think that was real?" Natalia asked once they were out of earshot.

Emma said, "It better be. Besides, he can't lie to save his life."

"You sure about that?" Natalia smirked, "I feel like to be a leader, you have to lie."

"Well, he can't lie to me, at least," Emma said, "Tali, this is good." Natalia smiled. She was never one for nicknames, but it didn't bother her when Emma referred to her as Tali. It sounded soft, a word that could never describe her or Emma, yet it somehow worked.

"So when do peace talks start?" she asked. To this, Emma just sent her an annoyed glare. The two girls had spent enough time together over the past few days for her to know just how opposed the Raven girl was to structured negotiation. Emma believed that the moment Sebastian and Donovan tried to impose a real leadership institution, one side would come out unhappy, and their teamwork would dissipate. With the two boys as their unofficial leaders, they were doing great, and it would only get better if her brother could put his ego on hold and learn to work with the Riot. "You know it has to happen eventually."

Emma stopped walking, frustrated, "Not if nobody ever brings it up."

"It wouldn't be such a bad thing," Natalia shrugged, "If we're all one people, then your friends aren't gonna be as pissed at you for trusting us."

Emma shook her head. It was true that some tensions had developed between her and the other Ravens. In a sense, she had become a stranger to them. After her dark time with the Condors and weeks in the woods, pretending to be dead, she had come back stronger, more independent, greater than ever before. However, she came back with the declaration that they needed to leave their home. She came back with Kamai, and the moment they'd arrived at Peregrin, she had joined the Riot's cause. The Emma her camp knew was gone, and in her place stood a person whom they didn't quite know they could trust.

"They'll see us as one people over time," Emma said, "An official label won't change anything. Only time or a catalyst."

And what perfect timing, for their catalyst had just arrived. Jacob came running out of the Riot's cabin, blowing a small air horn he'd found in one of the camp's abandoned offices. It was their emergency signal, a sign that they needed to congregate at once. Emma and Natalia dashed up the hill, along with the rest of the camp.

"What's going on?" someone asked, everyone pushing to get into the crowd and hear the announcement.

"Cameron radioed," Jacob said, ice blue eyes wide with fear, heart racing.

"Shit," Donovan muttered, "What'd he say?" This concerned the Ravens especially, since they had heard of Cameron, although the details on him were still fuzzy. Even Emma knew very little about this other boy, but they knew he was their source of information.

Jacob took a deep breath, "They're coming. Someone tipped them off, I don't know who, but they're coming here."

"What about the forest?" someone shouted.

"They've fallen," Jacob announced, "They surrendered in four days."

"It'll take them three days to get here," Kamai said, "Maybe less than that if they move fast. We don't have time to get somewhere else."

"We can't," Donovan declared, "I mean, you can leave if you want, but—"

Sebastian nodded and finished this thought, "But this time we hold our ground and fight."

XXVI. lull

Two Days. Two days until the City came to Peregrin. Two days to organize their ragtag team into a force strong enough to resist. They realized quite quickly that true resistance was impossible. The City had guns. Peregrin had some knives, and only a couple people actually capable of combat. The City had an army, Peregrin had twenty-five people, one of them only twelve years old, and one of them with a screwed up leg. Should the conflict turn violent, they all knew which side would lose.

So the solution? Not let it turn violent.

The hardest part with this was simply that they could not prepare. They could gather all the weapons they owned, take apart any systems that may be of use to the intruders, sketch escape routes and battle plans, should the extremities become necessary. The most important thing they could do, however, was unite. They were stronger as one people. One Peregrin. There could be no more six and eighteen. No, it was twenty-four, and twenty-four alone.

While they were all acutely aware of the need to come together, Sebastian was once again put on edge. He had good reason, of course. Every time he began to trust someone, something bad seemed to happen. He'd done it again—jinxed them all.

"Who tipped them off?" Sebastian approached Donovan and Jacob once the camp had cleared out, beginning the preparations.

"Yeah, if only we knew," Jacob muttered.

"It wasn't us, if that's what you're implying," Donny sighed, realizing what the Raven boy was likely suggesting.

"You said only you guys and that Cameron kid knew," Sebastian pointed out skeptically.

Jacob shook his head, "Cameron didn't know about you guys or Kamai, but he said that they were coming here in search of the Ravens. He told us that the Riot had to run, and let you guys fend for yourselves, but we're staying. If anything, you should be thanking us."

"Oh lord, Jacob, stop talking," Donovan muttered. He realized the importance of their teamwork in these difficult times, and from what he'd heard from Hayden and Yasmin, Sebastian was not exactly the best at handling guilt.

Sebastian murmured, "Not all our people chose to come. Those snakes ratted us out."

"And yet, we are the ones you can't trust," Jacob rolled his eyes, receiving another harsh glare from his friend. "What? It's the truth."

"You're not helpful, Coby. I love you, but you need to shut up," Donny smiled, staring his very best friend in the eyes. "Did Cameron say if Harper's army included people from the forest?"

"Yeah," Jacob nodded, "He said that there was some girl that could negotiate an alliance, and then this other forest girl is Harper's new right-hand, or something and wants to kill all of us."

"Goddamnit," Sebastian shouted, kicking the stones at his feet, "It's Megan, isn't it?"

"And who is this Megan?" Jacob asked, searching for clarification.

"My psycho ex-girlfriend who's already tried to destroy us," he sighed, "She's a ruthless bitch, sounds like she and Harper would get along great."

"Wow," Jacob muttered, "You really are a mess, Sebastian."

"Do you know her weaknesses," Donny cut off his friend, "Anything we can use against her."

Sebastian paused, an idea flickering into existence. It was a bad idea, dangerous, but based off what Emma had told him, it seemed to be their best bet. "Megan has a second, some little girl she's been training to succeed her. From what I've heard, this kid feels crazy guilty for tricking our camp and getting Ellie kidnapped. We might be able to use that to our advantage. If Megan's coming, she'll bring that girl along with her."

"We're putting the child in danger?" Jacob gaped, looking between the two other boys, "No, that's ludacris."

"It is," Donovan nodded, "But guilt is a weapon if we play the right cards. We'll get Mai hiding nearby with our gun. If this kid attacks Ellie in the slightest, she'll shoot."

"Shooting kids?" Jacob shouted, "No, this is insane."

"That would be a last resort," Sebastian said, keeping eye contact with Donny only. He hated this plan; it would only result in Murphy's Law, where everything that theoretically could go wrong would. "Should I brief

Ellie?" The other boys nodded, knowing very well that only the Raven leader could convince one of his own people to undertake something so dangerous.

"This is ridiculous," Jacob rambled once the oldest boy had walked away, "We can't do this. We should leave, run while we still can. We could be at the coast by sundown tomorrow, probably. There are lakes all over this area, there's bound to be other old camps, old towns, anything."

Donovan shook his head, "We're gonna stay. This is our battle too, Harper's our enemy."

His friend frowned, "They're willing to put a twelve year old in danger, and possibly shoot another child. What the hell do you think they'll do to us? How long until Harper proposes a trade? They would gladly hand us over if it meant that they'd leave them alone."

"Coby—" Donny began, but was quickly cut off.

"Don't call me that," Jacob snapped.

"They wouldn't do that," Donny sighed, trying to finish his original claim.

"How can you be so sure?" the other boy retorted. When his best friend didn't have an immediate answer, he simply frowned, a wave of disapproval splashing over his face. "See you in the City of the Forgotten, Donny Boy."

A nervous Sebastian walked over to the cabin that had become the makeshift Med Hut. Ellie was sitting there with Serena, organizing bandages and the other supplies they'd brought from the Grove. They hadn't officially unpacked it all yet, but now there was pressure to be ready.

"Hey," he said, walking up to them, "Ellie, can we talk for a moment?"

"Yeah!" she smiled, jumping up. Serena examined the leader closely, able to tell just how anxious he was. She worried what his message entailed.

"You remember that girl Hannah, right?" Sebastian asked once they were a little ways away from the Med Hut.

Ellie's face dropped, a mixture of anger, betrayal, and embarrassment flooding her eyes, "What about her?"

"The Condors are coming with the City," Sebastian began, "Which means she's coming."

This time, a new fear spread between her eyes, "The-the Condors?"

Sebastian nodded, "We'll be alright though, but we'll need your help. Emma said that it seemed like she felt bad for deceiving you. We're gonna need you to guilt her into betraying her people."

"What?" Ellie asked, "That's your best plan?"

"We're not exactly equipped to fight," Sebastian sighed, "If we can tear them down from the inside out, we can win this thing."

"We're really screwed, aren't we?" she asked, although it wasn't much of a question. The answer was apparent in the sweat that highlighted the leader's hairline, the way his shoulders slouched inward. "I'll try my best."

"Thank you," he breathed out a sigh of relief, "We'll have Mai stationed nearby. If Hannah dares make one move against you, she'll be able to protect you."

Ellie nodded, thankful that they'd thought of this precaution. She felt the need to mention something else, however. "Her name is Cora, by the way. She lied about that too."

Sebastian nodded, "I'm glad you knew that. You got this, kiddo." Ellie smiled, a slight new spark coming into her eyes. As nervous as she was to have to face that girl again, she was honored to have such a responsibility. She'd expected that she'd be pushed to the sidelines the moment their enemies arrived, but no. She would be right in the center of the action, carrying out a mission only she could perform. Yes, she was nervous, but more important than ever.

Emma and Natalia were stationed at the bottom of the hill as the sun was setting. They had spent the afternoon helping Mai improve their weapons, sharpening and cleaning the blades. Natalia revealed that she had never experienced any armed fighting; she was good with her fists and kicks, but never had she wielded a knife against another person.

"Well, you need to fix that," Mai smirked, "Emma, go teach her. I can handle this." Emma smiled, grateful for the opportunity to anything less static than their previous activity. She led Natalia down to the grassy area near the miniscule beach where they would have this lesson.

Suddenly, a metal rod with a texture like sandpaper landed at Mai's feet. She looked up, glaring at the perpetrator. "Marley, what are you on? What is this?"

"I'm sober, Mai," the girl smirked before adding, "That's a knife sharpener, genius."

"You wanna help?" Mai shrugged, gesturing to the empty space on the stone beside her.

"Can't, looks like my boy Jacob is freaking out," Marley sighed, gesturing towards the boy stressing in front of his cabin. He seemed livid, a side Mai had never suspected could exist in him.

"Go talk to him," Mai nodded, and she returned to her work, now using her friend's gift from the dining hall.

By the time the sun was setting, Emma and Natalia had been hard at work for almost an hour. They'd been scrimmaging with sticks instead of weapons themselves, since neither girl wanted to risk hurting the other. In truth, it was simply that Natalia didn't want to hurt Emma. Emma was not afraid of injury, nor did she think she could possibly hurt her friend. Her abilities were above that, she believed.

Their most recent trial had ended with Emma standing over Natalia, her stick pricking her opponent's neck. Natalia had yet to beat the other girl, but it was no longer easy for Emma to win. She did have to fight back now, although so far she'd continued to come out on top.

"You're getting better," Emma smiled, helping her friend up, "But you left your chest exposed. I could have stabbed you in the heart if I wanted."

"Glad you didn't," Natalia smirked.

"Don't think this stick is sharp enough," Emma responded. "Do you want to give it another go?"

"Just because you want to beat me again? I'll pass," the other girl laughed, tightening her dark ponytail.

Emma just frowned, "We're going into battle in two days. Seb says it won't get violent, but it will. I don't want you to get yourself killed right away."

"Breathe, Emma," Natalia sighed, putting her arm around the other girl, "The lake is gorgeous right now."

"We can talk about sunsets later, Tali," she muttered, pushing her friend away, "We have a war to win."

"It's a sunset, not a matter of life and death."

"You can't work once the sun goes down," Emma looked down, "Besides, I think the stars are prettier."

"So will you stargaze tonight?" Natalia asked.

"Find me when the war is done," the Raven muttered.

"There's always going to be a war," the other girl smiled softly, "You're always going to be fighting someone. It's who you are." Emma Gail Harlem did not respond, for there was nothing else to say.

XXVII. enter the peregrines

As surely as the sun rose, two mornings had passed since Cameron's news when they heard from him again. He had wandered from the group slightly, using the excuse that he needed to relieve himself, which nobody dared question. This gave him the opportunity to radio his friends quickly with their current location: forty-five minutes away. As their undercover spy had to return to his group, Jacob sounded the air horn to alert the rest of Peregrin that their time was running out. They had to be ready; everyone had to be armed and in position, ready to guard the cabins they had claimed.

"They're going to start with negotiations," Jacob explained, repeating the words Cameron had told him. "They won't resort to violence if we give up our land. We just need to draw them out until they lose patience and give up."

"They're not just going to give up," Mai protested, "We're going to have to fight them."

"He's right," Sebastian nodded, "We have to sustain peace for as long as possible, and somehow manage to tear them apart from the inside."

"So we just let them walk on over us?" Mai shouted, "That's bull, Seb. You can't be serious."

"They have around eighty people, Mai. Eighty people with guns" Sebastian sighed, "We have twenty-three that can fight." He did not include Ellie and Hayden in that number, which bothered them both. Although they were either too young or injured respectively, they hated feeling like dead weight. At least Ellie had her responsibility with coercing Cora to betray her people—Hayden had nothing.

"Alright," Donovan declared, "Everyone head out, get ready. No matter what happens, I love you all, and we're in this as one. One Peregrin, right?"

"One Peregrin," the camp repeated. Even Sebastian muttered this line.

The Raven's old leader clapped and shouted, "Let's go!", and the camp began to get to work. Sebastian used this time to approach Emma, who seemed to be fiddling with her shoe outside one of the empty cabins. "What are you doing?"

She looked down slightly, feeling like this answer should be self-explanatory. She had torn out the sole of her shoe, revealing a small compartment. In her hand, she held the smaller of her two knives, "I've been doing this for two years, how have you not noticed?"

"That you walk around with a blade underneath your foot?" Sebastian raised an eyebrow, smirking slightly.

"It's never been stolen," she shrugged.

"I want to talk to you," her brother sighed. She gestured for him to continue, as she was busy situating her blade in its secret compartment, "You can't be out here when they come."

"To hell with that," she muttered, "I'm one of the best fighters we have, you need me."

"The Condors are coming, Emma," Sebastian frowned, "Megan is coming. She wants you dead."

"She already knows I'm alive," Emma said, "The other Ravens are the ones who ratted us out to the City. You don't think they've told their best friends that I'm here?"

"I can't let them see you, Em," Seb bit his lip, tears flickering in his eyes. He was genuinely afraid of the actions Megan would take when she saw her. She wanted her dead to begin with, and now she had been humiliated. Megan Martins would seek vengeance.

Emma's face dropped, and she looked at her brother as though what he was suggesting was ludacris, "I'm not hiding. I didn't go through all that shit just to hide the moment I faced danger."

"I'm sorry, Emma," he brother whispered, and before she could react, his hands were on her shoulders, and he was shoving her back onto the floor of the empty cabin. She was much smaller than people often realized, and it did not take much force to knock her down. Before she could get back up, he had locked the door behind him, trapping her inside with nothing but the knife in her belt. She was even missing her other shoe, as she had put it down when she stood up to face her brother. She was wearing that sneaker with the secret blade the whole time she was in the Condor's cell, yet this was the moment when she lost its protection. The irony, she thought.

Standing outside, Sebastian could hear his little sister pounding on the inside of the door, cursing at him to let her out. He sighed, resting his forehead against the splintered wood as a small tear trickled down his face. He could feel her rancor, her sense of betrayal. Should his sister think rationally, she'd come to understand how he did what he had to, but reason was hard to achieve. He knew her. Time would pass before she could forgive him. After the war, perhaps she'd understand.

Turning his head, he saw her clever shoe lying on the grass outside. He wanted to give it to her, provide her with that second weapon in case the danger followed her regardless, but if he dared open the door, she'd be freed. So instead he took the shoe and hid it beneath his bed, hoping to keep the knowledge of this secret weapon between as few people as possible.

Sure enough, as fifty minutes had passed since Jacob's announcement, Yasmin came sprinting down the hill. It was her job to bring the news of their arrival, and when they saw her return from the outlook near the entrance, they filed into formation. Sebastian and Donovan stood at the center of the camp, awaiting the intruders. The rest of the camp's fighters were dispersed nearby, ready to attack if necessary.

As the first people began to wander down the gravel road, all of Peregrin held their breaths. They watched in silence, hearing nothing but their hearts pounding in their ears and the sound of stomping boots on pebbles. In the lead was a small girl with a tight blonde ponytail, brown eyes fuming. She glared at the two boys as she approached, and Sebastian tried to view Donovan in his peripheral. The boy had closed his eyes slightly, letting out a tired sigh, and his face fell into a tight scowl.

"Donny!" the girl exclaimed, her voice sounding unbelievably fake. Sebastian could tell she sounded too excited, too happy to see him, for this to be genuine. No, this was all an act, and he could see right through it. "What are you doing here?"

Donovan made eye contact with a boy standing to her right, who seemed to be searching for someone. Sebastian thought this might have been Cameron, the one who'd supplied them with information.

"This is my home now," Donny said, "Different city, different forest."

"That's silly," the girl said, "This place is a mess. I can't imagine you'd leave your life behind for this wasteland. Whatever, it will be easy to incorporate into our territories."

Donovan stepped forward, "It's my wasteland, Harper. Not yours."

"Why don't you let your friend speak?" called another voice, walking to the front of the group and taking Harper's side. Sebastian's heart sank. "It's been awhile, Sebby, hasn't it?"

"This is Peregrin," he declared, trying to avoid staring at the new girl. The moment he looked at her face, he saw her and his old best friend in his sister's bed the night of his Halloween party. He could picture them right now: naked and cuddling underneath her light blue blankets. Neither Harlem had seen it happen, but the younger one put the pieces together. Megan had spent enough time at their house for Emma to recognize the purse she left in her bedroom, and the rest of the evidence soon fell in line.

But how had Megan Martins come to trust Harper, the girl who came to take over her forest? Why, she offered the Condor leader power. The two groups did not need to fight; a simple negotiation was all it took. If Megan would support the City's conquest of the Grove, then she would be protected in the aftermath, although they could not guarantee the same fate for the rest of the Condors. But Megan had a different plan. The news had spread that half of the Ravens had disappeared, including her long-lost lover Sebastian. Should the remainders fall to Harper's rule, their new location would be flushed out, and she could finally get the revenge she always wanted. She wanted to destroy them, destroy Sebastian from right where it hurt the most. That was why she'd taken Mai, and why she'd taken his darling Emma.

The Raven girl, Megan believed her name was Dylan, soon told her all the secrets. Mai was alive, which she had suspected. But Emma—Emma, the girl whose blood she'd seen splattered along the cell's walls, the noble warrior who she had whipped and burned and tortured, had somehow returned. Well, she'd declared, Little Miss Harlem would not be so lucky this time around. This time, Megan would make the final move herself, watch as she took her final breaths, relish in her brother's misery as he would watch the life fade from his sister's vibrant eyes. Then, and only then, would she be satisfied.

"Here's the problem," Harper began, "Your camp is a little too small and a little too far away for us to effectively appoint a viceroy, so whatever agreement we can come up with will take time. My suggestion is that we join your camp, and our negotiations can happen after we've learned the way of the land. If you can't agree to this, then we'll turn to violent actions, which I know you don't want.

"And we already know exactly who we'd start with. Sebastian, right?" Harper turned to the boy who had barely spoken since they'd arrived, although fire flared behind his eyes, "I think you ought to be especially concerned. My girl Megan's pissed."

Donovan gulped, realizing exactly who the invaders were referring to. He could tell in the way Sebastian froze, the way his jaw tensed and sweat began to dot his hairline. "Trade regulations," he nodded, "That's it."

"We'll take it," Harper smiled, "They all say that at the beginning. You'll come around, don't worry. Now, where should we unpack?"

"Ellie!" Sebastian called into the Raven girls' cabin, "You're up!" The little girl ran out of the structure, her blonde hair up in a wavy ponytail. Mai followed her out, the gun situated in her holster. "Mai, get into position.

In three minutes, Ellie, you need to get Cora up by the bench. That'll give Mai enough time to hide." The older of the girls nodded and snuck into the woods behind the cabin, giving her enough cover to reach the bushes without being seen.

"What if it doesn't work?" Ellie asked, biting her lip. She was excited to participate in their silent war, but at the same time, she couldn't deny her nerves. The last time she'd seen Cora, the girl was tricking her into a kidnapping plot. Ellie may not have been injured in the experience, she may not have faced the same torture as Mai or Emma, but she was still livid at this other girl. She had been forsaken, and she had not forgotten.

"Then we'll figure it out," Sebastian sighed, "But if Cora is in fact steadfast, it's not your fault. Nobody expects this to really work, it would just be nice if it did."

"So you don't think I can do it?" Ellie muttered, looking down, "Great, just give the kid something to do so she feels like she matters."

"Oh my God, Ellie, no," Sebastian shook his head, "This plan is a longshot, but if it works? You just saved a lot of bloodshed."

"Got it," she nodded, "I'm just teasing you. I know this is important."

"Not the time for jokes, kiddo," the leader sighed, "You ready?"

"Ready as I'll ever be," she shrugged.

"Knock 'em dead," Sebastian smiled, patting her on the shoulder as she began to approach the cabins on the other side of the camp where the City and the Condors were setting up. Her heartbeat began to pick up as she got nearer, when suddenly she froze. It was Dylan, leading some of the old Ravens into a cabin. What were they doing here? They had chosen to stay behind—for what reason would they have allied with the Condors, of all people, to chase after them? Dylan seemed to see Ellie, and quickly ushered the others inside, shutting the door, as if they didn't want the younger girl to see them.

"Ellie?" called a small voice from behind her. She whipped around to see the girl she was in search of.

"Hey!" Ellie smiled, trying her hardest to sound happy to see the little spy. "How are you, Hannah?"

She frowned, "It's Cora, actually. I lied about that too. Um, do you want to go talk somewhere else? You know, where there aren't people around?"

Ellie nodded. Everything seemed to be working according to plan so far, assuming Cora didn't have a specific location in mind. It was possible that the Condor group had developed the exact same plan, banking on Ellie's old nativete. Well, she wasn't naive anymore. They couldn't fool her again. "Follow me!"

The two little girls soon approached a bench behind some trees and shrubbery: the perfect secret meeting spot. Ellie's eyes darted around, looking for Mai, but she was unsure of where the girl was hiding. They agreed that it was for the best if not even Ellie knew where her protector was. Should her eyes wander towards her, it could give away their cover.

"Ellie, I'm really sorry," Cora began, "I didn't want to bring you back to our camp, it was just my mission."

"You were going to let them kill me," Ellie muttered, her personal feelings starting to come out now. She was trying her hardest to maintain this friendly persona, but acting innocent could only work for so long.

"They wouldn't have killed you!" Cora protested, "They were only going to hold you there as bait. They weren't going to hurt you!"

Ellie smiled, "You could make it up to me, you know."

"How?" The other girl paused, as if she was actually considering this proposition. "Ellie, I want to be friends with you, really. I haven't been around anyone remotely close to my age in years. I feel so, so bad."

"You were a spy for the Condors, right?" Ellie began, "What if you were a spy for us now?

Cora's face dropped, her head shaking, "No. No, you liar. You only brought me out here to convert me to your side. That's not happening."

"Then never talk to someone your own age again!" Ellie snapped, "That's my offer. Take it or leave."

Suddenly, the other girl had pushed the Raven to the ground. "I'm not a traitor!" she screamed, "I'm going to tell everyone that you've all tried to solicit us, turn us against our people. We came in peace, but you've ruined it!"

Now was the moment that Mai appeared from her hiding spot, yanking Cora off of Ellie and pinning her onto the ground, pointing the barrel of the gun at her forehead. Cora's eyes widened in fear as she saw Mai's glaring demeanor and the dangerous weapon pointing right at her. She looked over to Ellie, hoping the other girl would tell her friend to stand down, but the twelve year old had nothing to say. Mai could shoot Cora right then and there and she wouldn't object.

"You won't tell your friends anything," Mai hissed, "Mark my words, they find out about this meeting, then you can watch me kill your people, and I'll kill you last. I promise you that."

Cora nodded, eyes fixated on the finger pressing slightly into the trigger. She had no doubt that Mai would shoot her or her friends, and she had not survived the past two years just to get killed now. She was a spy, lying was in her blood. This could be remain her little million dollar secret.

With that fandango over, Cora had returned to her side of the camp, and Mai and Ellie returned to theirs, walking at separate intervals so nobody would suspect they'd been together.

Sebastian was seated with Donovan at an old picnic table when Mai approached. She shook her head slightly, enough to signal that their plan had failed. The boys sighed, having hoped that the youngest girl could pull over their rival, but understanding it's unlikelihood of success.

"So what's the plan now?" Mai asked, taking a seat. The two boys made a slight eye contact, causing the girl to send them an impatient glance.

"Exactly what Seb's been doing since you all got here," Donovan smirked.

"And that is?"

"Avoiding peace talks at all costs."

xxviii. shifting sands

Trigger Warning: Lots of language in this chapter. Moreso than usual

While the sun had begun to set on Peregrin—which now held more people than it had in years—the kids were just getting started. Harper's army had settled into the empty cabins on the western side of the camp, but she didn't feel they had reason to celebrate just yet. Yes, this would be comfortable for the time being, but until they could truly assert authority over the land, she had to keep working.

But Harper had a secret weapon: the Ravens who had stayed behind were on her side. They had joined her cause, which she had to admit was in their own best interests. Uniting the forest under one common ruler, herself, meant that the old factions had dissipated and they could finally be at peace. Sure, they now had to follow her rules when before they had complete freedom, but it was a small exchange for all that they would gain.

"Find him," Harper instructed to the brunette in front of her, "He'll listen to you."

And so, Dylan Alexander took a deep breath and crossed the border into the other side of the camp. The Ravens who were once her friend stopped and stared as she walked across the dying grass, but all she received were a multitude of glares and disapproval. Nobody smiled or even bothered to say hello. They were pissed. She could understand why.

"Sebastian," she said, approaching the boy from behind. He whipped around, but his expression when he saw who was speaking didn't change. If any part of him was at all happy to see her, he suppressed it well. "You found a nice camp."

"Are you surprised?" he asked.

"Can we talk?" she changed the subject. He nodded, but gestured for her to drop her weapon. She did so, and he left his knife on the steps outside the boys' cabin. The room was empty, but after taking one step in, Dylan could feel the life that used to flourish in the Grove. She missed that energy. Without Hayden's smile, and Nathan's remarks, or even Corey's infectious laugh, her camp had felt empty over the past week. She'd missed them all.

"Thought you said our camp was worth fighting for," Sebastian said, crossing his arms and leaning against one of the bunks.

"We gave in to Harper for the same reason you gave Hayden your jacket, and the same reason he gave it back to you," Dylan said.

"And why is that?" Sebastian raised an eyebrow, not actually interested in anything she'd have to say. He saw no way he could forgive her for falling in line with their enemy, for betraying their legacy.

"Because stepping down gave us our best shot," she said, "I thought you'd understand that."

"What did she offer you?" he sighed.

"Everything," Dylan smiled, her eyes soft and charmed, "We're at peace with the Condors, Seb. Isn't that amazing?"

"You were always at peace with them," he muttered, "Emma and I weren't. You'd have never had problems with them if we weren't there. Harper didn't give you that."

"Sure," she rolled her eyes, but continued, "Don't you realize that it helps us to be apart of a real civilization? We can trade, we can be a part of their economy. They have so many resources, Sebastian, it's wonderful. It's like we're in the real world again."

"This is the real world," he shook his head, "Do you have any idea who Harper is?"

"She's not demonic, if that's what you're suggesting," Dylan said, "She saved our people."

"She didn't save mine."

"Seb—"

"She threatened to kill my sister if I didn't submit to her terms," he snapped, "She put a kill order on her best friend because she wanted to explore. She let my friend take a grenade for her, and paid no attention as he was comatosed. She tried to conquer three thousand acres worth of forest."

"She's trying her best," Dylan pleaded, "She's human, she's not perfect."

Sebastian stepped forward, glaring down at his old partner. He only had a couple inches on her, but his wrath made him appear more menacing. It radiated off his body, its tendrils wrapping around her. He hissed, "She brought Megan here to kill my sister. Not a chance."

"No, that's only an incentive," Dylan tried to explain, begging the boy to hear her out, but his mind was made.

"Get out of my cabin," he declared.

"Sebastian, listen to me," she urged, but there was no reaching him. He was too far gone, too stuck in his own beliefs to even consider her argument. He simply repeated his command, and this time she listened, exiting the cabin.

In the now empty room, Sebastian sighed and took an exhausted seat on his bunk, cradling his head in his hands. The silence of the airy cabin rang a warning in his ears. He had checked on his sister earlier, who was still locked safe in the empty cabin. He had knocked on the door and asked if she needed anything, but she had adopted what seemed to be a hunger strike. She had stopped making noise the moment she'd heard the foreigners arrive, realizing that although she was stuck in there, she didn't have to make the poor decision to draw attention to her situation. With the hectic events of the day, he had yet to hear any rumors of her disappearance, and he had only told Mai and Donovan his plan to keep her safe. Neither of them liked it, and neither did he, but they realized its necessity. They realized there was no changing his mind.

He knew that Emma was hurting, and it hurt his heart to cause her pain, but Megan wanted her head. He thought he'd lost her once, but he was given a second chance. Now was his time to redeem himself, not make the same mistakes he had before. She could only cheat death so many times; someday she would understand.

Outside of the cabin, Dylan breathed in the night air, feeling distrusting eyes track her move. Everywhere she seemed to look, there were Ravens staring at her. She tried to smile, avoid eye contact, but eventually she passed Hayden, whose look of disgust hit her right where it hurt the most.

"Go back to your Condors," he spat, "See how badly they still want you now that you've brought them here."

"It's for the best, Hayden," she smiled.

"Bet Napoleon said that too," he said, "So did Stalin, probably."

"Why don't you get the hell out of here, you bitch," said another voice, walking up from behind Hayden. Dylan's eyes widened as she saw Mai, her face livid and determined.

"I'm not here to bother you," she promised, "I'm on my way out. You don't need to get so angry."

"I don't need to get angry?" Mai snapped, and Hayden simply sighed, predicting the following events. She repeated her last comment, enunciating every last word, "Get the hell out of my camp."

"It doesn't belong to you, Mai," Dylan said, "It's called Peregrin for a reason. It's for the strangers, the foreigners. Sounds like it's for everyone, right?"

Mai did not respond with words. Instead, her fist connected with the other girl's cheekbone, causing her to turn away and gasp in shock. When she raised her head again, a red imprint had appeared on her pale face, and she stared at Mai as though she was an animal. She lived up to this expectation. Snarling, she attacked the girl again, knocking her to the ground.

"Mai!" Hayden shouted from behind her, knowing very well that if he tried to physically step in, he'd soon be taken down. His knee prevented him from successfully holding his own against another, and Mai was far stronger than him to begin with. His call seemed to go unnoticed, as Mai continued to hit the Raven.

However, the tide soon turned, as Dylan was able to kick Mai in the stomach and flip onto the top, suddenly gaining the control in this battle, although her short burst of power would not last for long. As the two girls wrestled on the ground, a small crowd began to form, nobody sure if it was in their best interest to pull the two apart. It was Corey and Yasmin who made the move to separate the two, trying to keep the clashing girls apart.

"Mai, you need to chill," Hayden said, "We're trying to keep the peace, remember?"

"They invaded our camp!" she screamed, "She betrayed us, ratted us out. She deserves it."

"Yeah, Dylan's a snake, nothing new," he muttered, "But the last thing we need to do is make matters worse."

"I came here to save your asses," Dylan said, but again, only received glares, "Harper is your best option, I'm telling you!"

"Coming from the same person that didn't want Sebastian to know his sister was alive, that's not saying much," Hayden said, "Go back to your own cabin, Dylan." She glared at him coldly, but ripped herself out of Yasmin's grip, returning to Harper and the Condors. Once she was gone, Corey let go of Mai, and the circle began to disperse. Hayden sighed and went to inform Sebastian on what had gone down outside, and Mai stormed down the hill, looking for a spot to clear her head.

"Impressive," said a voice. She closed her eyes slightly, not in the mood to put up with anyone else's nonsense. "You really do hate everything."

"What do you want, Marley?" Mai sighed. The other girl's laidback and witty attitude felt inappropriate at this time, but this was one person that could not easily be pushed away. She really was a parasite—she would crawl under your skin and never let go.

"That's the girl who screwed you over?" Marley smirked, "She looks like a rat."

"She is," Mai said.

"No, but she literally looks like one. How was she your leader? Who decided that was a good idea?" the dealer laughed.

"You're not funny, Marley," Mai said.

"I'm not trying to be funny," she said, "I'm genuinely confused. Even Emma would be better than her."

"Please don't start talking about how great Emma is," Mai groaned, "This isn't about her, and she's not that great."

"She's a narcissist."

"Again, not the point," the other said.

"Calm down, girlfriend," Marley said, "I'm gonna go. You're not in the right mood."

"You noticed, I'm impressed."

As Marley turned to walk back up the hill, she called, "You're not funny either, Mai!" Mai did not respond, but a rare soft smile pressed lightly against her lips.

It had been at least ten hours since Emma had last seen another person. Ten hours since her brother threw her onto the ground, trapping her inside the cabin. With nothing but the empty bunkbeds, it might as well have been another cell. Sebastian might as well have been Megan. She had spent the first hour searching for escape, fiddling with the lock, searching for anything to break a window, cause enough commotion that someone would realize her brother had acted no less tyrannical than the intruders they feared, but it was to no avail. She would have no rescue, and she had no way out.

Sebastian had first come by a few hours after she'd heard their enemies arrived. Knocking on the door, he'd asked if she was alright, if there was anything she needed.

I need my freedom, you asshole.

The next time he came around, he had grabbed her some leftovers from whatever sketchy meal they'd eaten at four in the afternoon. She had refused. He offered her water, which she did not accept. She was a prisoner in her brother's own camp; she wanted to make him feel that power, that dominance. He could never stomach it, and so she vowed to starve herself.

The sun had gone down when she heard the handle on the door begin to shake. It wasn't a soft tapping on the wooden frame; it was someone trying to enter. Someone trying to invade. Breath picking up, she scrambled over to the wall adjacent to the doorway. If someone were to come in, this would be the last part of the open room they'd see, and she could prepare to fight, should that prove necessary.

As the door creaked open, she moved into a crouched position, gripping her knife tightly. She had taken her left shoe off long before, leaving it strewn in the back corner of the cabin. With her right sneaker and secret blade gone, she was left unbalanced. Her best bet was barefoot.

The intruder carried a flashlight, which confused her. Any batteries must have died out long ago, but then again, the City was described to have a surplus of supplies and resources. The faint light illuminated the figure's silhouette: a boy, although anything more than that remained unclear. Emma slowly pushed herself off the ground, rising to a standing position, ready to attack. This was the moment the figure turned around, shining the light right on her, and reflecting his own face as well.

"Thank God," he sighed, "Emma, are you alright? What did they do to you?"

"Get the hell away from me, Mason," she snapped quietly, neither of their voices daring to reach higher than a whisper, "I swear on my life, I will slit your throat if you come any nearer."

"Let me guess, they locked you in here to keep you away from Megan?" he said, although he listened to the girl's threat, and did not take a step forward.

"What do you want?" Emma said.

"Your help," he said, "I saved your life, now you owe me."

She shook her head, "I don't owe you anything." Lifting up her sleeve, she pointed to the dreaded 37 that still held residency on her skin, "Saving my life made up for this alone. Not the other shit you put me through."

"I betrayed my people for you," Mason scowled, "Do you really not care at all?"

"I don't think we should reward each other for just following morality," she shrugged, "So what do you want?"

"To take down the City. Are you in?"

"Is Megan?"

"No," he said, "I have a plan, but I'll need your people."

Emma just kind of laughed, "Give me one good reason I should trust you."

"I saved your life," he said, amazed by her incredulous greed.

"Again," she repeated, "It's called morality."

"Like you're so righteous," he said, "You made me cheat on my girlfriend. Don't go preaching morals when we both know you don't have any."

"Never said I did," she shrugged, "You, on the other hand?"

"I cheated on Megan," Mason said, "You want proof that you can trust me? There it is. There's the blackmail."

"Good," Emma smiled, her brown eyes glinting in the darkness with that mischievous spark she wore so well,"I'm in."

xxix. blood lines

Mason and Emma had agreed that, much to Emma's disdain, she did in fact have to stay in the cabin. When Sebastian was to come around in the morning, she must let him in, let him talk to her. She hated this, truly wanting nothing to do with her brother at this time, but she understood that he was the key to Mason's plan succeeding. If she could make him believe that they had their spy, they had their eyes on the inside, they could oust Harper's army. Should Emma come to her brother outside of the cabin, he would be too flustered to think rationally. They would lose all chances of success instantly. So no, she would have to wait out that night, although Mason left her with the small bobby pin he'd used to enter. She was no longer captive.

Emma had not slept that night. She'd watched as the sun rose, illuminating the dust particles floating in the hazy glow. Her stomach had begun to hurt and her head ached, a sign of the starvation she'd forced unto herself. It had been almost twenty-four hours since she'd last eaten, and while she'd gone longer without fuel, her body still panged for nourishment. However, when Sebastian came by this time around, she still would not eat. Her fasting might force him into trusting her and Mason's plan. She knew how much he hated to see her hurt.

Eventually, she heard a soft rapping on her door. It was time. She had taken a seat on one of the lower bunks, picking the dirt out from underneath her fingernails. Her biggest enemy in this new cell was the boredom. With the Condors she had at least had the pain to distract her.

"Emma," she heard her brother whisper from outside, "You okay? Do you need water?"

"Fine," she muttered, knowing this would bring him inside. She still had no intention to drink. Sure enough, she heard the scratching sound of the key being inserted, and he slowly entered the cabin.

"I know you hate me," Sebastian sighed, handing her a red solo cup of water.

"You're right," she said, taking the cup and placing it on the ground beside her. She wanted to pour it out, spill it all over the splintering wood, but she knew that her brother was not the one working their hydration system the day before. It may have been Natalia carrying the buckets up and down the grueling hill. She wasn't going to be that wasteful.

Sebastian stared at her, eyes full of sadness and regret, "I'm just trying to keep you safe, Emma."

"I know," she muttered, "I'm guessing Cora failed?"

"Yeah," he nodded, "And Megan also has made it very clear that she wants to kill you, so don't even suggest I change my mind about you."

"We have our spy," Emma said, "Assuming you'll trust him."

Sebastian just shook his head, looking down, "How the hell do we have a spy?"

"Mason," she revealed, "He came by last night."

"Is that a Condor?" Her brother gaped at her, "No, Emma, you're insane. Look what they did to you! You can't trust any of them, you know that."

She shook her head, "Megan wants me dead, right? You don't think her boyfriend would have told her where I'm hidden by now?"

"You want me to trust Megan's boyfriend," Sebastian just kind of laughed, "You're wrong, Emma. You're delusional. You need to eat something. Drink that water, now." His sister simply stared at him, crossing her arms in a sign of refusal. She was not as crazy as she sounded, and instead was thinking clearly.

"You need to listen to me," Emma pleaded, "We have nothing else to lose."

"I do," Sebastian sighed, "You." The angered girl before him didn't fully know how to respond, but their moment was soon cut off by a scream outside. Both Harlems flew over to the door, although the older tried to hold his sister back.

"You can't," she shook her head, "You need me to fight."

He simply nodded, "Your other shoe is in my cabin, by the way."

"Don't need it." And so the two siblings exited the empty cabin. Emma squinted as her eyes adjusted to the natural daylight. In the room, all the light was provided by a couple of dirty windows—now she was seeing the camp in its reality. It was the opposite of the great allegory: she saw the truth only after she became its prisoner.

Halfway down the hill, two people were hugging, causing a crowd to form around them. It was a surprising sight to see in the midst of all this chaos, and the siblings instantly became skeptical. As they got nearer, they saw the faces of the duo. One of them was Nova, the Ravens' resident mechanic who had gone on the original search for Peregrin. The other a stranger to Sebastian, a reminder for Emma. He was a Condor prison guard, one she had seen in her cell numerous times. In fact, she believed him to be the one who carved the dreaded branding into her forearm, although she could not be sure. In that moment, all she'd felt was pain; tied to that pole, she was unable to see what her captors were doing. But oh, could she feel it.

"You—you're alive!" Nova exclaimed, separating from the boy.

"What about you?" he laughed, "You've been a Raven all this time?"

"Yes! And you were a Condor?" she examined his body, staring him up and down. Sebastian came to notice how similar the two looked. They shared the same slim figure, slender nose, and messy curls. He recognized the glimmer between the pair's eyes, it was the one he saw in his own little sister, and he could only imagine existed in his own. Nova had a brother, that much he'd known. They all thought he was gone.

The newly reunited siblings stood on the dying grass, clutching each other's forearms, listening for the pulse of the blood they shared. Nova was a girl known for her hard attitude, realistic take on the world, but here she stood in a mixture of wonder and amazement, emotions they had never even fathomed could exist.

Sebastian turned to his sister beside him, remembering the fateful morning at the Rogue Lily's cabin, the moment they found each other once again. For the first time since their father's death, he had seen his sister cry. Oh, how he had held her in his arms, how badly it hurt to let her go. All he felt for Nova and her brother was sympathy. He had lost Emma for two weeks. They had gone two years.

Emma, however, did not appear touched by this sweet encounter. Instead her eyes had turned to slits, her jaw tensing, her body as though she was about to pounce. She was a lioness, brimming with anger, hatred pulsing through her veins. With one glance, Sebastian realized that this Condor was no stranger to her, but the girl beside him was. This was not the Emma

Gail Harlem he'd grown up with. Not the little girl he'd walked to her first grade class. Not the girl who came to him in tears when their father showed the earliest symptoms. This fire did not live inside that girl, but the Emma beside him now was up in flames.

"Give them space!" Sebastian called, gesturing for the crowd to separate. Nova was a friend of his; she deserved some privacy in this emotional moment. They deserved a chance to speak to each other, come to terms with the amazing truth that yes, they were both alive, without the pressure of wandering eyes staring them down. The circle, consisting of both Ravens and Condors alike, all listened. Not because they liked Sebastian, in fact, many of the Condors weren't even aware of his identity, but simply because they understood the need for these sacred moments. That thread of humanity had survived through them all.

As the hill began to empty, Emma used this opportunity as a chance to sneak away from her brother's watchful eye. She knew that he had no problem locking her up again; he wanted to keep her safe. She understood that, but she also understood that she did not need his protection. It suffocated her, that stillness, that security. She had learned that with comfort came carelessness, and with negligence came vulnerability. His actions only limited her movements. She would not let him take her captive again.

She had made eye contact with one Condor boy across the crowd, and after her brother called for their dispersion, he'd given her a slight gesture, enough to signify he'd follow her. In the midst of the commotion, she journeyed towards the woods on the Eastern side of the camp. The forest here was thicker, and there would be more cover.

"Did you talk to him?" Mason asked, entering the small clearing. Emma simply nodded, biting her lip softly. "How'd it go?"

"Not well," she sighed, "Turns out dating my brother's psycho ex doesn't help your cause."

"I take it he's not going to help us," Mason muttered.

"Shocker," Emma rolled her eyes, "So what now?"

"There's a back-up plan, but I don't like it," he hesitated. Emma stared at him to continue. "You still have your knife, right?"

"Of course," she said, a little bit dubious.

"Good," he said quickly, "You need to kill Harper."

"What?" Emma quipped, eyes widening.

"It's the only way."

"No," she declared, "I'm not going to murder her. I don't even know her."

"Please," Mason shrugged, "It's not like you've never killed someone before. Those bounty hunters right after I saved your life? You weren't so concerned about taking theirs."

"That was different," she shook her head, "That was to save myself."

"This time it's to save the forest," Mason frowned, "This is bigger than just you, Emma."

"Then you can do it," she shrugged, "I'm out."

"Emma, I can't," he pleaded.

"And why not?" she snapped, "Is it just too immoral for you? But since I'm Emma Harlem, the forest slut, your fragile ethics obviously mean nothing to me. Clearly I don't have a heart."

"You kind of don't," he shrugged, "But that's not why, I promise."

"Oh, really? Then tell me why," she demanded. Stomping her foot into the ground, her stance radiated confidence and control over the situation. She was unafraid, yet insulted.

"I hooked up with her cousin, alright?" Mason revealed, kicking the dirt up in frustration, "That's why I can't kill her. He'd never speak to me again."

"You have a girlfriend, Mason," Emma pointed out, confused by this turn of events.

Mason shrugged, "That didn't seem to matter when you were kissing me."

"Again, different rules when you're saving your own ass," she said, "Harper dies, and then what? You can live happily ever after with her cousin, all the while knowing you were behind the death of his loved one? That's hopeless, sorry."

He simply sighed, "Will you do it or not?"

"We'll see," she frowned, and the two went their separate ways. Mason returned to Cameron and the hidden flower, blossoming between the two, while Emma was off to her own side of the camp, where the age-old flower between her and Sebastian had begun to die.

XXX. the road to hell

Emma's lucky streak was over the second afternoon following Sebastian's approval of her freedom. Her brother was not happy with her ability to run rampant in the camp, but she wasn't dumb. She never planned to leave the half that belonged to the Ravens and the Riot, but not because she was afraid. She simply had nothing to gain by venturing towards the other side, but far too much to lose.

However, Megan eventually came to her rivals' side, seeking negotiations with Sebastian. That was her cover, to say the least. Her true purpose in coming to visit her enemies was known only to her, and even then, she may not have fully known. Motives can be hazy, and sometimes you just walk where your feet carry you. How else had they all come to the Grove in the first place?

Megan's eyes landed on a long, dark ponytail she recognized in a heartbeat. Her eyes turned to slits, a fierce fire boiling in her blood, as she chased the girl. Her hand wrapped around her hair-tie, and she pulled the girl down to the gravel path, moving so that she stood on top of her. But Emma Gail Harlem did not miss a beat. Pulling herself out from beneath her attacker's legs, she was able to administer a swift kick behind her kneecap, giving her the slightest advantage.

The girls wrestled for a while, the person in power changing by the moment, drawing a nearby crowd. The bystanders were Peregrin, yet none of them moved to assist their fighting friend. Emma did not seem to need help, and to see her battle skills in action was strangely beautiful. Everyone had heard that she was a warrior, that her abilities in combat were outstanding, but she fought her battles in the wild, in places where no onlookers would see.

Eventually, Emma had pinned the Condor onto the ground, blood covering both of their faces. Megan glared up at her, but she did not move. Her body had given out, the fight stealing her of the remainder of her strength. But Emma? Oh, Emma was just getting started. She drew the knife out of her back pocket, stroking it gently. One slash, she thought, One slash and she'll be gone. It could be so simple, so fast.

Standing over her, the memories began to replay through her head. She was fifteen again, still in high school, still weak, coming across the evidence that revealed what had happened in her bed the night of her brother's party. She was watching him cry as he learned the truth about his two best friends. She was watching him vomit the evening Megan came forward and told the world about how Sebastian was a liar, how she would never cheat on him, going so far to accuse him of cheating on her. She was holding her brother's hand, letting it clench around hers as Mai was taken away to the Condor's camp, feeling his racing pulse as he feared that the monster in Megan would destroy another person that he loved. She was sitting in the Condor's cell herself, bound and bloodied and overwhelmed with more pain than she had ever felt in her life. She was standing shirtless for Mason, providing him with whatever he could want in hopes that he might save her sorry ass from destruction. She was examining her branded arm for the very first time, rubbing the scars with her dirty fingers.

She looked down at the number on her wrist, and began to adjust her grip over the knife. The camp was still, everyone frozen in the somber moment. Sebastian was dumbfounded. The Emma he saw before him now was nothing but a stranger. The Emma he knew did not contain this violence, but the Emma he knew had died long ago. This Emma Gail Harlem was a wildfire, a stack of tinder only beginning to burn. He wanted to save the underbrush from her flames, save her forest from a self-imposed destruction, but the scars on her skin marked a fence of barbed wire. He could never get through to her.

But Emma looked up, and she turned her head slightly, as if contemplating her next step. She had won, and now, with one quick movement, she could win forever. But at the last moment possible, she saw Natalia. Natalia, whose eyes were filled with fear and disgust, who did not recognize the murderer in front of her. They had scrimmaged in this very spot, but back then, it was just a game. This time around, Emma was on the verge of the greatest theft imaginable. Was this the girl she'd grown to know? Could this be the same voice who advocated that the two groups of strangers in Peregrin learn to work together?

Emma saw the shock in her friend's eyes, and it struck all the disappointment she'd been storing up for years. She'd let them all down, even Natalia. When had she become so wrong? When had all the good left inside of her dried up and blown into the wind?

For a moment, the rage that flooded her veins seemed to dissipate, and she was left with a cold emptiness. She lifted her knife, placing it back into her sheath, and simply turned away. She did not help Megan to stand, and instead left the battered girl on the ground, very much alive. Too much alive, as they would all soon come to realize. Perhaps she should have killed her right then and there; perhaps the lives of the innocent would be saved. But who in this forsaken world could be called innocent?

Emma soon found herself in the small clearing where she had spoken to Mason the previous morning. He had asked her to become a murderer, pointed out that that was what she already was, but for some reason, she'd refused. Could it be that one rose petal of her humanity had yet to fall? She pondered on that heavily, and came to one conclusion: all that was good inside her must have disappeared. It was not that she feared killing Harper, or that she even feared killing Megan. She simply did not want to disappoint the people who still saw her suitable for love. She could not understand why Sebastian thought she was worth his affection, or why Natalia thought she was worth her time. She was a ticking time bomb, and eventually, she would snap. Emma could not fathom why her brother and friends would put themselves in the path of her destruction.

"What happened out there?" asked a voice, coming up behind her. It was Natalia. Emma could recognize her sound anywhere.

"You saw it for yourself," she muttered in response, "You think I'm a monster now."

"Maybe if you'd killed her," Natalia shrugged, moving forward so that the two girls stood side by side, "Which you didn't."

"I wish I did," Emma simply sighed.

"No, you don't," the other girl smiled softly, "You act on instinct, Emma. You listen to your gut, and it told you that taking her life was the wrong thing to do."

"I saw you close your eyes," she said, her voice monotonous and flat, "You were disgusted."

"Because a killer isn't who you are, Em," Natalia grabbed her hand, clutching it supportively.

Emma simply shook her head, squeezing her eyes shut for just a moment, as if to block out all the world around them. "Yes, it is," she said, "You barely know me, Tali."

"Tell me your story then," Natalia prompted, "You looked at your scars, and then you looked at your knife. If I don't know you, then introduce me."

So Emma took a deep breath and began to speak. She started with Cora's arrival into the camp, how she had deceived Ellie into becoming the Condor's prisoner. She told how Mai had arrived, and carried in a hurricane to their camp. How she had snuck out in the mayhem, been betrayed the slippery Adrian, and ended up in the cell as well. The way she'd stayed in the cell while Ellie was freed, however, she did not mention the negotiations involved. She brushed over the pain, the scars, the torture which she had endured, but included her manipulative moves towards Mason. She told her about the bounty hunters she had murdered in cold blood, how she had taken advantage of Lily's hospitality. The way she'd snuck into her camp to give Hayden a warning, and up until the moment she'd met Kamai underneath that eternal sunset.

And when she was finished, she barely had the moment to breathe before Natalia's lips were pressed against her own, and all the fiery teardrops were released unto the dying embers of the ground. They were kissing, yearning for each other's flames to intertwine and burn a hole in the forgotten fabric of the sky. The wave of adrenaline that pulsed through Emma's body was foreign. She could not remember the names of all the people she had kissed, she had forgotten the way they felt. In this moment, all she could feel was Natalia, all she wanted was Natalia.

"You're not a monster, Emma," Natalia whispered, holding her close, as if to protect her from the wild winds swarming in her mind.

"You're wrong," she confided, "All of you are wrong about me."

"Look at me," Natalia pleaded, lifting Emma's chin slightly, "Everything inside of you is good. You're just trying to do what's right, but there are no easy answers anymore. Every move you've made has been for good intentions."

"And so is the road to Hell," she muttered, quoting the old saying.

"Emma Harlem, you are good."

"I wanted to kill her," Emma looked away, "I would have done it." Natalia cooed, pulling the other girl in, comforting her racing heart, and a new sense of clarity overcame her. Emma Gail Harlem did not deserve Natalia Sanchez, or Sebastian, or Hayden or Kamai or any of them at all. She would not be the cause of their demise. She had brought them to Peregrin, and her mere existence had brought the Condors and the City. Well, now it was time she saved her friends again. Moving her right arm away from Natalia's shoulder, she rubbed the handle of her blade. It was time she retrieve the peace.

Megan pressed the wet washcloth up to her forehead, wiping away the drying blood. Never had she been so humiliated. It was even worse than the moment she discovered Emma was still alive; this time she'd been beat again.

"Fool me twice, shame on me," she muttered, looking up as a duo approached her.

"What happened out there?" Harper asked, taking a seat beside her. Next to Harper was Phoenix, her twin brother.

"That bitch Emma," she frowned, "She started attacking me unrelentlessly. I swear, I didn't do anything wrong this time."

"Revenge, probably," Phoenix added, although neither girl acknowledged him, "I mean, you did try to kill her."

"Harper, she's dangerous," Megan declared, "She will burn this entire camp down to ashes if we don't act soon. She'll destroy everything we've accomplished."

Harper nodded, gulping as she saw the scratches on her friend's face. She had yet to see this violent Emma Harlem, or at least, she was unable to recognize her. Harper expected her to be a giant, covered in blood and screaming bloody murder at all moments. She did not believe this conniving killer could be someone so small, so put-together, or at least who appeared to be whole. "You want to kill her, don't you?"

"Precisely," Megan hissed, and Harper began to nod.

Phoenix, however, stepped in. As he was closer with Cameron than either of the two girls, he was consequently closer with the Riot. He knew exactly who Emma was, and he saw her as a human being. Megan's antagonizing descriptions did not affect his view.

"We can't kill her," he protested, "But we can use her to force Sebastian's hand."

"What are you suggesting?" Harper turned to her brother, hoping he had some sort of plan in mind. Although her image of Emma may have been skewed, she did not want to call herself a murderer. Perhaps there was another option.

"We use her as blackmail," he declared, "Sebastian will hand over his power as ransom. Nobody dies." Harper nodded, approving of this scheme, and Megan slowly came to agree as well. And so the strategy was set, and would all be underway by the following nightfall.

xxxi. the trade and fall of the birds

Trigger Warning: Torture and Abuse. This chapter is very intense, and if this puts you at risk, please stop reading asap.

It was the following afternoon when the unstable world in which they lived came crashing down like broken glass.

The plan began with Megan, Harper, and Phoenix, accompanied by the two strongest members of their camp, entering the side that belonged to Peregrin. This was an odd sight to see, their three most important personnel going to visit their enemies together. The entire camp was put on edge, the air growing noticeably cooler.

"Don't," Natalia whispered, placing her hand on Emma's knee. Seated at an old picnic table that looked like it could break at any moment, she could see the darkness rise in her friend. With the sight of the Condor leader, her skin grew hot and her expression hardened. However, the group of intruders began to approach the two girls, and Emma was swiftly lifted into the air by the larger boys. One of them placed his meaty hand over her mouth, silencing her, yet she continued to kick and squirm and fight her way out.

"What the hell?" Natalia screamed, jumping up and punching the brutes. They quickly pushed her backwards into the table, but it was alright, for the commotion had grabbed Sebastian's attention. He, Mai, and Donovan came sprinting up the hill, and he tackled Megan. This was a smart move, because with the fall of their leader, the group's plan was suddenly thrown off track. The sequence of events was forced to change.

"What the hell do you think you're doing?" Sebastian snarled, "Put her down, now, or we shoot your asses." Just for effect, and to show that he was deadly serious, Mai began to stroke the gun in her right hand. Megan sent the boys a small nod, and the girl was dropped onto the ground. Sebastian scrambled down to help her up, but she simply slapped his hand away.

"Emma almost killed Megan yesterday," Harper began, "And attempted murder is a criminal offense." With a quick gesture, one of the boys quickly had a knife around her neck. Emma did not move, nor did she complain. She simply closed her eyes and exhaled, although she was nothing but exhausted of fighting for her life. "Either we take her back to our camp for punishment, or she dies on your turf. Your decision."

"A trade," Emma began to speak, but the boy muted her again, as well as pulled the knife up higher, raising the threat he posed.

This was enough for Mai, however, as she understood exactly what Emma was suggesting, "Emma can be brought to you camp, but Phoenix stays at ours. If Emma dies, Phoenix dies. Those are our terms." The two girls made a stoic eye contact, just enough to show that they agreed on this plan.

"No," Harper laughed, "No, you're the side that committed the crime. You don't get to make the rules."

"We don't have rules," Donovan added, "We're not your people."

As Harper looked like she was about to protest, Mai raised her weapon, "Those are our terms. You agree, or I'll shoot you right this instant."

Harper turned to her brother Phoenix and sighed, "Fine. Tomorrow morning they'll be retrieved. Until then, nobody from either side can visit the other." Phoenix rolled his eyes slightly, regretting ever coming up with this sort of plan, and a new fear resonated within him. Harper may have been his twin, but her motives could be unclear. Should Megan convince her that Emma's loss of life was worth his as well, then he'd be gone by morning. The same fear plagued Emma.

Sebastian shook his head, "This is dumb. Nobody is switching sides, alright? Megan tried to kill Emma, Emma tried to kill Megan. They're even. She stays here."

Harper smirked slightly, "She could stay here if you were to recognize our power." Emma's eyes widened, hoping she could convince her brother that Harper's new suggestion was the worst option possible. Yes, she was terrified of what Megan might do to her now, but she would not be the reason for the end of her camp. She was willing to be a martyr.

Sebastian recognized his sister's urgency and sighed, "Tomorrow morning." He added one last threat, "If she's dead, then Phoenix isn't the only one on your side who will pay."

The burly teenage guards hoisted Emma up so that her feet barely touched the ground, her weight being carried by the boys. This felt unnecessary to her, as she had agreed to not fight back or struggle, but her freedom to walk across the camp was not worth causing commotion for. They had, however, lowered the knife and moved their hands away from her mouth, allowing her to breathe again. Her gaze met Sebastian's, whose were filled with fear and emotion. She sighed slightly, and smiled softly, promising that Megan would not dare take her life that evening, especially what with the trade between her and Phoenix. Should Emma die, Phoenix would die, and Megan and Harper's alliance would shatter.

Harper hoisted the knife out of Emma's belt and tossed it to Sebastian. Megan looked like she was about to protest, believing that they deserved to keep their returned prisoner's weapon, but was quickly cut off.

"Phoenix," Harper turned to him, "You're going to be fine, assuming Sebastian wants to keep his sister safe. She'll make it through the night, unless Sebby here makes the first move, which is highly unlikely. We have nothing to worry about."

Looking at the knife in his hand, Sebastian turned to his sister, "You're barefoot. Do you at least want your shoes? I can go grab them."

"I don't need them," she said, "Never really helped me all that much."

"Let's go!" Megan yelled, cutting them off, "It's one night. Save your incest for the morning."

"You've got to be kidding me," Donovan muttered. The others seemed surprised to hear him speak, as though they'd forgotten he was apart of the conversation. Nobody responded, however, as they set to work to instigate their plans. Megan turned around, beckoning her cronies and their new hostage to follow. Harper stayed behind for just a moment, embracing Phoenix in one last hug.

"Don't kill her," Phoenix pleaded, "It won't help anyone."

"That would be Megan's move," she sighed, looking at all three of the boys, "And she knows that it would destroy our teamwork. I don't think you should worry."

"Thanks," Sebastian muttered, rolling his eyes slightly. He was fixated on the four people marching away from him. Somehow, he had put his sister right in the hands of their enemy, and once again, he felt powerless. He wanted to run, chase after her, tackle the brutes down, but they had made a deal. He had to let her walk into their trap. It was time to accept that someday, perhaps not that evening, but someday, Emma Gail Harlem would meet an untimely death, and there was nothing he could do to stop it.

When she was brought to the cabin shared by Megan and Harper, she was thrown onto the floor, and one of the guards stepped on her chest to force her down. Megan had whistled for assistance, and four more people came into the room. Among them was Dylan, who did not appear at all fazed by who this prisoner was. This did not surprise Emma, since she was the one who had ratted her own people out, but it caused a deep rage to boil in her blood. The foursome carried a multitude of supplies: ropes, belts, and some rusty old chains they had likely stolen from a fence somewhere along their journey.

They began to move with impeccable organization, as though they had predicted this job that evening. There was clearly a set plan, an agreement as to what each person's responsibility was.

"Remember guys!" Megan announced, "Complete immobility. We can't let this whore slip out of our hands again, now can we?" This phrase made Emma's heart sink. Complete immobility. The last time she was in a Condor prison, by the end of her two weeks, only her hands were bound. She feared that this time she wouldn't be so lucky.

As Emma was still pinned onto the ground, her captors began to secure her hands by firmly tying her wrists with a long rope that was then wrapped around her waist. She was hoisted off the ground and slammed against the pole of an empty bunk-bed, where a padlocked chain quickly wrapped around her forearms, tying her tightly to the wood. They had moved through this first stage in about two minutes time, and there was always some person's weight holding her down; even if she wanted to fight back, she never stood a chance.

Almost as though to taunt her, Megan placed the key to lock right at the top of the pole. A spot so close to Emma, yet out of reach. The Condor leader snickered as she worked, and praised her helpers for how effectively they had subdued this threat.

"We're not done yet, Emma," she laughed, "Don't you worry." They were onto stage two: her feet. Her ankles were initially bound by a thick wire that dug into her skin. A rope was then used to secure them to the pole.

"Try to break free, Emma," Megan demanded. The prisoner just stared at her, refusing to move. Complete immobility, right? Why would the captor simply wish to reveal a flaw in her system? With a quick nod to the guards, a blade was soon held to Dylan's neck. "Try to break free, Emma. Or else this will be your brother, and you don't want that, now do you?"

Emma sighed, closing her eyes and taking a deep breath before pulling on the restraints. Her arms and feet were hopeless; Megan's plan had gone accordingly. She gestured that the old Raven leader be released from the knife, and Dylan picked up a belt from their pile of supplies, tightly fastening Emma's waist to the pole. Her head was now the only area that had some amount of free range, which Megan of course had to limit. Tying a dirty rag around her mouth as a gag, she stepped back, examining her masterpiece.

"Fight it, Emma!" she screamed, and the girl obeyed, pulling against the restraints with all her might. They only part that seemed to move were her shoulders and head, but Megan quite enjoyed watching her struggle. Perhaps it was not complete immobility, but there was no chance the girl could ever escape, and that was good enough.

But this wasn't all. Megan reached down and picked up a thin leather strap off the ground. Attached to it was a small bell that jingled as she picked it up. She had no idea where this item had been found, but it was the perfect final step to her plan. She secured the collar around Emma's neck, making it so that she could hear whenever the girl moved.

Harper then stormed into the cabin, beckoning for Megan's helpers to evacuate. She froze when she saw what had become of Emma, mouth gaping at the extremities her friends had taken.

"This is a little much, don't you think?" Harper asked, eyes widening as she began to see the craziness that dwelled inside the Condor.

"This one's tricky," Megan shrugged, "We thought we'd killed her, but to no avail. Somehow she made it out. I won't make that same mistake again."

"We aren't killing her," Harper protested, "We can't."

"Sebastian won't kill your brother, if that's what you're worried about," added Megan, "He's too weak."

"His girlfriend would," Harper said. At this, both of the other girls, the captor and the captive alike, looked up, confusion settling in both their faces. "Maybe they're not dating exactly, but that girl he's always with? The one with the gun? She'd kill Phoenix in a heartbeat."

"I don't plan on killing Emma tonight, if that's any consolation," Megan sighed, "I just want to make her suffer. Once the deal runs dry, we can work from there."

Harper nodded slightly, still becoming increasingly skeptical of her Condor ally. On their journey, Megan had made Sebastian and his sister out to be dangerous. She described them as a couple of stonecold renegades who would kill anyone and anything in their paths. She stripped them of their humanity, turned them into immoral beasts. They would come ravage the Grove, she said; it was in their best interest to take over their new camp. The Harlems she had met at Peregrin, however, were quite the contrary. Emma was fierce. Without a doubt could she be pose a threat, should the proper occasion arise. Little did Harper know that this very conversation turned Emma into less of an enemy, that her critique of Megan's tactics bought her respect. Little did she know the tied down girl's original plan for the evening, a plan she would not live to learn.

"I have work to do," Harper sighed, leaving the cabin. Her eyes shone with guilt; she could hardly look at their prisoner. What they had done to Emma seemed morally unjust, and a sinking fear told her that Phoenix might be facing the same fate. However, she did not believe the Raven boys to be as cruel as Megan. Regardless, there was no way for her to find out her brother's state. Their terms explicitly stated they could have no visitors from their respective sides until the morning.

Inside the cabin, Megan snickered, finally alone with Emma. Emma, the freshman girl who had humiliated her in front of their entire old school. All her peers would go down thinking she was the slut that had sex with her boyfriend, the golden boy Sebastian Harlem's, best friend. Emma, who had revealed her lack of control over her own camp by somehow escaping death. This time, it was clear that Emma had no power. She could not talk her way out of her problems again, she could not fight. Finally, she was forced to submit.

Just because she could, Megan slapped the girl forcefully along the cheek, causing her head to whip to the left. The little bell sang its happy song, and Megan couldn't help but laugh as she saw the fear rise in Emma's eyes. Before, the prisoner hadn't understood the contraption around her neck, but now the truth was inescapable. It was a collar. She was nothing but an animal. Her degradation was complete: she was branded, tied down, and now that tinkling sound provided her captors with her every movement. 'Twas the fall of Emma Gail Harlem, for she had become nothing.

Megan continued to beat her, securing her victory after their squabble the previous morning. Every hit was for Sebastian, for Mai, for Emma, for every person who had ever tried to tell Megan who she could or couldn't be. She was on top now. She was the lioness. She was in control. And so she continued, pummeling hit after hit on a defenseless body, cackling at the jingle jingle of a girl who had finally submitted.

xxxii. down goes the cape

Harper did not return to the cabin that evening; she was too disgusted by Megan's actions, but lacked the power to end the trade. She simply had to stay away. This was good for Megan, to say the least, and dreadful for Emma. Neither girl had slept that evening, and by the time the sun rose, the prisoner was covered in her own blood, barely strong enough to stand any longer. However, the bonds covering her body forced her up, but with her unattached upper body weak, the bell was constantly jingling. It was music to the twisted girl's ear, and to Emma's? At first it was pure ignominy, but after two hours of the pain she had begun to go numb, begun to lose her consciousness. She was unable to feel or comprehend what was happening anymore, all she could think about was darkness.

Your presence keeps them at bay.

When she was in the cell the first time, this was her mantra. This was the phrase that kept her going, helped her to endure. It was just the same situation, just the same results. If she was in their cabin, she'd be able to hear their plans. And since Megan had yet to leave the small building, she knew that nothing important had been accomplished that evening between the convoluted duo.

The commotion, however, began around nine in the morning, as it appeared to be to Megan. There was screaming in the camp, chaotic wails piercing into the sky. As concern began to settle, the Condor leader took one last look at the defeated Emma, threw over a blindfold, and left the cabin. For the first time since her arrival as their prisoner, she was left alone, but she could not even process that. To be deadly honest, she thought perhaps those screams were her own. Perhaps she had lost control over her body. Yes, she was still gagged, but that detail seemed to elude her.

Soon after, the cabin's door flew open, and she heard footsteps scrambling towards her. Soon hands were pressed against her face, against her arms, and she heard her name being repeated and repeated. The gag was ripped out of her mouth, but she couldn't find the strength to speak. The new bandana was removed from her eyes, but she couldn't find the strength to see. She couldn't register who it was in front of her, what they were saying. She felt the weight around her waist loosen as the belt was released, and she heard the person curse when they realized they would need a key to unchain her hands.

"Up," she whispered softly, using all of her strength to force out that small sound, yet it was still barely audible. Her rescuer, luckily, was able to understand just what she meant, and found the small key at the top of the pole.

"Stay with me, Emma," he begged, but his words meant nothing to her. She was slipping away, slowly but surely her world was turning black. Her feet were then released, causing her to fall forward. There was no strength left in her to stand, hardly even strength left to think, to breathe. She felt the pressure loosen around her neck, heard the faraway tinkling sound of the demeaning collar. Her arms fell down along her sides, the rope tying them must have been cut loose. She felt herself being held in this boy's arms, collapsing onto him. She could feel his strong arms around her, feel his racing heartbeat.

"Seb?" she managed to whisper, looking at the boy. Her vision was blurry, her ability to discern what she saw was even worse.

"Yes, Emma," he cried, tears landing on his sister's weak, bloodied face, "Oh my God, Emma. Emma, I love you." It was as though repeating her name made her more alive, as though those two soft syllables could keep her from slipping out of his fingertips.

"But-but the deal?" she said, her voice little more than a hoarse whisper.

"It's over," he assured her, "They got Phoenix, which means you're free too. I'm so sorry, Em. God, this is all my fault." This was when she lost consciousness, and was unable to respond. Sebastian lifted the limp girl, holding her protectively in his arms, and carried her back to her proper side. She could have hardly weighed over a hundred pounds, and yet all of her body was muscle weight. He had never realized just how small she was, just how frail. The fact she had managed to survive over all this time was a miracle in itself.

"Serena, we need help!" he called, carrying his sister into what had become Peregrin's Med Hut. She was seated outside, having promised Sebastian earlier that she'd be there to help Emma once she was freed. They had suspected something like this might happen.

"Do you have any idea what's going on over there?" she asked, ushering the siblings into the cabin. They laid the unconscious Emma onto a bunk, and Serena began to place a wet washcloth over the wounds, clearing up the blood just enough that they could see where the damage was. "There's so much commotion."

"I have no idea," Sebastian shook his head, "I just had to get her back, I couldn't figure out what was happening."

"One-track mind, huh?" Serena sighed, smiling softly.

"Fatal flaw," he muttered, "Is she going to be alright?"

"I think so," she said, "There's some swelling in her knees, but her head seems alright. Maybe some broken ribs."

"That's good," he nodded solemnly, "She won't be like Hayden though, right? She'll be able to walk normally? They'll heal?"

"We'll have to see," Serena admitted, "We don't have x-rays. I can't see what's going on. Her knees don't feel like they're broken, which is what happened to Hayden. It seems more like a stress fracture? All of the pressure was being forced into her knees and shins, it happens to runners all the time. I think it'll be okay."

"Okay," Sebastian sighed, taking a seat beside his sister. He stroked her hair, its follicles caked with drying blood. This was the image he'd seen looming behind every tree, painting his eyelids when he tried to sleep, haunting his every movement while she was in the Condor's cell. It was his worst nightmare come alive, his paranoia proving real. Staring up at the bright blue sky through the cracked old windows, he began to pray to whatever God might be watching them. But what God would do such a thing? Leave the youth out to die, to kill one another? The sky was too blue, he thought. There was nobody watching them.

When Emma opened her eyes, she was instantly confused by her surroundings. She did not recall being brought to the Medic Hut, or even being freed from Megan's chains. Her body ached, and she could feel her blood pulsing all throughout her body, felt every weak rush flow through her veins. Every heart beat pressed against her chest, and the thumping racked her brain. Never before had it been so loud. But she had endured worse, had she not?

"Sebastian?" she whispered. Her body was turned away from him, and she was too weak still to move. She did not truly know her surroundings, but there was no fear trickling through her body. The first thing that crossed her mind was that perhaps this was the afterlife, for she did not remember ever being saved. It did not cross her mind why her brother's name was the first one she called out.

At the sound of her voice, he raced over to her, kneeling down where she'd be able to see him. He grabbed for her hand, holding it as supportively as he could. "Emma," he smiled, "Emma, can you hear me?"

Emma blinked slowly, "Am I dead?" What a silly thing for her to ask, but her rationality was too far out of grasp.

Sebastian laughed slightly, "No. No, Emma, you're alright. We got you back. The trade is over, they can't steal you again."

"There was screaming," she recalled the last thing she remembered, "Megan blindfolded me. I don't think that was me screaming."

"You were gagged, Emma," her brother said, "You're right, it wasn't you screaming. You were so goddamn strong." There were tears forming in his eyes now as he stared at her. His heart was bursting out of his chest, relief overcoming him that somehow his sister had made it out alive. Somehow she had stared death in the eye and forced it to turn the other way.

"Then who was it?" she asked.

"It doesn't matter," Sebastian assured her, "You're safe, that's all that counts right now."

"No," she muttered, "No, we need to know. I need to know if they're all safe." She began to try and push herself up, but her brother's comforting arm held her down.

"Everyone is safe, Em," he promised, "They all know I'm here. If there was a problem, they'd have come found me right away. Everyone we care about is safe."

"Dylan was there," Emma said, "She tied me down." She watched as her brother's disposition hardened, as the shaken force of betrayal and vengeance swarmed behind his eyes. She knew just what he felt inside, for it was what she almost always felt. They were just the same. They were gunpowder waiting to explode.

"Did she hurt you?" Sebastian asked, his voice growing darker.

"No," Emma said, "Only Megan. But Dylan— she looked right at me and she didn't care, Seb. Like she didn't even know me."

"She disowned us all," he sighed, "It's not your fault. You did nothing wrong."

"I did everything wrong."

"Don't say that," he said, more forcefully, "You saved us all. You didn't break. You didn't break the first time, and you didn't break now. You're the strongest fighter I know."

She shook her head slightly, "I'm tired of fighting, Seb."

"Me too, Emma, me too," he whispered, brushing her hair out of her bruised face, "We can't always play the hero."

"I'm no hero," she murmured.

"Keep telling yourself that," Sebastian smirked, wrapping his arms around his fragile sister. Seeing her so weak shattered his heart, and reminded him that he himself must remain strong. He couldn't seem to listen to his own advice. He couldn't seem to put down his cape.

By the time it seemed to be four in the afternoon, Emma had regained enough strength to stand again, and both her and her brother could not contain their curiosity any longer. Nobody had come by to visit the Medic Hut, and Serena's frequent visits out did not provide them with any true information. It seemed as though she was hiding the truth from the struggling siblings, as though she didn't want to break some tragic news.

With enough persistence, Emma was finally approved to leave the small cabin, assuming Sebastian remained with her at every moment. This was not simply for protection, but for physical support as well. She was limping heavily, and could only last for so long. He was her crutch.

And so the duo left the Med Hut, Emma squinting as the sunlight stabbed the space between her eyes. She shivered in the cool October breeze, her light jacket and leggings hardly providing the necessary insulation. Sebastian sighed, wrapping his own outer layer around her shoulders.

"You pulled through," said a voice from behind them. They turned around, and Sebastian quickly pushed his sister behind him.

"Get away from her," he hissed. His entire body tensed as he took a step forward towards the boy.

"It's alright, Seb," Emma assured him, and, much to his disapproval, stepped out from behind him, "What do you want, Mason?"

"I knew you'd do it," the Condor smirked, "So much for morals, am I right?"

Emma's face dropped, and Sebastian looked to her in concern, "I didn't do anything. I was tied up in Megan's cabin the whole night, you knew that."

"What?" Mason stepped back, alarmed.

Sebastian retorted to his sister, his hand resting on her shoulder, "Don't listen to a word this asshole says. He knew."

"Mason, what's going on?" Emma snapped, beginning to lose her patience with both the boys. She was still weak, yes, but the old spark was returning to her eyes. The match was beginning to light.

"Harper was found dead in the forest," he revealed, "And if neither of us killed her, then who the hell did?"

xxxiii. murder boy

Trigger Warning: Gun violence

With Mason's news ringing in their ears, Sebastian brought Emma back to the Med Hut, much to her dismay, so that she could rest. The commotion could not be good for her at this moment, as she would be too weak to fight back, and he knew well enough that fighting seemed to follow her. He arrived quickly to the center of the hill, where almost the entire camp, Ravens and Riot and Condors and City alike, had congregated, everyone souring the crowd for the one person who may be missing. They'd all been out there for hours, lost in a sea of confusion and an inkling fear that should they stray far from the madding crowd, they may be subject to the very same fate.

"Look who decided to show up," a snapping voice said from behind him. He turned around to see a cross-armed Marley, "Where've you been all day? Not like this is some new phenomenon."

He rolled his eyes, "With my sister. In the Med Hut. You can ask Serena."

"And where's your sister now?" Marley challenged, "Forgive me for finding it strange that the most uncontrollable person in this camp has been missing since the moment that gun went off."

"There was a gunshot?" Sebastian's head perked up. When he'd heard the screaming that morning, it was just as Phoenix was being retrieved from his night spent with the Ravens. He had not paid any attention to the commotion, as he was now able to save his sister. His mission had been Emma, and nothing else.

Marley simply clicked her tongue and began to walk away, calling out behind her, "Be careful, Sebastian. They'll be on to you soon." He simply sighed and walked away, knowing that neither he nor his sister were at all responsible for Harper's death, and that there were plenty of witnesses to support that they were both innocent. That was simply Marley, seeing the world through her untrusting, sarcastic lense.

Perhaps it was Marley covering her own tracks, blaming others to divert attention from herself. But then Sebastian shook the thoughts out of his head, and looked around the world surrounding him, the sky growing darker by the moment. Someone in their camp had died, someone important had been shot. Now was not the time to throw accusations out like falling leaves. It was time they put the facts together.

Someone had shot Harper Smith. Careful, now, or they might strike again.

Sebastian whipped around to a face a turbulence across the crowd. There were four people turned against a fifth, their face hidden from his angle, but a visceral feeling urged him to approach. As he neared, he saw exactly who it was in question, and his stomach dropped. MaiLinh Walker was in for a fight.

"I didn't kill her, alright?" Mai snapped, glaring her opponents down.

One of them groaned, "You're the only Raven with a gun. You want us to think one of our own people killed our leader?"

"If I was planning on killing someone, it wouldn't have been while my friend was being held captive by their allies," Mai said, "Do you have any idea what your people were doing to Emma last night?" She looked up and saw Sebastian, and shook her head slightly, signaling that he go away. She could see the stress resonating within him, and worried that being around this much tension would only make things worst. She had gone by to visit the siblings that morning when Emma was still unconscious. While was no secret that Mai did not particularly like the other girl, she still hated to see her in such a weakened state, hated to see the effect it had on her brother. Mai had assumed that she herself had suffered more, as she had spent more time in the cell, but she was slowly coming to realize that there was no point in competing. Why did it matter who had the toughest trials—why could they not support each other?

"Emma deserved it," one of her opponents said, "I mean, she volunteered. Or no, you volunteered her."

Mai paused, as she was the one who suggested the trade between Emma and Phoenix. However, it was under Emma's jurisdiction, and she would never condemn another to that fate had it been unnecessary. This sort of comment was the exact reason she did wanted Sebastian to avoid the conversation. He was already standing on the edge of a cliff; one wrong comment would be enough to push him over.

"So if you didn't kill her," began one of the other Condors, "Then who did?

"Like I would know," Mai said, "Have you even counted your own weapons yet? We have one gun, and it's mine, and I was in the cabin all night. We're done here, if you'll excuse me." She did not wait for their answer, and simply stormed away from her rival group, now approaching Sebastian.

Should she lead the conversation, she could steer all topics away from anything that might prove to be a trigger.

"You didn't do it, right?" Sebastian asked hesitantly, as though he did not want to hear the answer.

"Of course not," she assured him, "How's Emma?"

"Better," he said, "She's awake, she's walking, sort of."

"Does she know about Harper?"

"Yeah. That asshole Mason thought she did it," he said.

Mai sighed, "I bet a lot of people thought she did it."

"That's bullshit," Sebastian said, "She almost died last night, and everyone knows it. They're just looking for a scapegoat."

"Seb," Mai began, lowering her voice, "We kind of have a problem."

"What do you mean?" His face dropped, anticipating whatever bad news she may be carrying.

"My gun was stolen," she said, "It was hidden in my stuff this morning when I went to collect water, then we heard the gunshots. When I went back, it was gone. I've checked it like ten times, Seb. It's not there anymore."

"So you're saying it has to be one of our own?" he asked grimly, "Couldn't a Condor have snuck in and stolen it? Trying to frame us?"

"It's possible, but we would have noticed if there was a Condor on our half this morning. The only stranger there was Phoenix, and it wasn't him. He left our side right after the shooting," Mai said.

"Has anyone been missing out here? Anything suspicious?" Sebastian asked, turning to examine the crowd around them.

"Only you, your sister, and Serena. I've been counting all day, everyone else has been outside," she said, "Someone in our camp shot her this morning. They're in here now, and they still have their weapon."

He did not mean to kill her. At least, he did not think he meant it. When he fled his cabin in the earliest hours of the day, he thought they would return to the camp, with a new alliance formed and a blanket of peace finally covering the dying grass. However, his plan became irrelevant the moment they stood face to face, the moment he felt the weapon in his hand, the moment he let anger cloud his judgement.

He'd long noticed the girl's tendency to travel towards the top of the hill—the entrance towards the camp that faced the deserted highway. From that beige and dry spot, she could feel the wind rush through her hair, not obstructed by trees or buildings or the pressure. Here she could see no people, hear nobody calling her name, ignore the incessant voice of her ambitious mother, living as president of a fortified city, reminding her that she must do better.

And so when morning came, the boy decided to meet her. He stole his friend's gun. She would never forgive him, but perhaps she would never find out. The gun was solely a backup plan, in case the expected sequence of events went haywire.

"Who's there?" she asked, turning around. She had heard a twig snap, some rustling leaves, and felt a pit drop in her stomach as she realized she was being followed.

The boy slinked out of the forest, revealing his identity. He did not try to hide his face, nor conceal the stolen gun. The weapon was his only form of protection. It was common knowledge that he was a weak fighter, but his decent aim was his own secret. He'd shot someone dead before. He could do it again, if need be. Hopefully Harper would realize he was unafraid to kill her, and she would negotiate. He did not want to shoot.

"We need to talk," he said slowly, leaning his side side against a nearby tree, attempting to maintain this aura that he was confident, or that knew exactly what he was doing.

"What do you want?" she snapped, "And you might as well put that weapon away because your friend is still tied up in my cabin, and if you even try to attack me, she'll be the one who pays."

He paused at this, and even considered taking her advice and removing the weapon. Emma had done a great justice to him, helped him more than he had ever deserved. But he could shoot, could he not? There would be no Harper left to declare Emma's death sentence. Besides, the sun had risen now. The trade would soon be over.

"I want to make a deal," the boy began.

"Your terms?" she asked, her eyes glued to the pistol in his holster.

"You leave this camp," he declared, and she just laughed and shook her head, "You leave, but we won't interfere with the Grove. You can do whatever the hell you want in the forest, and we won't step in. As long as you stay away from Peregrin, there shouldn't be a problem."

"No," Harper said, "Peregrin could hold so many more people than just you twenty—"

He cut her off, "Twenty-five."

"Doesn't matter," she said, "This camp could hold three hundred. Everyone in the Grove could come, build a real, functioning civilization. Peregrin could thrive, don't you see that?"

"That's impossible," he said, "The Ravens and the Condors could never live peacefully in the same camp. Everything that's happened between us will never become water under the bridge. It's too late for that."

"You're making it work now," Harper said.

"You're wrong," he almost laughed, "The Condors have our leader's sister tied down in your cabin, presumably torturing her. She could be on the verge of death right now. In what world are we going to make peace?"

"One that's civilized."

"We stopped being civilized the day they sent us out here to die."

"You can get that back. We just need to work together," she pleaded.

"If your City is so holy, then why are people running away from it?" was his response. He paused, and then added, "You take your people out, or I shoot."

"You wouldn't," she shook her head, smirking slightly, as though she was challenging the boy in front of her.

"Just watch me," he snapped, yanking out the weapon. He lifted it, the barrel aimed directly at her forehead. He watched her gulp, realizing that he was serious. There was a murderous look in his eyes, a darkness that she had only ever seen in Megan.

Harper pulled a whistle out of her back pocket, and raised it high enough that he could see. "If I blow this, Emma dies. You don't—you don't want to kill her," she threatened.

"She'd be a martyr," he shrugged, "That's how she'd want to go out anyways."

"You don't get to make that call about your friend," she began, but was soon cut off.

"Neither do you," he hissed, "You agree to this deal, you take your people out of this camp for good, or I shoot." They stood at a stalemate, neither one willing to move. Emma's life was held in the whistle in Harper's mouth, and her own life was held by the boy's steady hands. They were not shaking. This would have surprised even himself, although he was too focused to think outside his mission.

"Fine," she broke eventually, "We'll leave. But by kicking us out, you're no better than the fortified cities. You're just the same."

He shot.

She fell back, blood seeping from her stomach. Her eyes widened as the unthinkable happened, as she fell to the ground, pain washing over her entire body.

The boy just stood there, and he lowered the gun. He felt satisfied. He felt as though his revenge was complete. Harper was dead, and it was time the City and the Condors left their camp to be. They were at peace.

But then he stood back, and he saw the terrified life fading from the girl's eyes, and suddenly he began to shake. He had killed her. He had killed another person. What kind of monster had he become?

He threw the gun across the field, covering it with dying leaves and whatever waste he could find. This gun could not kill someone else. It must be hidden. They must not have this power.

Oh, God, what had he done?

And so Hayden James Barrels returned to the camp, his hands shaking and heart racing and guilt throbbing in the back of his mind, but now was not the time to flee. Now was the time to hide in plain sight, and run away when the moment was right.

xxxiv. tyrant number two

It took four days for the kids to decide it was time to take a step forward. It was as though the camp was frozen, nobody quite sure what their next move should be. For four days, the Condors and the Ravens had no defined animosity—what a strange sight to see.

On the dawn of the fifth morning, however, Phoenix was the first to act. He told Jacob to sound the blow-horn and grab the camp's attention as the brother of the dead girl made his way towards the center of the hill. Slowly, the others started to approach, concerned about what details his great announcement may contain.

"What's the plan, guys?" he asked, his voice tired and dull, as though the life had been sucked right out of his lungs. "We can't just sit here. We need to reorganize, figure out what's going on. Someone needs to go back to the City, assume power there. Send the rest of us back to the Grove, restore the natural order. This isn't your pity party anymore."

The crowd was shocked by his assertiveness, the cold edge in his voice. He didn't sound angry or upset, just empty. Sebastian recognized that heavy vacuum consuming his soul, and everything inside of him yearned to help the other boy, but he realized it would be unappreciated. Unlike

Phoenix, Sebastian got his sister back. Harper's body was found; there was no escaping death.

"We'll go to the City," Megan volunteered, and the Ravens' hearts dropped. "We were Harper's closest allies. It's what she would have wanted."

Phoenix shook his head, "Did you kill my sister?" This was quite the paradox. No answer was acceptable or could justify a Condor rule over the City. If she pleaded guilty, then she had broken their alliance. If she was innocent, then she had no claim to power.

"It was a Raven," Mai interjected, and eighty heads whipped towards her, this new information shocking them all. She continued, "I don't know who, but my gun was stolen. I'm sorry."

"Someone stole your gun?" shouted a Condor, "Damn, you're guilty."

"I didn't kill her!" Mai retorted, feeling Sebastian's hand meet her shoulder protectively. She pushed it away. She could very well fight her own battles, and her partner knew it. "If I was guilty, I wouldn't be denying it, you dumbass."

"That's nothing new," Phoenix muttered, "I counted all of our ammo time and time again. Nothing was missing. It had to be a Raven gun."

"And that's it?" Megan screamed, "They need to get out of here! They're guilty of murder, Phoenix, they deserve to die for that!"

"Like you've never killed anyone," Emma spat, receiving a sharp glare from both her brother and the Condor leader, as well as from Natalia and Serena.

Phoenix continued, "The Ravens didn't break an alliance. By the same standards that put Harper and I in power to begin with, the person who killed the leader gets to take their spot. Sebastian?"

His head shot up, confusion resonating in his eyes, "What? No—this wasn't a Raven attack. Whoever killed her was acting on their own; we don't have anything to do with this. I don't have any claim to the City."

"Doesn't matter," Phoenix shrugged, "They're still your people. Unless one of them wants to step up and admit to it, it could be any of you."

"What's the point of this?" Yasmin cut in, suddenly skeptical, "Why do you want us to come take over your city?"

"Because there are people there who have no idea what's going on, and they just need someone to come take charge. Will you come or not?" he sighed.

Sebastian appeared hesitant, "I had nothing to do with your sister's death, Phoenix. What are you trying to do?"

"I'm trying to move on," he persuaded, "We can't just mope around this camp for the rest of our lives. We need to figure out what happens next."

"And you want your sister's killers to take over your city," Sebastian pointed out, "Phoenix, this doesn't make any sense."

He sighed, "You said yourself you personally didn't kill her."

"Bro, you're kind of contradicting yourself," Cameron said from behind. His expression seemed just as perplexed as those of the Ravens.

"Look, Sebastian," Phoenix began, "If you don't assume control over the City, then who will?"

"I don't know," he shrugged, "Someone that's actually from the City?"

"That's how we ended up with Harper," the other boy explained, "Besides, nobody else there knows the first thing about being a leader, and not only do you know that, but you know people in the Grove well enough to set up trade and communications. You're the perfect candidate."

"What about Donny?" Mai added, "Everything Seb has to offer and more."

Donovan stepped in, "I can't. They'll never accept someone who left."

"But they'd accept Sebastian? He has no reason to be there!" Mai protested. However, there was very little that protesting could accomplish. As the argument continued, it became exceedingly clear that a stranger was the only one who could truly assume the City's throne, and that Sebastian Harlem fit the bill. After hours of debate, both sides agreed to return to the damned City of the Forgotten, with Sebastian and Cameron at the head. As far as the group could tell, there was no other way to proceed.

The Condors had long left the crowd, and were packing their bags to return home to their forest. Dylan had gone with them. For the first time in years, their threat was out of the picture. Finally, it seemed that the Ravens had won.

"I'm not going back there," Marley declared, slamming the door of the cabin she shared with the rest of the Riot. "We ran for a reason. Why the hell should we be going back?"

"We left because of Harper," Donovan sighed, "But clearly she's not a threat anymore."

"So?" Marley snapped, "Harper was a tyrant. She killed Dana Pruitt to gain her power. How is Sebastian any different?"

"Sebastian didn't kill Harper," Emma snapped. She had been sitting with Natalia on the floor of their cabin, resting her head on the taller girl's shoulder. "You wanted the difference? Well, there it is."

"Sorry, Emma, but your brother doesn't have any right to that crown," Marley shook her head, "It's ridiculous."

"I know," she shrugged, "I never said I supported this."

"What do you want to do, Marls?" Natalia sighed, looking up at her best friend.

"We should stay here," the girl proposed, "Cameron can run the underground transport thing we'd discussed before we even left, raise our numbers. Establish trade with the City if we want. Run our own camp, with our own rules for once in our lives. Is that not why we left in the first place?"

Kamai nodded, "I'm in."

"Guys," Donny warned, "We don't know how to run a camp by ourselves."

"Didn't seem to be a problem when we left," Marley shrugged.

"Things were different then," he pleaded, "Harper was dangerous. Sebastian and Cameron are good people. They're our friends."

"You said the exact same thing during the first coup," Jacob muttered. "I'm with Marley. I'm not going back there."

"History is repeating itself, Donny," Marley preached, "Sebastian's a good guy right now, but just wait until he's used to the power. He won't be the same person in two months, let alone a year. They never are."

"He's already been in power for two years," Emma cut in, "The world has changed him, but ethically, he's still the same Seb. He won't become a psychopathic dictator, I can assure you that much."

"Em," Natalia frowned, "You should probably go."

"No," she refused, "You're right about one thing, Marley. Some of us need to stay here. The City will need trade, alliances, I don't know. Megan is still out there, she'll come after the City eventually. We need to keep this camp."

"Great," Marley smiled sarcastically, "Real insightful."

"She's supporting your cause, Marls. Why are you fighting her?" Jacob muttered, although he was quickly interrupted by Donovan.

"Sebastian won't want anything to do with this camp," he claimed, "He'll be overwhelmed with the City, the last thing he'll think about is the group of delinquents that were just too cool to suck up their egos and move on with their lives."

"This is moving on," Marley stressed, "We're moving on from the City completely. Why don't you get that?"

"Why would Sebastian want anything to do with our camp? What makes you think we'll have some alliance?"

Emma stood up, shaking the dust off of her dirty leggings, "Because I'll be here. That's all the incentive he'll need."

By the evening, Emma had gathered Serena and Yasmin to discuss the Riot's plan to stay in Peregrin. Much to her friends' dismay, they did need these two Ravens to join their cause. Their closest bet to medical expertise was Marley, and they all knew what a disaster that could be. And besides Emma, none of the Riot kids really knew how to fight. Serena and Yasmin were necessary assets.

At first, the Ravens seemed skeptical, but soon they became convinced. An alliance between the City and Peregrin was necessary to their survival, and they would be integral parts of the precarious game of chess. With Serena and Yasmin's help, Peregrin had a real chance at succeeding. Without them, they'd be left with two knives for protection and damnation at the first sight of injury. The alliance depended on their choice, and so they agreed to choose Emma's side.

"Hey," a fourth person approached the trio. It was Hayden. He continued, "I need to talk to you guys."

"What's up?" Yasmin asked, opening up the circle slightly. She could see concern taking over the boy's body, guilt eating him alive.

"I screwed up," he said, "Big time."

"Hayden, what did you do?" Serena sighed, eyes widening as she began to suspect the unthinkable. It was at the forefront of all the girls' minds.

"I—I shot her," he said, "I didn't mean to, it wasn't part of the plan, but it just kind of happened and I was holding Mai's gun and my finger was on the trigger and she agreed to leave but I just shot her anyways because I could and because I was powerful and I don't think I wanted to do it but—"

"Hayden, stop," Yasmin frowned, "Are you out of your mind?"

"I wish I was," he shuddered, "I wish I didn't kill her, I don't know what the hell I was thinking."

"So what's your plan?" Emma asked, seemingly unfazed by his announcement. She had to admit, it seemed a little bizarre for a boy like Hayden to murder another in cold blood, but she could she truly judge him? She'd come to believe that humans were inclined to kill one another, that they were savages who tried to cover up their violence with so-called love and fancy clothes.

"I'm leaving," he admitted, "Now, actually. I thought you three deserved to know."

"You don't have to do that," Emma sighed, and Serena gave her a worried glance. It definitely concerned her that Hayden was the secret killer. If he had come to kill Harper, what would it take for him to choose his next victim?

"It's for the best," he promised, "I can't hurt anyone else." At this, Emma nodded, understanding and respecting this decision. It was the same choice she'd have made herself. Serena and Yasmin both seemed more uncertain, yet they realized there was no hope in persuading him otherwise.

And so, as the sun began to set over Peregrin, the killer slinked into the forest, disappearing from the people he had once called his friends. He had no place to go, and so he simply ran.

XXXV. fare thee well

As the sun rose the following morning, the twenty-seven left at Peregrin gathered in the center of the hill. Most of them carried backpacks and small duffels that they'd stolen when they ran to the Grove to escape disease. It reminded Emma of the morning she and Kamai had led the Ravens to their new camp, only this time, she was Dylan staying behind. She had yet to tell Sebastian that only nineteen were following him. She wasn't quite sure what to say.

"Hey," She approached her brother. "Can we talk?"

"Of course," he nodded, "What's up? Are you ready? Have you packed?"

"I'm not coming," she said, not wasting a single moment or sparing a single breath.

"Emma, what are you talking about?" Sebastian's face dropped, "Of course you're coming. Have you eaten anything? You sound crazy."

"Stop saying I'm crazy whenever I disagree with you," she snapped, "The Riot is staying, along with me, Serena, and Yasmin. You need this camp for your own protection, and so you need us in charge to keep an alliance. Is that clear?"

"Fine, they can stay, but Emma, I'm not letting you go again," he said, grabbing her wrist, but she yanked her arm out of his tight grip.

"I'll be safe," she promised, "But I can't go with you."

"What happens when Megan comes back?"

"I'll fight my way out. I always do."

He bit his lip, eyes darting to the ground so as to hide the inevitable tears pressing behind them. "I can't lose you, Em."

"You won't," she said, pressing a small black box into her brother's hand, "Cameron's walkie. I'll have Donny's. If anything happens, you'll be the first to know."

"I can't do this," he said, "You're all I have left."

"That's not true," she said, "What about Mai? She'll be with you every step of the way."

"I'm supposed to lead two hundred people, and you're not even one of them," he muttered, "I'm not qualified for this. I have no idea what I'm doing."

"You think anyone else does?" she asked, "You'll make the right calls, Seb. You've done it before, you'll do it again, and this time you're not alone."

"What the hell did we get ourselves into, Em?" he sighed, looking at his precious sister through tired eyes. He had not slept the night before, his mind keeping him awake with thoughts of the new terrain he was somehow supposed to lead.

"It's the wild," she smiled softly, "It's all we've ever been."

"You used to not be wild," he sighed.

"I think I just suppressed it."

Across the camp, a similar interaction was occurring. Marley had come to Mai to say her goodbyes to a friendship that had flamed for so little time, yet burned bright into the open sky.

"You sure you want to leave?" Marley asked, leaning against a tree.

Mai simply sighed, "I have to. Someone needs to keep Sebastian sane."

Marley scoffed, "Why don't you and Emma just switch places? I don't think I can handle her being the freaking princess all over this camp."

"Wait, Emma's not coming?" Mai's eyes widened, "Shit. Seb's gonna lose it."

"Great!" Marley said, "Convince her that she needs to go."

"You know that's impossible," Mai said, "You could always come with."

"That's impossible too," she said, "So is this it? Goodbye?"

"Seems like the most affectionate thing you've ever said," Mai smirked.

"Probably was," Marley said, "Don't get used to it. I'd still throw a knife sharpener at you any day."

"I'm honored."

"You should be."

The next farewell came between a more surprising duo: Emma and Mai. Despite their rivalry and disdain for each other, they shared one commonality—Sebastian.

"Does he know?" Mai asked, interrupting his sister's conversation Corey.

"Seb? I told him," Emma said, not turning her attention away from the other boy.

"And he's alright with this?" Mai snapped, slapping her on the shoulder, forcing her to move her focus.

She sighed, "He will be. You'll need to help him."

"You think?" the other girl muttered, "He's a disaster whenever you're gone."

"He'll be alright. He has Cam's radio, he can talk to me whenever he needs to. If anything, he'll be smarter without me there."

Mai nodded, "He won't have to worry about how his measures might affect you."

"Exactly," Emma said, "Good luck out there."

"You too," said Mai, and the girls embraced in some awkward sort of hug that was foreign to them both. Some might have found it odd how these two girls could not get along, as they had gone through the exact same trials and tribulations, but that was what caused their deviation. They were lone rangers, wild cards. Their games belonged on separate battlefields.

Finally, they were in control of their own chessboards.

"I heard Emma broke the news earlier," said Donovan to Sebastian, "I thought we should have told you earlier, but it was her call."

Sebastian sighed, "You'll keep her safe, right?"

Donny laughed, "She keeps herself safe. She doesn't need protection." The Raven boy glared, and the other added, "I'll be there for her. She's one of us now."

"God, I hate that," Sebastian sighed.

"What?" Donovan asked, slightly concerned.

"That she's 'one of you.' She's still a Raven, whether she likes it or not," he said.

"Are you still Ravens?" Donny asked, "I mean, Dylan went back to the Grove under the same title. Some of you are staying here at Peregrin, the rest going to the City. Don't you think your old identity is slipping?"

"It doesn't go away that easily," he said.

"You're not going to screw the City over, right?" Donny asked cautiously.

"I'll try not to."

The other nodded, "Listen to Cameron. He's a good person. You won't be alone."

"And who do you get to listen to?" Sebastian sighed.

"Emma."

"Well, I guess this is it."

"We'll miss you."

And just like that, Sebastian turned around and faced the camp at Peregrin for one last time, everyone looking at him for direction. He saw his sister hanging near the back with Natalia, and the she smiled softly, as if to suggest that this would never be goodbye. I love you, she mouthed, and he nodded back, a sign that he had understood her message.

"You ready?" Cameron asked, approaching Sebastian.

"Lead the way," he stated, taking a deep breath and shaking the scattered thoughts out of his hectic mind.

There were eight left at Peregrin: the five in the Riot and the three Ravens. They watched as their friends abandoned the camp, the dust flying into the air. It was silent, a sound they had all but forgotten.

Silent, at least, until Emma Gail Harlem shattered the pristine glass, "Let's get to work, Peregrin."

epilogue

- -

Two months had passed since Sebastian Harlem arrived in the City of the Forgotten. The people were not pleased to have a newcomer assume such power, nor were they upset that he was a stranger. It seemed at first that they did not care. That the system meant nothing to them.

Phoenix left the City after two weeks. The remnants of his sister were left scattered along the office walls, her footsteps omnipresent on the concrete ground. It became too much, and though Sebastian and Cameron wished he would stay, Peregrin would mark his fresh start. This left the other two boys to manage the affairs of an entire civilization, what a job for two children who had yet to reach twenty years of age.

"Ever thought you'd be a politician?" Cameron had asked his partner one day.

"Never," Sebastian had laughed, "Is that even what we are?"

On a typical day, Mai would be found in the office alongside the two boys, having been promoted to military supervisor. She was responsible for organizing protective measures around the City, as well as training sessions to teach the others the skills needed for defense. Cameron was thoroughly concerned about the Riot when they'd first travelled to Peregrin, for none of them had any experience in combat. The Ravens in the City aimed to change that. Mai had appointed Nathan to be the main teacher in these sessions, as he was an accomplished fighter himself, and well trusted by her and the leaders.

Ellie was beyond pleased with this situation, as her older friends were finally trusting her enough to learn to fight. She was constantly training in classes, and was improving quickly. Mai was especially impressed with the younger girl, and was soon to start putting her in actual positions along their defenses.

Much to everyone's surprise, Nova's brother had opted to leave the Condors behind, and instead accompanied her and the Ravens to Peregrin. He was the only one to leave all of his people, and still his welcome could only be described as cold. As time passed, however, the Ravens grew to accept him into the fragile fabric of their new society, and he was soon a member of the City. Just as Nova was the Ravens' mechanic, she soon took the same position in their new settlement.

Corey, along with others, had fallen into the line of travelers who traded between the City and Peregrin, or the City and the Grove. Having lived in both the other camp and the forest, the trio was highly valued among the other merchants. Every time they returned, Sebastian was adamant about receiving updates on the situation at Peregrin, constantly asking for details about his sister and friends.

Across the abandoned highway, a three day trek over fifty-two miles southeast, the camp at Peregrin had grown to thrive. Not long after their founding, Marley opted to return to the City and operate the underground transport for the renegades who craved that open air and independence. Thanks to her, already fifteen people had joined the camp, and their numbers were only on track to increase.

Emma and Donovan had stepped up as leaders. The natural option, of course, since neither teen had any intention of listening to another's orders. Perhaps this was what sent Marley overboard. Perhaps she was still nurturing that free spirit inside, desperately searching for the way to fulfill its demands.

As Mai led the defenses in the City, Yasmin was her parallel at Peregrin. Whenever there was a new arrival, they were subject to at least two full days of training, preparing them so that they could defend their camp should trouble arise.

Jacob and Natalia were unsurprisingly the right hands to the leadership. It was the sort of job Jacob had expected to receive after assisting in the overthrow that placed Harper at the head of the City, only now he felt that Emma and Donovan truly did deserve their power, and that they were working towards the benefit of the camp. He felt no qualms by helping them. Natalia simply found it strange to be important in the camp. After spending two years as a nameless stoner in the City, she had somehow become something. What a turn of events.

At times, Kamai and Natalia would pressure Emma into finally watching the sun set over the pristine lake, and they would admire the vibrant colors that streaked across the empty sky. Yet Emma would then stand outside for longer, and watch as the night sky took over. Counting the infinite stars, tracing the bodies of Orion and Andromeda, a hidden voice told her that fifty-two miles away, another boy was staring at the same constellations, and maybe, just maybe, the other Harlems living in the fortified municipalities were watching them too.

The whole world was staring up at that one sky, she realized. Never before had she felt so small. That was, of course, until she looked around at her camp, and remembered that the rest of her world had cast them out, and while they shared the same sky, they were living in a separate dimension. She did not examine the stars again.

Two months in, and Hayden James Barrels was on the run, a trail of blood following him wherever he stepped. He was a killer. Through and through, the blood in his veins was a mixture of his and the lives he'd taken. His skin had held a gun and pulled the trigger on his father. His hand had shot a girl he hardly even knew.

He didn't mean to kill her. When he'd entered the woods that fateful night, he'd had no intention of taking her life. But as he watched her bleed, as he watched the life fade from her fearful brown eyes, he had felt absolutely nothing. It wasn't until he stepped back and realized the horrendous thing he'd done that he'd begun to feel.

He had stolen two lives. Who was to say he wouldn't steal more?

Eventually, his feet took him back to the Grove. The forest was just like the back of his hand; he could hardly recognize it against all the blood. Fires had ransacked the underbrush, a sign of the army that had swept through. That army was gone now. They'd gone home to their city, learning to survive under a new government that had no claim to their throne. Sebastian did not belong in the City of the Forgotten. He was there because of Hayden's mistakes.

He could not make things right, but he could stop them before they just got worse.

"Adrian!" He called as he approached a clearing he had spent two years trying desperately to avoid. He always knew that he would end up there, however. He could only run from the truth for so long. He could only dodge fate so many times.

The other boy appeared from the top of a hill nearby, and stared down at the intruder with surprise. The two had not seen each other in years. Last time, they were both learning what the post-plague world was. Adrian seemed to figure it out; Hayden was still falling.

"Why'd you come here?" The taller of the boys asked, confused by his cousin's sudden appearance. He knew the other boy was aware of the threat he posed. There had been an anger burning inside him for years, but as he looked at his visitor, Adrian realized that he didn't see a murderer in front of him. He saw the same boy he'd grown up with. The boy he used to race on their tricycles down his torn up driveway.

"Time to make things right," Hayden muttered, not breaking eye contact with his cousin. There was no fear in him. Not anymore.

Adrian smirked, "Your voice got lower."

"I hit puberty," Hayden shrugged, "Are you going to shoot me or what?"

"What?" His cousin stepped back, surprised by this request.

Hayden didn't look away, "Make my mom proud, or whatever it was. Avenge my dad."

Adrian sighed and pulled out the gun he'd carried for years, "I don't want to do this."

"You should," the other boy protested. Adrian took a deep breath and pointed the weapon at his cousin, and for a brief second, they were children again, playing catch in the backyard. Adrian was far better than Hayden. He was always taller and more aggressive. Hayden never stood a chance.

He lowered the weapon, "I can't do it." Before he could say anything else, however, Hayden's fist had collided with the side of his head, and the gun was suddenly in his cousin's hands.

"Shoot me, or I'll do it myself," Hayden pleaded, bringing the gun to his neck, the barrel resting underneath his chin.

"Hayden—" Adrian screamed, but it was too late. The trigger had been pulled, and the boy fell over, weapon still in his hand. As the blood began to seep out, his cousin was left staring at the limp body in front of him. The body he was meant to kill.

It was the same gun that Hayden had once held, almost three years before. Hayden James Barrels. Never had a name been more appropriate. His cousin stood there shaking, watching as his blood seeped into the minefield they called the Grove.

www.ingramcontent.com/pod-product-compliance
Lightning Source LLC
Chambersburg PA
CBHW071432200726
48294CB00002B/603